Spring
Upon a Crime

by

ML Erdahl

A Seattle Wilderness Mystery,
Volume 2

This is a work of fiction. Names, characters, places, and incidents are either the product of the author's imagination or are used fictitiously, and any resemblance to actual persons living or dead, business establishments, events, or locales, is entirely coincidental.

Spring Upon a Crime

COPYRIGHT © 2021 by ML Erdahl

Cover Art by *Abigail Owen*

The Wild Rose Press, Inc.
PO Box 708
Adams Basin, NY 14410-0708
Visit us at www.thewildrosepress.com

Publishing History
First Crimson Rose Edition, 2021
Trade Paperback ISBN 978-1-5092-3460-8
Digital ISBN 978-1-5092-3461-5

A Seattle Wilderness Mystery, Volume 2
Published in the United States of America

Behind them, the rumble of the truck's diesel engine grew. Not focusing on the treacherous path in front of her, she risked a quick glance backward. The truck halted next to the job trailer. The door creaked open and Crystal stumbled over a blackberry vine, the beastly bush sliding up her leg and raking her shin with thorns. Seizing her arm, Conner steadied her. The sound of the truck door slamming urged them on.

"Hey! What the hell are you doing on my property?" The furious, raspy bellow startled them into redoubling their pace.

Another ill-advised glance showed Crystal they were almost to the tree line. "Keep going. We're almost there."

An ominous metallic click caught her attention, followed by another. A gunshot blasted through the serene wilderness and Conner fell, gasping and swearing.

Praise for ML Erdahl

Dedication

To those who help polish the early versions
of my stories before they ever see the light of day.
My family, Jann, Dennis, Evelyn, Charisse,
my editor Ally,
and most of all my wife.
Your editing, proofreading, and
impromptu therapy sessions keep me grounded.

Chapter One

"No!" Crystal's heartbeat started again, but now with a furious pounding, filling her ears with intensity. "No, no, no." She chanted the mantra as she approached the pile of leaves with trepidation. Gouge marks, still present in the soil despite the persistent precipitation, made it clear someone frantic had flung forest debris over what lay beneath.

Crystal trembled as she stared at the mass, afraid to uncover what she had stumbled upon. If it was Olivia's body, how could she ever face her best friend's mother, much less live with herself? Falling to her knees in the damp soil, Crystal forced herself to shift the top layer. Piling it to the side, she scooped two more handfuls. Picking up speed, she found herself casting armfuls aside in her pursuit to find the truth.

She wished she had never boarded the ferry to the Olympic Peninsula, but how could she have foreseen the events that had transpired to bring her to this unimaginable reality?

****

Crystal stood on the foredeck of the vessel *Wenatchee*, her back to the water. The wind whipped her chestnut hair in a wild flurry, and she raised her voice over the rumble of the ship's engines. "The Puget Sound ferry system links the area's islands together with the cities on the mainland. Bainbridge, Whidbey, and the San Juans can be accessed by ferries from Seattle, Edmonds, and Anacortes." She addressed the twelve college students in her care, who had finished their spring quarter and were taking this opportunity to have an adventure, before heading home to their parents and starting jobs to pay for the next year's tuition. At least, that was what Crystal had done in college. However, the high-end clothes and newer generation phones several of her charges possessed indicated summer work might not be a necessity in their near future. One girl raised such a phone and snapped a shot of Crystal, momentarily breaking her concentration.

Crystal still hadn't adjusted to being worthy of a virtual stranger's picture. However, since she had taken the position of wilderness guide, she was fast learning that as part of people's vacations, she was one more memory they wanted to capture on their omnipresent devices.

After a pause to compose her thoughts, she continued. "The locals use the ferries to commute, but they can also allow us to access more remote areas of the state, like our destination, the Olympic Peninsula. We'll be docking at the Bainbridge terminal in thirty minutes, so enjoy the trip. Meet belowdeck at the vans when the Captain makes the announcement of our imminent arrival. In the meantime, feel free to explore the ferry. One more thing, Orcas, also known as killer whales, hunt in the Puget Sound waters this time of year, so keep a look-out. They have been known to swim along this route."

Excited murmurs ran through the crowd, and everyone rushed to the rail to peer over the edge in search of the black and white whales.

Crystal joined her fellow guide, Suzy Hawkins, in the rear of the group, who nodded at Crystal in appreciation. "I wish I was as good at those speeches as you." The compliment made Crystal swell with pride. Half a year after bluffing her way into the wilderness guide job, she still suffered from imposter syndrome. Meanwhile, Suzy was the consummate outdoorswoman. The short haired blonde packed a prodigious amount of strength into her wiry five-foot frame, earned from a lifetime of summiting mountains and scaling vertical cliffs.

"Fill me in on this trip we're going on. I've never done this particular trek." Crystal kept her voice down to not be overheard by their clients.

"We're taking them on what the ECO Adventures brochure calls the 'Olympic Rain Forest Experience'." Suzy waved her hands in an expansive manner at the grandiose name. "We are heading to the western portion of the Olympic National Park near the Pacific coast for a hiking and camping trip in the Hoh Rain Forest."

"Are we going through Forks?"

"Yeah. It's the small logging town near our starting off point."

"If we're lucky, we'll see a vampire or a werewolf." Suzy's blank stare told it all. Crystal sighed. "I'm guessing you never read the *Twilight* books."

Suzy nodded in understanding. "Nope, but I've heard of them. Maybe I should have read them if we're going to be infringing on their turf. I bet bear spray would stop a werewolf." Suzy stared into the distance, mulling over the concept before bringing her attention back to their conversation. "Supernatural monsters aside, we'll start at a trailhead in the Park and hike several miles to a small lake, where canoes are waiting. It's a short paddle, and on the other side of the water is private property owned by none other than your old friend Frederick Baranhof."

Mr. Baranhof owned unique properties across the state and rented several of the exotic wilderness locations to the company that employed Crystal for their excursions. His holdings included a chalet in the Snoqualmie forest Crystal had visited last winter on an ill-fated snowshoe weekend, where one of the guests had been murdered.

"I imagine this can't be any worse than my last visit to one of his homes." Crystal had come within a hairsbreadth of losing her job when Emerald City Outfitters had suffered the initial blame for the death.

Suzy glanced around for anyone who might have a question. "Gathering from what you and Conner told me about the group on your snowshoe hike, this lot doesn't seem to have the same homicidal tendencies."

Watching three of them flash peace signs for a phone extended on a selfie stick, Crystal smirked. "I don't think we have to worry this time. They'll be too busy struggling with poor cell phone coverage and coping with not being able to post to social media."

Suzy's hazel eyes focused on a point behind Crystal. Following her line of sight, Crystal spotted a bald eagle perched atop a towering fir tree, surveying the inlet they were passing through.

"You're on." Suzy urged.

"Looks like I am." Stepping into the center of the college students, Crystal spoke in what she had come to think of as her lecturing voice. "I want to bring your attention to the right. Scan the tops of the trees, and you'll see a bald eagle hunting." Crystal pointed, directing them to where the regal national bird perched.

Twelve heads swiveled to follow where she indicated. All of them raised their phones, trying to capture the distant eagle as anything but a grainy blur.

The eagle, seemingly fed up with being the center of attention, launched itself into the sky. Gasps followed the enormous bird of prey as it took flight.

"Well, there may not be any Orcas, but an eagle isn't a bad way to begin a trip," Suzy said with satisfaction.

Many of the party enjoyed the remainder of the ferry ride on deck watching for more wildlife. Crystal's eyes watered in the persistent wind tugging at her hair and clothes. A few half-hearted pictures were taken of seagulls coasting alongside, but their commonality took away from being worthy of photographs. Before long, the Bainbridge Island dock approached as the Seattle skyline retreated. Crystal wrangled her locks and wound them into a ponytail to prevent herself from looking like an eighties rock star.

Abruptly, the captain's voice rang out over the loudspeaker. "We will be docking in ten minutes. Please return to your vehicle at this time. Do not start your engine until directed by a crew-member."

"ECO Adventures, follow Suzy and me," Crystal called to the remaining members. ECO was short for Emerald City Outfitters, the outdoor gear and wilderness guide company where Crystal and Suzy worked. By trading a nine-to-five office job to explore the beautiful Pacific Northwest, Crystal had hit the employment lottery. She couldn't believe anyone would pay her to live out her dream job with next-to-no experience.

Suzy, in contrast, had grown up as the daughter of famous mountaineers who had been one of the first married couples to complete the seven summits, climbing the highest peak of each continent. She had been hiking, camping, and climbing since before she could read. Her skills and toughness made her an ideal candidate for the position.

On the other hand, Crystal had hiked and camped with her parents when she was young, like many Northwest families, but had no extraordinary skills to set her apart. However, Crystal had found herself to be a people person. At least she was when it came to guiding, where the individuals she interacted with were on exciting vacations and in perpetual good moods. This had been an enormous relief to Suzy, who had a short temper and sarcastic disposition. In unspoken agreement, the two had fallen into an easy partnership where Crystal did the talking during the educational segments, and Suzy took the lead when technical skills needed to be demonstrated.

Crystal had feared the other guides would resent her lack of outdoor acumen. The truth was quite the contrary. They had welcomed her into their ranks with open arms. Crystal had a sneaking suspicion a portion of the warmth was due to her solving the murder that happened in the Baranhof Chalet. The incident had precipitated the suspension of ECO Adventures guide insurance, and they hadn't started working again until Crystal had unraveled the crime. She had also managed to rough up two of the perpetrators involved, earning her extra points in Suzy's book.

Ever since, Suzy and Conner had been giving her lessons and on-the-job training to bring her up to speed. Thinking of Conner still caused tiny wings to take flight in her stomach after knowing him for almost six months. He had accompanied Crystal on her first trip and they had begun dating shortly after. Several months ago, he had introduced Crystal as his girlfriend to an old friend of his they had bumped into, and she couldn't be happier. His kind and quick-witted nature, not to mention his rugged outdoorsman good looks, made her feel like the most fortunate woman in the world. She was often paired with him for tours, but this time he was busy covering a beginning rock climbing course for Ethan, the company's resident climbing expert, who had broken his leg while teaching the same course. According to his doctor, Ethan wasn't ready for serious strenuous physical activity, but he itched to return to the outdoors since the Pacific Northwest had begun its transition into prime camping and hiking season.

Crystal navigated her way down the steel stairwell of the ferry to the car deck. Parked near the front were two vans with ECO Adventures painted on the side. The troop climbed into their seats, and she did a silent head count as they loaded to ensure none were left behind.

Crystal joined Suzy for a quick meeting as their charges made themselves comfortable. "Just follow me. It's a four-hour drive from the dock to our trailhead. We'll stop in Forks for a rest before we hit the forest," Suzy told her.

"Are we getting lunch in town?"

"I'll hand out a few granola bars. We'll want to save our appetite for Roxie's cooking." Suzy patted her belly in appreciation.

"Roxie is hosting this trip?" Crystal could feel the grin spreading across her face.

"She sure is. I can't wait for her delicious Southern cooking."

"You do know she isn't from the South."

"Of course she is. I heard she's from Savannah." Suzy snorted at Crystal's ignorance.

"Oh, yeah. That makes sense." Crystal repressed a grin. She wasn't going to blow Roxie's cover. A former theater actress, Roxie had opted to imitate a Southern accent once for fun. Her comment cards had raved about her hospitality, so she opted to go full-blown Southern when playing hostess and chef, despite being from Vancouver B.C. Already an accomplished chef, she had thrown herself into Southern cuisine and referred to her hostess personality as a role she adored playing.

Aside from the meals, Crystal looked forward to seeing Roxie herself. The hostess lacked certain social filters and either enjoyed pushing boundaries or didn't recognize what they were, making the conversations memorable, to say the least.

Promising to stick close to Suzy's bumper, Crystal retreated to her van. The ferry coasted into the dock, heavy lines were tied off, and a ramp dropped between the shore and the ship's deck. With a signal from a crewmember in an orange vest, Crystal started the engine and tailed Suzy off the ferry and onto Bainbridge.

A brief drive passing the lush vegetation of the picturesque landscape tricked several of the tour group into believing they were already in the rain forest. As they passed over an unremarkable bridge on the western edge of the island, Crystal made an announcement. "Welcome to the Olympic Peninsula, everyone, which encompasses the entire northwest region of Washington State." Crystal had prepared her speech the night before with more than a little help from the internet.

"Where's the rainforest?" asked one guy she had seen taking a selfie earlier.

"The Hoh Rain Forest makes up the western portion of the park and averages an astounding twelve feet of rain per year. To put that amount of precipitation into perspective, the city of Seattle, with the unofficial nickname 'Rain City', averages a little under three feet a year."

"Wow," the same guy said. "But it's not going to rain on our camping trip, right?"

"The forecast says it will rain tomorrow morning, tapering off in the afternoon," Crystal informed the crestfallen occupants of her van.

"Won't we get wet?" complained a lanky girl, tugging her long red hair.

"We've got you covered. Literally. There's rain gear for all of you."

"But we wanted to cook s'mores over a campfire."

"Well…" Crystal trailed off, waiting for a name.

"Janice," she filled in, "and this is Pete." She gestured to the dark-haired guy in the adjacent seat. His silver nose ring and black spacers in his ears attempted to portray edginess, but his budding beer belly and whining over rain were not screaming tough guy.

"Janice and Pete. We are going to a *rain* forest. I hope it doesn't live up to its reputation for all of our sakes, but the name is a give-away."

The other twenty-somethings in the van laughed, and even Janice and Pete acknowledged her words with rueful grins.

"Do you all know each other?" Crystal had been working on her small talk as well as her lectures. A guide was half-instructor and half-entertainer and needed to possess the ability to keep a conversation going to make for happy customers.

"We do. Some of us recently graduated from Nevada State College, others have another year to go. This is our last hoorah before we go our separate ways." Janice continued in her role as the spokeswoman. "Most of us haven't been camping before, and we thought it would be exciting to have an adventure somewhere different than where we're from."

The van filled with a happy buzz as they discussed their hopes for the upcoming trip.

Crystal interjected when she was asked a question but let the group of friends talk among themselves as she followed Suzy's van down the highway. After several hours of driving, they passed a pair of signs, the first proclaiming, "The City of Forks Welcomes You." The next portrayed a wolf howling at the moon, and announced, "No Vampires beyond this Point. Treaty Line."

"I didn't know we were near Forks!" a girl exclaimed. "Pull over. I want to get a picture by that sign."

Crystal flashed her lights at Suzy and swung into the parking lot of a local burger joint. Suzy's van looped around as Crystal's entire vehicle emptied of its passengers.

"What are we stopping for?" Suzy grumbled as she hopped out. "There's a rest stop a quarter mile down the road."

The sound of her own van's door sliding open caused Suzy to spin and see her passengers flocking to join the festivities in front of the sign.

"I told you *Twilight* was a big deal." Crystal laughed at Suzy's sour expression.

"It's just some vampire movie, right?"

"Well, it was a book series first, but they made it into movies, all set and filmed here. They were a huge hit."

"Here?" Suzy looked out at the town. The forest crowded a pocket of buildings lining the highway they had been traveling on. Even from the beginning of the town where they were standing, they could see where the buildings tapered off in the distance and the forest's edge marked the end of the unpretentious town.

"I suppose we're stopped now and they all seem happy. When they're done taking pictures, we'll dish out some snacks and hit the road." Suzy stretched her arms to ease the tension of the long ride.

However, as the selfies in front of the sign came to a close, the pack of graduates, drawn by the tempting scent of patties on the grill, wandered into the restaurant. Suzy muttered under her breath, glanced at her watch, and opened her mouth to say something, but Crystal reminded her that their guests' happiness was the whole purpose of why they were there. After some cajoling, she convinced her coworker to relax and enjoy a cheeseburger and fries. They joined the others and settled down at a small table, draped in a plastic red and white checkered tablecloth. The wood paneling and rust tinged steel signs on the walls bespoke the age of the place, but the meal was on point, with the right amount of grease and salt to satisfy Crystal's desire for indulgence.

By the end, Suzy was laughing and joking. As she dumped the wax paper the food had been served on into the trash and nestled the red plastic basket in with the others on top of the bin, Crystal couldn't help but tease her partner. "You were just hangry. You shouldn't have been starving yourself for Roxie's cooking."

Suzy conceded the point. "I feel better, but, as tasty as that was, I know Roxie's cooking is *so* much better."

"You do realize we have a three-mile hike *and* a canoe trip ahead of us. You might get hungry again."

"I suppose I will, smarty-pants," Suzy said with her characteristic flippant nature. "Now get your flock in the van, and let's get going."

Crystal hollered at the lingering group. "We're leaving in five minutes. Finish up, and let's hit the road. We've got some hiking to do."

Chapter Two

Turning into the Olympic National Park, Suzy shot down dirt roads at alarming speeds. Crystal did her best to keep up but kept thudding through potholes she couldn't see until the last instant, disguised as they were by the constant changes of sun and shadow, not to mention the dust cloud kicked up by the leading vehicle. Suzy slalomed around the obstacles as if she were practicing for a future career in off-road racing.

After an intense, jaw-rattling ride, they arrived at a small dirt parking lot. The crowd behind her let out relieved sighs as the uncomfortable trip ended.

By the time Crystal jumped out, Suzy already had the back doors of her van open. Crystal followed suit, revealing a series of backpacks.

"Grab your packs and some rain gear if you didn't bring any," Suzy announced to the milling crowd.

Nudging Crystal, Suzy pointed at their bags resting in the corner. "I split up the necessary safety supplies between us."

Crystal nodded and grabbed the strap of hers but staggered under the unexpected weight. She started to mention something, but her friend launched into speaking. "Listen up, everyone. I know several of you have never been hiking, so I wanted to go over a few things before we begin." The eager crowd quieted and gathered around Suzy. "Don't drink from the streams running beside the trail. You can get giardia from tainted water. If you get it, I'm abandoning you and everyone else will thank me." Her threat earned a few snickers. "Don't leave the trail. The rain forest is sensitive and can be damaged by our footfalls, but more importantly, you can get lost, and I feel guilty when that happens. It takes me at least an hour or two to get over it." This elicited a few more chuckles. "Also, streams and waterfalls are fed with snowmelt this time of year, so while they are perfect for taking snapshots, they can be dangerous to enter due to strong currents, so don't do it. Most of all, don't complain about the weight of your pack. I carry three times as much equipment up Mount Rainier every year during ECO's annual ascent, so I don't want to hear you bellyaching over this piddly thousand-foot climb."

Dead silence greeted her stern announcement. Crystal, holding her pack, bit back the objection she had been about to voice. Suzy continued after sharing a stern glance with the group. "It's time to tell you about the route we're taking. We're starting in the National Park, but we'll end the day at a campground on private property. Both the park and our campground are old growth forest and filled with wildlife, including black bears, who are particularly active in the spring. With the noise generated by a group this big, I'm sure they'll come nowhere near us. Still, watch out for them, as well as cougars." Suzy did not excel in broadcasting a we're-on-an-adventure tone but leaned more toward a we're-all-probably-going-to-die vibe in her speeches. Downcast faces and shuffling feet from her audience showed they were having second thoughts in regard to their simple hike in the woods.

Oblivious, Suzy started for the trailhead. The group struggled into their packs, including Crystal. She still couldn't believe how heavy it was. *How much safety gear did they need for what amounted to a brisk walk?* She would have to gut the three miles out, but made a mental note to hit the gym harder when she got home. If she ever wanted to ascend Rainier with Suzy, she needed to be a whole lot stronger.

Their trek began in a stand of lofty trees with little undergrowth, rays of sun shining through the canopy. The beautiful scene stretched for a hundred yards in every direction.

She fell to the rear to help any stragglers, while Suzy took the lead. The hikers captured everything with their phones, including trees, a mushroom cluster, and even attempted to capture a woodpecker in flight. As the trail began heading up in elevation, Crystal found *herself* the straggler as she huffed after everyone. She wasn't sure what her pack contained, but it must be heavier than everyone else's. She wiped the moisture from her forehead with the sleeve of her long T-shirt and dug deep to keep up.

The trail switched back several times, and the forest closed in tighter. The trees still extended upward out of sight, but dense brambles packed both sides of the trail. A rivulet of water trickled down the hillside, and it was all Crystal could do to not splash some on herself to cool off. The humid, earthen scent of the forest was refreshing, but by the time they crested the hill, sweat streamed down her face and she couldn't stop wheezing. Several of the other hikers turned to stare at the noise. Embarrassed, Crystal forced control over her body by drawing air with calm, steady inhalations. She managed a few deep breaths, but her body's craving for oxygen re-commenced her panting.

"You'll notice a remarkable difference as we continue," Suzy announced from the front of the line. "We're leaving the second growth forest behind and entering old growth." Suzy must have the conditioning of an Olympic athlete because her words rang clear. Bracing her hands on her knees, Crystal lifted her head to take a peek. Not even a drop of perspiration showed on Suzy's face.

Janice raised her hand like she was still in school, and a bemused Suzy nodded in her direction. "What's the difference between old and second growth?"

"Old growth has never been logged. Second growth has. They are both considered rain forest, but the old growth rainforest is special, and you'll soon see why."

Ignoring her discomfort, Crystal focused on what Suzy was saying. That task was a lot easier since they had paused at the top of the hill. However, the break was way too brief for Crystal's liking, and they set off. Thankfully, the trail leveled to a pleasant stroll. The straps of the pack dug into her shoulders, but Crystal no longer sounded like a dog sunning on a scorching August day. The underbrush grew denser as they traveled, filling the space under the forest canopy, even as the size of the trees increased exponentially.

The sheer variety of the green amidst the expanse of the woods astounded her. From the lime-hued moss carpeting the ground to the olive tops of the fir trees, her vision was awash with the color. Crystal called a halt as she stumbled upon a point of interest. The group stopped and returned to where she stood. Under the pretense of freeing her arms to better demonstrate, Crystal shrugged off her pack, setting it on a dry patch in the trail. Her muscles ached, but the relief of being free of the cursed weight was unbelievable. The day's gentle breeze passed over the sweat on her back, shocking her as she transitioned from over-heated to frigid. "If you'll take a closer look at this fallen tree, you'll notice a baby cedar and several ferns sprouting from the rotten section. This is called a nurse log. They not only provide nutrition for the next generation of plants in the forest, but the added height gives them a chance to reach the sunlight on the crowded forest floor." A quick round of pictures from everyone, and it was time to put on the wretched pack.

Crystal hefted it, stifling a groan and berating herself. She was a wilderness guide, for crying out loud. With her job, she should be managing this better than any of her clientele. Many of them were huffing and puffing as they started another ascent, but none came close to her exertion level.

Finally, after what felt like hours of hiking, Suzy called a halt. Crystal had been focusing on her feet, willing one ahead of the other, but now glanced up at a small lake.

"Everyone take a little break." Suzy set her pack down with nary a care in the world and unscrewed the top of her water bottle. "Drink some water and have a snack if you're hungry."

Crystal made her way to stand by Suzy's side and stifled a relieved sigh as she set her pack next to her co-guide's.

"I'm surprised none of them complained." Suzy kept her voice low.

"You did call them out at the beginning of the hike." Crystal surreptitiously attempted to work some relief into her arms.

"I'm even more surprised you didn't complain." Suzy sipped her water with a slight smile.

Feeling a little insulted, Crystal plastered on a puzzled expression. "I don't know what you mean. I feel great."

"You sure? Even after carrying a giant rock up here?" Suzy's smirk widened into a full-blown grin.

"Are you serious?" Crystal ripped open her pack and sure enough, nestled under her clothes on the bottom was a round stone, the size of her head. Grunting with the effort, she hefted the offending weight from the pack, while Suzy broke into gasping laugher. Crystal dropped it with a thud on the soft forest floor and slugged the laughing prankster in the arm.

"I am so getting you back. If this trail had kept going uphill, I'd have hyperventilated," Crystal grumbled.

"You fell for the oldest trick in the book," Suzy managed to say through her laughter.

Several of the party who had been watching grinned at their antics. One even snapped a picture of the rock.

"My friends and I are always trying to pull that trick on each other whenever we go hiking." Suzy dabbed at her eyes. "We tear our packs apart making sure no one snuck anything in. It was time for you to join the Sisterhood of the Traveling Rock."

Flattered to be included like this, Crystal couldn't help but smile. "I'll have to meet these hiking partners of yours someday. I'll chalk this up to a learning experience and will watch any of you like a hawk if you get near my pack."

"Just know the best way is to sneak little ones in, bit by bit, so they don't notice the change until they unpack for the night."

The hiker who had taken a photo of the rock tried posting the image but was surprised at the lack of signal. He wandered off, holding his phone in the air.

Suzy and Crystal both snorted in disbelief, and Crystal refocused on her friend. "Well, now that I've caught my breath, I have a question. What's up with Baranhof's property? I didn't think you could own land in a National Park."

"He doesn't own land in the park. It just happens that his property is adjacent. His family has held and protected it for decades. They were conservationists before it was popular."

"That's amazing."

"Even more so considering how much the timber is worth. This whole area outside of the park has been logged several times over the decades, and the acreage he owns is worth millions. However, I've heard rumors he's considering selling off his properties. He's seventy-two years old and doesn't have any children. They say he might cash in his chips and travel the world. It's all gossip, though. Who knows what's going to happen?"

"I bet I know who has a pretty good idea. Roxie. She's worked under this guy for years and always keeps her ear to the ground," Crystal mused. "Let's ask her tonight."

"Great idea." Suzy stretched once and nodded at the lake. "We aren't going to get there gabbing. Let's get in the canoes."

Crystal nodded and returned her attention to the resting hikers. "Time to start the next phase of our adventure. Now that everyone, but me, had a nice stroll through the woods." The crowd laughed and one girl toed the rock Crystal had cast aside. "It's time to see if you can paddle a canoe."

Suzy took over speaking. "By the lakeshore, are five three-person canoes. Has anyone canoed before?" Three hands were raised.

"Perfect. You three will take the stern position of the canoes, and Crystal and I will do the same in the other two. It's easier to control the direction from the stern than the bow. All you have to do is place the paddle along either side of the canoe and trail it in the water to steer."

"Remember to communicate to maintain a comfortable rhythm, determine proper direction, and decide on each action of the canoe. Let the inexperienced bow paddler set the cadence and the other two can match the pace by watching," Crystal interjected. She had canoed a few times in her life and was confident offering advice to novices.

They stared at the guides, a little unsure. "Is that all there is to it?" Janice scowled in the direction of the tippy watercraft.

"The best way to figure out how to do this is on the lake," Crystal explained. "It will start making sense once you begin paddling."

"Oh, and don't stand up or you might flip over. We're going to be wearing life vests, but I can guarantee your fellow passengers will not be happy if you dump them in the lake," Suzy finished with her standard comforting words.

Everyone grabbed their gear and trooped down to the lakeshore. Crystal's pack was a fraction of the weight, now that the hitchhiking stone was ditched.

Lashed to a tree were the waiting watercraft. Suzy had the first group position the baggage throughout to balance the load. After a firm shove into the water, Suzy held it steady as the selected three climbed into the rocking boat, causing the bottom of the canoe to touch on the lake bed, holding them in place. They found paddles under the seats and waited as the others were loaded.

Crystal repeated the same technique with the second and third canoes before situating herself in the stern of the fourth. Suzy oversaw the final canoe and stood alone on the shore. Stripping off her boots and socks, she tossed them alongside her pack before rolling up the bottom of her pants.

"Here we go," she exclaimed, and launched the canoes, one by one. She splashed through the water when pushing her own canoe, slinging herself aboard as it glided into the lake. The next ten minutes were chaotic as the inexperienced canoeists attempted to familiarize themselves with paddling. One girl lost her paddle and Crystal had to steer over to retrieve it. Another drifted to the left and Suzy coasted over to offer tips.

Eventually, everyone managed to get pointed in the correct direction, and Suzy's canoe struck off to lead the way.

After getting the knack, the tour group embraced the experience. Leaving the lush rainforest behind, the late May sun broke out over the lake. The rays warmed them as they glided across the serene water. A pair of mallards drifted to land twenty yards from the canoes and fish jumped to feed on insects alighting on the lake. Calling a halt to the paddling, Crystal slipped into educational mode. "If you'll look where we came from, you can examine the many layers of an old growth rainforest. The tallest Sitka spruces and western hemlocks you see are between three hundred to seven hundred years old. Mixed in are snags, which are dead trees, an important part of the ecosystem. These create homes and food sources for a multitude of creatures, including the spotted owl and several species of woodpeckers. Farther down, you'll see younger trees filling in any empty spaces, and below them are the nurse logs and smaller foliage. Throughout all of this you'll note lichen and moss covering virtually every surface. This dense canopy creates an incredibly bio-diverse ecosystem. Hundreds of animals, birds, and insects make their homes in the flora above our heads while we stroll along underneath, oblivious. This vantage from the lake allows us to appreciate the complexity of this ecosystem." Crystal did her best to be heard by everyone floating in the water. Suzy nodded her head in appreciation before calling out for everyone to resume paddling. Once they put their minds to it, the group did an efficient job. Not thirty minutes later, a small dock and several buildings came into view.

"Here we are," Suzy called. "Home sweet home for a few nights, Camp Baranhof."

They glided to a stop alongside the dock. Suzy and Crystal clambered out, and with quick twists of the ropes, lashed the canoes to the cleats. Once secured, they assisted with offloading the packs and passengers.

"I figured ya'll got lost or crashed in a glitzy hotel somewhere." Striding onto the creaking dock was the ponderous figure of their camp hostess.

"Roxie," cried Crystal. "I'm so happy to see you."

The camp chef beamed. "You, too, darlin'. How've ya been? How's our boy, Conner?" Her accent was spot on, and Crystal smiled at her dedication to the role.

"He's doing great. He'll be disappointed to have missed you."

"I'll see him next time, I'm sure. How are you Suzy, dear?"

"Happy to see you, and I can't wait to eat."

Roxie spread her arms in greeting to the rest of the bystanders. "Welcome to Camp Baranhof. We've made it as comfortable as possible for you. I'll be serving dinner in a few hours, but I invite you to explore the grounds. We have tents set up, the lake to play in, and hiking trails crisscross the property. If you want to relax, there are Adirondack chairs and a lounge in the main house, packed with books and games." She pointed at a lakeside building. Built in a log cabin style, its immense windows commanded a view of the property, and an immaculate exterior with a wrap-around covered porch promised luxury rather than rustic.

Roxie led the group like a mother duck, chattering the entire time. "If you want to skinny-dip, I have to ask you do it after sunset. We had a few fishermen get an eyeful last time, and they lodged a complaint. All I can say is I might not have the curves of my youth, but I still think it was rude to kick up a fuss."

Crystal had a hard time not laughing. These stories

were what she had come to expect from Roxie. The strangers trailing after her, though, were at a loss for words.

Taking the silence in stride, Roxie continued, "I'm fixin' to get supper ready for ya'll. I'm sure Suzy and Crystal will be happy to show you where you will be sleeping." With her pronouncement, Roxie lumbered off in the direction of the log cabin.

"Your accommodations are this way." Suzy took off down a gravel path arcing around the home. Slinging packs on their backs, the group followed.

As they rounded the cabin, Crystal was stunned. She had expected cramped tents and sleeping bags. Instead, a large expanse of white canvas had been tied taut over the top of a rustic log frame. The floor was a raised platform covered with wide hardwood planks and lavish rugs. Two single beds, plush comforters, and soft pillows gave the impression of a sultan's bedchamber rather than the tents of her youth. Past the first structure, eight similar units were positioned throughout the sparsely wooded area behind the main cabin.

"Pick wherever you want to sleep. Crystal and I will share this one closest to the cabin." Suzy took several steps and tossed her pack onto the closest bed.

The enthusiastic group broke apart and separated into pairs. Gasps and calls of appreciation showed the opulence was not lost on them.

Crystal followed Suzy to their quarters and set her pack down at the base of the bed on the right.

"This is stunning." Crystal couldn't stop herself from gushing along with the clients.

"I take it you've never been glamping before?"

"Glamping?"

"Glamorous camping. You get the feel of being in the great outdoors, but the luxury of all this." Suzy waved at the scene before them. Noticing small fairy lights strung up throughout the interior, Crystal couldn't wait to enjoy the effect at night.

"I have never experienced anything like this in my life."

"This is why we work with Frederick Baranhof. For an older guy, he keeps up with current luxury trends. Some of our clients like the true roughing it experience, but many prefer a taste of ritziness to go with their outdoors."

Crystal kicked off her boots and fell backward onto the bed. It was even more sumptuous than it appeared. "I can get used to this. What do we do the next few days?"

"We make it up as we go along." Suzy followed Crystal's example, and with a little leap, landed on her own bed, sighing in appreciation. "This is better than my mattress at home."

"What do you mean we make it up?"

"We offer guided hikes, lead canoe trips around the lake, get the evening campfire lit, that sort of thing. For the most part, they run wild and entertain themselves. These next few days are as cushy as they come."

****

The Nevada State graduates had found two horseshoe pits and were busy shouting and laughing as they flung horseshoes back and forth. As soon as she was sure the tour group was entertained, Crystal left to catch up with Roxie.

Opening the front door of the log cabin to a

spacious dining area, the plunk of something being dumped in a metal bowl let her know where to find the hostess. The sweet aroma of baking filled the cabin, and Crystal took an appreciative breath to savor the scent. A sliding glass door on the back wall, covered in condensation from the warmth, was cracked to let in fresh air. Through the misty glass was an expansive deck overlooking a path trailing into the dense, green forest.

A hallway led away from the main area toward the bedrooms and bathroom. Stepping around an impressive dining table hewn from a single slab of wood, Crystal turned a corner to spot Roxie humming as she busied herself at the stove.

"Hey, Roxie. Whatcha cooking?"

Roxie whirled around with a masher in her hand, flinging potatoes across the kitchen counter. "Land sakes, hon. You 'bout gave me a heart attack."

"Sorry to sneak up on you. Does something have you on edge?"

"Actually, yes. My boss is supposed to be coming by and plans on staying tonight."

"Is he the type of boss where that's a bad thing?"

Roxie patted her chest, and even though it was just the two of them, continued in her character. "Not in the least. He's a sweetheart, and we've gotten along tremendously since he first hired me, but he was cryptic when he called. He said he wanted to meet and discuss the future of the company. I'm worried he wants to shut it down and retire. He's getting up there, so I knew this would come to an end eventually. I suppose it's got me a little anxious." Waving her free hand to dismiss the subject, Roxie pointed her potato masher at a woven basket covered with a tea towel. "Go ahead and grab a cornbread muffin."

Lifting the edge, Crystal snatched one. "Don't mind if I do." Crystal sat at a small breakfast table situated in the corner of the kitchen and stretched for the butter. "Suzy said something similar, but who would be interested in a place like this other than a logging company?"

Roxie snorted contemptuously. "Loggers aren't going to get the time of day from Freddy. He doesn't want to see this beautiful forest ruined after his family has protected it all these years."

"That's a relief. There isn't a lot of old growth around anymore."

"He's been talking to a developer, though. I know what they would do. They'd carve out the heart of the estate and put in luxury condos, vacation homes, and a golf course like they did a little farther down the highway. Their pitch is they'll keep most of the forest intact, but Freddy's too smart to believe them."

The tender cornbread's crisp outer layer and moist interior tantalized her tastebuds with a touch of sweetness. "These muffins are delicious," Crystal said through a mouthful. "How's all of this going over with the locals?"

"As far as I know, no news has been leaked regarding anything happening here. Thank goodness, too. Nothing riles the local eco-conscious souls more than a threat to old growth. There are environmental activists who will tie themselves to trees if they catch wind the logging companies might get a crack at this forest, and the locals have mixed feelings dealing with the developers. Some welcome the opportunity for work, but others hate the idea of luring a bunch of tourists to their quiet town. It's a pretty jumbled mess."

"Wow, has there been any trouble?"

"None, but like I said, Freddy has kept it pretty hush-hush."

Crystal braced herself and asked the hard question troubling her. "What are you going to do if Mr. Baranhof sells off his holdings?"

Roxie put her palms down on the table and took a deep breath. She gave a hefty sigh, and when she spoke, it was without a hint of her accent. "I have no idea. This is all I know. I don't have enough to retire, so I'd have to figure out something. Maybe I'd go back to working in a restaurant."

"That wouldn't be so bad." Crystal could feel the unhappiness this proposition caused and wanted to cheer her up. Having recently gone through an unstable period of employment, Crystal sympathized with the stress it could wreak on a person's mental health.

"Let's just say I'm not employable for a wide variety of reasons. Freddy saw past all of that. He's been a friend to me for decades, and it's tough to imagine life without him."

"Maybe you could work with ECO Adventures?"

"I'm a hostess and a chef." Roxie gave a wan smile. "Your company is dedicated to wilderness guiding, not hosting luxury getaways. Unless they change how they do things dramatically, I don't see me working with you."

Sighing, Crystal admitted the truth of her words. Trying to break the melancholy mood, she changed the subject. "You still haven't told me what's for dinner, other than these delicious corn muffins." She took another generous bite.

Just like that, Roxie's hostess persona returned along with her accent. "Country ham, spuds, and black-eyed peas are on the menu. To finish the evening, peach cobbler. I even brewed some sweet tea. It's in the fridge if you want a glass." Crystal helped herself to the tea, and Roxie recommenced mashing the potatoes. "How're you and Conner doing?"

"Conner and I are perfect." Crystal took a sip and reeled at the overwhelming sugar. Despite the name, she hadn't expected tea-flavored syrup. "I can't believe how much I love spending time with him."

"Oh, is it love? Have you told him?" Roxie winked at Crystal as she added sour cream to the bowl and gave it a final stir.

"Actually, he told me months ago and I told him the same."

"Good for both of you." Roxie beamed. "And especially for you. You never want to be the first to put yourself out there and say it, but land sakes it feels good to hear it when you feel the same way. Nothin' worse than hearin' 'I love you' when you don't feel likewise. Talk about some awkward moments."

Crystal stared at Roxie in astonishment. "How often have men professed their love to you?"

Roxie grimaced as she started peeling peaches. "Hasn't happened for a few years, but you know what I mean, right?"

"Roxie, I believe you and I have had very different love lives. Suitors haven't exactly been throwing themselves at my feet. My mother had convinced herself I was going to be a spinster at the ripe old age of twenty-seven."

"Has your family met Conner?"

"My parents met him, once. I keep thinking I'm going to invite him to Sunday brunch, but they're a lot to handle. My parents have asked me to bring him, but so far I'm avoiding the situation."

"Crystal, you aren't doing this for them, but for Conner. If he told you he loves you, you need to invite him into your family to show you're serious."

Crystal mulled over the advice. "I never considered it from his perspective. My family was so nosy even when I had nothing going on in my life, it became second nature to block them out. You know, you're right. I should take him to next Sunday's family brunch." The decision brought on a bout of queasiness and the food abruptly went tasteless.

Roxie nodded in sympathy. "From the way you turned green and put the muffin down, I can tell you're nervous. You know why you're feeling this way? It's because you care. You wouldn't feel so ill at ease if you weren't worried it might go horribly wrong."

Crystal nodded silently.

"Tell me this, Crystal," Roxie said softly. "Are your parents terrible human beings?"

"What? No." Crystal was put off by the question.

"Is your sister? Do you think she will embarrass you to the point Conner won't want to be with you anymore?" The absurdity of Roxie's questions made her smile. "You see? It'll be fine. Before you know it, he'll be part of the family."

Crystal's nerves eased. "Thanks, Roxie. You've helped put it into perspective. I think I might have been making a mountain out of a mole hill."

"It's all in a hostess's job description. Make your

guests comfortable and happy." Roxie threw her another wink as she poured an absurd amount of sugar onto the peeled peaches.

The front door opened, and Crystal tilted back in her chair to peer around the corner.

A distinguished man in wire-rimmed glasses, impeccably styled hair, and a close-cropped graying beard stood in the doorway. His dark blue slacks and matching suit jacket marked him as out of place in the middle of the forest.

"May I help you?" Crystal used the helpful tone of voice she had cultivated for dealing with the public.

"My name is Frederick Baranhof. I'm here to speak with Ms. Roxanne Bloomfield."

Chapter Three

Crystal tilted her chair past the point of no return, but she managed to slap her hands down to brace herself on the table an instant before toppling over. Catching her balance, she stood and composed herself.

"Mr. Baranhof, it's a pleasure to meet you." Crystal extended her hand, remembering at the last moment that it was covered in butter and grease from the corn muffin. Retracting the offending limb, she wiped it on a napkin. Re-extending her hand, she thought better of it, and dropped it to her side.

Roxie saved her from further embarrassment by stepping by her and embracing him in a warm hug. In true professional manner, she refused to step out of her southern character. "Freddy! It's been too long. Goodness gracious, I haven't seen you in over a year."

Looking over Roxie's head, he nodded to Crystal. "Only two people in my life have ever gotten away with calling me Freddy. Roxie and my mother. Even my late wife called me Fred."

Roxie released her employer from the hug. "I'm being rude. Freddy, this is Crystal Rainey."

A Hollywood-worthy smile lit up his face, all straight and bright teeth. "Ahh…Ms. Rainey. I've wanted to meet you. I never did get a chance to thank you for assisting in clearing up the unfortunate matter that occurred at my chalet last year."

"I was happy to help." Crystal had never heard a murder described in such a casual fashion. Frederick Baranhof was the master of understatement.

"The police were beginning to create all manner of difficulties this past winter, trying to shut down the property during prime rental season. I was most pleased when you stepped in."

A timer on the stove chimed. Roxie opened the oven to check on the ham and pronounced it finished.

"What a stroke of luck. I'm in time for dinner," Frederick announced. "I have been missing your fine cooking. I need to make a point to visit more often when you're working."

"I'm always happy to put out another plate for you. After the ham rests a short spell, it'll be time to eat. Would you like to dine in the common area or in your room?"

"Crystal, do your guests know each other?" Frederick peered over his bifocals.

"They do, sir." She didn't know what made her say 'sir', but his aristocratic bearing demanded the honorific.

"Then I would hate to be a boor and interrupt their retreat by intruding. Roxie, would you deliver a plate to my quarters? I have some documents I need to go over before my meetings tomorrow. I would also like to speak with you this evening after you have finished your tasks."

"I'll pop in after I'm done cleaning up." Roxie pulled an electric carving knife from a drawer.

"Splendid. Crystal, it's been a pleasure." His brisk strides took him from the room.

"He's sorta impressive, isn't he?" Crystal dropped

her voice to a whisper.

"He is, dear. But he puts his pants on one leg at a time, just like the rest of us. When it comes down to it, I think he's lonely. The regal attitude serves him well in business, but not when it comes to happiness. It's one of the reasons I make a point to not let work interfere with our friendship."

"You're a pretty great person, Roxie." Crystal's heart swelled in admiration for her kind friend.

"That's sweet of you to say. Now, will you ring the dinner bell? By the time the guests wash up, it'll be time to eat."

"The dinner bell?"

"I bought a bell, just like the good old days, and I've been hankering to see if it works. I hung it on the back porch. Give it a ring and let's see if they come runnin'."

"Sounds like fun." Crystal found the dinner bell outside the door. A large iron triangle and its striker dangled from a hook in a rafter. Charmed with the quaintness, she poked the striker in the triangle and banged it around. Clear musical notes carried into the camp and Suzy popped her head out of the tent.

"What's going on?"

"What do you think is going on? Come and get it."

"Finally. I'm famished." Suzy rushed from the tent.

Pete strode around the corner of the cabin and spotted Crystal standing by the dinner bell. He shouted, "I told you it was time to eat. Come on, everybody."

****

Suzy prodded her belly. "I feel like I'm going to explode."

"It was the extra helping of cobbler," Crystal

groaned from her bed. "We shouldn't have done that."

"I bet this is what a bear feels like before it hibernates for winter," Suzy muttered. "I think I'll sleep for six months."

"We're going to need at least that long. I wish I could send Conner a text to see how his class went, though."

"This place has Wi-Fi, Crystal. We're glamping, not camping. Cell phone coverage may be awful, but Wi-Fi was added to keep the customers happy."

Crystal dug her phone from her pack and powered it on.

A text from Conner greeted her—*How's your trip going?*—

—*Outstanding. Roxie is here. Hope you don't mind a round girlfriend. Suzy and I are going to have to be wheelbarrowed out of here after a few more days of her cooking.*—

He responded a minute later—*Lol. I know that feeling. Tell her hi from me.*—

Suzy's breath deepened into sleep as Crystal carried on her conversation.

—*How was the rock climbing class?*—

—*Everyone learned a lot. You could say they reached new heights.*— Crystal bit back a sigh inspired by the pun.

Roxie's raised voice erupted from the log cabin. Crystal couldn't make out what was being said, so she ignored it and responded to Conner.

—*Glad to hear it. I'm heading into a food coma. Sweet dreams. Love you.*—

—*Love you, too. Sleep tight.*—

Crystal switched off her phone. Her eyelids

drooped, but the argument happening in the cabin kept her from drifting off.

"What's going on?" Suzy hadn't budged an inch, and her voice was groggy.

"I think Roxie and Frederick are having a disagreement," Crystal whispered.

"About what?"

"I can't make out any words." Crystal strained her ears for all she was worth. "Earlier, he said he wanted to talk to her tonight. Roxie thinks he wants to sell off his properties and retire."

"The rumors must be true. Why didn't you say so?" Suzy sat bolt upright.

"Is it a big deal?"

"It's huge. A lot of ECO Adventures overnight trips are planned around his properties. Without them, we'll have to restructure most of the excursions we do."

"I didn't know." Worry began gnawing at her abdomen. "I haven't been doing this long enough to realize how important the situation was."

"Did she tell you anything else?"

"Not much. He spoke with a logger and a developer, but—"

"What?" Suzy almost shouted, but Crystal made shushing motions with her hands and shot a glare at her boisterous companion. Suzy ignored the look, grabbed a glass from her nightstand, and flung the water out the tent flaps and onto a fern. "You coming?"

Crystal jumped up, unsure what Suzy had in mind, but willing to join in whatever escapade she was planning.

Suzy stepped into her boots without lacing them before glancing back and forth outside the entrance.

Distant conversations filled the campground, but they were quieting as dusk settled. However, the loud discussion in the cabin continued unabated.

Placing her finger to her lips, Suzy crept out of their tent in her sweatpants and T-shirt, tiptoeing to the side of the cabin. Crystal followed in her own pajama pants, T-shirt, and unlaced shoes, doing her best to mimic Suzy's burglar-esque walk. When she arrived at the wall, Suzy lifted her glass and settled it against the side of the cabin, laying her ear against it.

"What are they saying?" Crystal's curiosity had always been too strong for her own good.

"Roxie said, 'You can't come in here and sell the ham,' " Suzy murmured.

"I bet she said 'land'. You've got ham on the brain."

Lowering her voice to indicate it was Frederick. Suzy said, "I can do what I want, Roxie. It's my ham, I mean land, after all."

Crystal gasped, covering her mouth. "Roxie was right."

Suzy held up a palm for quiet. "Both of them will clearcut the forest. Can't you sell to someone who'll take care of it?"

"What are you two doing?" Janice's high-pitched voice rang out behind them. Suzy lowered the glass, and they spun to see the willowy redhead glaring down, judgement radiating from her expression. "You shouldn't be eavesdropping." She tilted her nose up and sniffed at their antics.

Stepping away from the cabin and heading toward their beds, Suzy played it cool. "What is it you think we were doing?"

Crystal walked in sync with Suzy, forming a moving barricade to the interloper.

"You were listening in on them. That's an invasion of their privacy."

Suzy snorted. "I'm sorry. I didn't realize you were a member of the privacy police. Are you going to arrest us for first degree snooping?"

The girl flared up. "You can't talk to me like that. I'll write you such a bad review no one will ever go on a tour with your company again."

Back in their tent, Suzy flopped down, unconcerned. "Go ahead, officer—"

Crystal shot a sharp glance at her touchy friend. "What Suzy meant to say," Crystal cut in hastily, "is we're concerned." She didn't let the ridiculousness of taking the moral high road while sporting pajama pants decorated with cartoon cats ruin her argument.

"Concerned? Why?" Suspicion infused Janice's words.

"Can you keep a secret?"

"Of course I can." She leaned in, eager to hear the gossip. It was astounding how fast she vaulted from her high horse when she was included.

"The owner of the camp is considering selling this property. The two most interested parties are a developer and a logging company."

"What? They can't do that. This is old growth forest."

"Nothing's set in stone, but we wanted to hear what's going on to see if we could...umm...help. I guess." Crystal winced at the lame finish of her self-righteous speech.

"Good for you." Janice bobbed her head up and

down, with more than a touch of condescension, in Crystal's opinion. "I didn't know what you were doing. I apologize for rushing to conclusions."

"Thanks. That means a lot," Suzy said wryly.

Hearing the subtle tones of sarcasm in her friend's voice, Crystal attempted to hustle the conversation to an end. "Anything else, Janice?"

"I'm wondering what your plan is."

"Plan? I guess we'll try to talk to Mr. Baranhof, the owner."

Janice snorted her disdain. "I'm sure that'll work. Sounds like it's going great for our chef."

"We'll think of something," Crystal assured her.

With a last skeptical look, Janice shook her head and left.

As she passed from ear shot, Suzy let loose, "If the girl were wound any tighter, her head would pop off. Who asked her to stick her freckled nose where it doesn't belong? You should have let me take her down a peg, Crystal."

Turning, Crystal admonished Suzy. "Like it or not, those type of reviews make or break our business. Do you want to explain to Amelia why we got torn apart by an angry client? I know I don't."

At Amelia's name, Suzy dropped her head. "I suppose you're right. I miss the good old days when you could rip an idiot a new one and not have to worry."

"You're not even thirty years old, Suzy. I think these are your good old days. Now, get some sleep."

****

A myriad of bird songs woke Crystal at dawn. She snuggled under her covers, enchanted as the first sporadic calls crescendoed into a symphony filling the forest. This, to her, was the best part of sleeping outdoors. Not wanting to wake her snoring tent-mate, she slid from her bed and changed from pajamas into a long sleeve tee and a pair of jeans. Tugging on a red fleece, adorned with more than a little hair from her cat, Elf, she left to walk the camp in the morning calm.

Stopping near the dock, she sat down on a bench overlooking the serene lake. Her meditative moment was ruined when a groundskeepers' truck towing a trailer full of equipment rattled to a stop in the dirt parking lot. Two guys in the cab emerged, laughing.

"Can you believe those weirdos?" the older one asked.

"What do they think they're going to accomplish? No one's trying to cut down their precious trees. You'd think we had a truck full of chainsaws instead of hedge trimmers," the second added. They both chuckled at the absurdity of the notion.

Curious, Crystal approached the two groundskeepers, "What's going on fellas?"

They both gave her a quick glance as they positioned a ramp at the back of their trailer. "Some tree huggers are at the front entrance to the camp, literally hugging trees. They blocked us by standing in the road until we explained we're groundskeepers. They have it in their heads someone is coming to level this place."

Feeling an unpleasant source of dread, Crystal ventured a nervous laugh. "How funny. I wonder where they got that crazy idea? How far is it to the entrance anyway?"

"Just a half mile up this road. You gonna go catch

the circus show?"

A circus show? That couldn't be good. "I think I'll check it out."

Leaving the two to their work, Crystal acted casual as she sauntered in the indicated direction. Once she passed the first corner, she double-timed it. As she approached the end of the road, music and voices filled the air.

Rounding the final corner, she froze in astonishment. Four cars were parked catawampus by the entrance of the camp. Ten or so people milled as a small stereo blasted Reggae.

Hippie was the only word Crystal could think to describe them.

The exception to the general flower child appearance of the growing throng was a passing tall, muscular man with short brown hair and a tie-dye shirt. She grabbed him and asked, "What are you doing here?"

"Saving the trees, ya know? Are you here to help us?" His deep green, piercing eyes and short, trimmed beard were captivating, especially when coupled with his impressive physique.

"No, I'm not..." she trailed off as two more cars arrived. Passengers spilled out to join the growing throng. Returning her attention to the conversation, she continued, "What makes you think something's going to happen to these trees?"

"It's all over Twitter. Someone named 'Stormy Janice' posted it on the Earth Warden Account. She said we needed to take immediate action to preserve this bastion of the rain forest."

Crystal dropped her head into her hands. Nosy,

pain-in-the-keister Janice had made a gargantuan mess of the situation. If word got out how Mr. Baranhof's private discussions had become public, Crystal and Suzy were in serious trouble.

"Heeeey." A statuesque blonde in a flowing sundress bounded up. "How've you been, Tyler?"

"If you aren't a sight to behold. It's been years, Misha."

Misha flung herself into his arms. Tyler caught her and swung her around. Her dress flared and Crystal stepped backward to avoid getting clobbered by the whirling feet.

She laughed as Tyler set her down. "What's the plan this time?" she asked.

"We're going to assemble a platform on that awesome hemlock over there," he said pointing. "I've studied how the artist Tadashi Kawamata used rubber sheaths to protect the tree trunk from damage when we build. I'm going to live up there *au naturel* until they agree to leave the forest intact. Everyone's ready to keep me supplied for as long as this takes."

"Why do you have to be naked?" Crystal couldn't help but ask.

Expecting some half-baked holistic answer regarding being in touch with his primal self, she was surprised to see him turn to her with a calculating look. "This stunt is an attention grabber. The more outrageous the scene, the more coverage the situation will receive. All of those gathered here have social media accounts with thousands of followers. If we get enough attention, we put pressure on the owner. Enough pressure, and he'll bow to society's wishes."

Inwardly, she wanted nothing more than the

animals and trees to live here, unharmed, forever. In the meantime, though, this was going to cause her a whole heap of trouble.

Chapter Four

Leaving Tyler and his friends behind, Crystal hurried back to the campground. People were stirring, probably due to scents of the waffle and bacon breakfast permeating the camp.

Inside their tent, Suzy sat on the edge of her bed, yawning and rubbing her eyes.

"Hey, Suze. We've got trouble."

Suzy dropped her hands and blinked several times. "Geez, Crystal. I just woke up. Did Janice blab to Mr. Baranhof?"

"Oh, she blabbed, but not to him. She posted it on Twitter and a bunch of protesters are gathering at the entrance of the camp. They're here because of what I told Janice."

Fighting a prodigious yawn, Suzy swore. "She's as obnoxious as a blackberry seed stuck in your tooth."

"What do you think we should do?"

Suzy gave a resigned shrug. "What can we do? I don't think we'll be able to hide it for long, so we better come clean."

"You're right." Crystal's heart sank. It made her feel like a child again, when she and her sister had made a mess they couldn't cover up, and the time had come to own up to their parents.

Crystal took off for a walk around the camp as the smell of breakfast continued to tease her nose. The guilt overwhelmed her, and she couldn't wait any longer to confess.

Inside the cabin, Frederick Baranhof sat alone, eating at the head of the large dining table. He pored over documents while absentmindedly cutting a waffle with his knife and fork. Her stomach rumbled at the sight of food, and Crystal willed her body from making any further unwanted noises.

Looking up from the stack of paper, he gave her a soft smile. "Good morning, Miss Rainey. Care to join me for breakfast?"

"Actually, there is something I need to discuss with you, first."

He raised his brows at the seriousness of her tone. "Certainly. What's on your mind?" He crossed his utensils on his plate and gave her his undivided attention.

"Suzy and I overheard you and Roxie speaking last night." No need to mention the whole listening at the wall. Confession was good for the soul, but there was no need to hang yourself when someone handed you a rope. "I may have mentioned to one of our guests you were considering selling to a developer, and she posted it on social media. Twitter to be exact."

Roxie returned from the kitchen with two cups of coffee. Frederic nodded his appreciation. "This explains why I have Bohemians at the entrance of my property."

"You know?"

"The Forks police called and asked if I wanted them removed. I didn't see any need to man-handle them, so I declined."

Roxie returned with a plate for Crystal, the waffle invisible beneath a mountain of strawberries and whipped cream. Roxie didn't even need to ask how Crystal liked her waffle topped.

"I am indeed considering selling, as you overheard last night. I have several meetings today to explore different options. I am reviewing the offers and wanted to discuss with prospective buyers their plans if I were to sell the land. This information was going to be revealed sooner or later, so please don't worry yourself."

Crystal felt the stress melt away like the whipped cream on her plate. She took a seat next to her food. "I won't bother you any further, Mr. Baranhof. I know you have a lot of work to do."

Frederick nodded and returned to his task. Crystal ate in silence and carried her plate to the kitchen as soon as she finished.

Dicing up ham from the previous night, Roxie greeted her.

"I only had a little waffle batter left over, as well as a rasher of bacon. If you come back in an hour, or so, I'll be making omelets to order."

"I'm stuffed, but I might join you anyway."

Roxie glanced up from her dicing with a twinkle in her eye, "Did I hear we have hippies in our camp?"

"You heard right. One of them said he's getting buck naked and living up a tree."

"Finally, a show worth seeing. The most interesting things seem to happen when you visit me."

****

After a second breakfast—Crystal couldn't help returning for an omelet with the others—Suzy and Crystal gathered the tour group and shared the options for the day. The sun had broken out of the morning clouds, causing several to opt for a canoe trip led by Suzy to the north shore of the lake. The rest followed Crystal on a hike through the property.

They split up, and Crystal, using a map provided by Suzy, led the four who had joined her into the surrounding trees. The trail of trimmed foliage showed the gardeners had been down the path this morning.

Striding through the lush forest, Crystal described items of interest along the way and answered questions. Several lichens, the size of a person's head, sprouted from the sides of tree trunks, and moss dangled from every available branch, imparting a feeling of prehistoric times. Janice had chosen to join the hike and was obsessed with learning as much as she could, asking numerous questions every time they stumbled upon a new plant or tree. The nosy troublemaker had seized the role of eco-protector with a vengeance.

At several points along the wider main path, smaller, overgrown trails merged. Curious, Crystal peered down them. They were marked on her map, so weren't game trails blazed by passing deer, but the verdant spring threatened to overtake them soon if someone didn't maintain them.

After completing a three-mile loop wending through the property, the hikers thanked her and chose to go for a swim. Crystal opted to head to the tent to ditch her fleece. Passing the parking lot, she spotted two pick-up trucks that hadn't been there earlier. The dented, older brick-red model displayed a tree silhouette logo and the name Forks Logging Company. A gun rack was mounted in the rear window, with two rifles on display. From the gleam of paint and chrome, the sleek black truck parked adjacent may have been driven off a dealer's lot the previous day, and had the name of the local developer, Evergreen Resorts, emblazoned on the door in green and white.

Frederick stood on the far side of the parking lot, speaking with two people as disparate from each other as the two vehicles. A grizzled man with a bushy gray beard and dressed in overalls squinted at Frederick. Beside him stood a woman in a dark blue pant suit, her wedges giving her an inch or two height advantage. She ran her fingers through the side of her dark hair to straighten non-existent flyaways that had no chance of getting loose from her flawless hairstyle. The three of them were talking and gesturing toward various points of the property. Crystal sat on the bench she'd occupied earlier in the morning and cast surreptitious glances at them. The businesswoman sported a permanent grin as she waved her arms in grand fashion during her sales pitch. The bearded codger scowled throughout her entire speech. After a few minutes of this, Frederick shook the woman's hand. He then proffered a handshake to the woodsman, but the gesture only earned a glare before the furious man stormed off. The angry logger spat on the ground with the vigor only a man chewing tobacco could muster and jumped in his company truck. Gravel sprayed behind him as he sped out of the parking lot. After he disappeared from view, the developer launched back into her spiel for another few minutes before finally taking her leave when Frederick's expression didn't budge.

Looking out over the water, Crystal spotted Suzy returning to camp with her group. Jumping up, she strode down to the dock and waited as they approached. "Did you have a good time?" The canoeists chorused their assent and flung her the ropes. Crystal cinched them tight and assisted everyone from the swaying watercraft.

Seeing several of their friends swimming in the lake, the others left to join in the fun, hustling away from Crystal and Suzy.

"I spied on Frederick talking to a logger and a developer." Crystal kept her voice low. Maybe it was closing the barn door after letting an entire herd of horses run free, but no need to spread even more gossip.

"You did?" Suzy gasped.

"The logger was as angry as a wet badger, but the developer was still trying to convince him up to the moment she left."

"I can't believe it. I hope they don't damage this breathtaking place too much if they buy it."

"Roxie's plight worries me, too. If he sells his properties, she'll be out of a job." As if summoned, Roxie appeared, strolling down the road toward the protester encampment.

"Let's go catch up with her," Crystal urged.

Roxie slowed when she spotted them approaching and spoke with her typical southern hostess drawl. "Are ya'll fixin' to check out the fun, too?"

"No, we wanted to discuss Mr. Baranhof selling the property," Suzy said.

"Oh that? The two of us talked last night, and I listened in on his conversation with Crystal this morning during breakfast. I know he's planning on retiring."

"Have you given any more thought as to what you're going to do when he sells?" Crystal hated pressing such a difficult subject, but Roxie didn't look upset at her words.

"I'll be fine. I came to terms with it last night. It's been a good run and I appreciate everything Freddy has done for me. I'll keep working as long as he needs me, and then I'll figure out what to do afterward. It's how I've led my whole life. I'm just a little rusty at flying by the seat of my pants after this cushy spell. Right now, I'm more interested in checking out what this naked guy I keep hearing about is up to than figurin' out my future."

Walking down the gravel road in companionable silence at Roxie's slow pace, Crystal pondered. Their lives were all going to change. Roxie was forced to contemplate a whole new future, while ECO Adventures would have to reinvent many of the favorite trips that had earned their company such a sterling reputation.

The familiar strains of Bob Marley grew louder as they approached the entrance to the campground. They froze when they made it around the final bend. The small gathering at early dawn had become full-blown bedlam. Nearly fifty eco-protesters were milling in chaotic fashion by the side of the road. One man with dreadlocks banged on a drum in sync with the music, while several others danced in a circle around him. Some pitched tents in a nearby clearing in the forest, while still others threw frisbees, sat on rocks, or smoked what didn't look like commercial cigarettes. Crystal gave a sniff, recognizing the odor from her college days. Definitely not tobacco.

However, some were carrying supplies to the tree in the center of the clearing Tyler had indicated would be his perch, and the epicenter of the protest. Despite the crazy scene, a lot had been accomplished. A shaky-looking platform had been erected fifty feet above the ground. Tyler appeared at the edge wearing a hard hat, tool belt, and nothing else.

"Whoa," Roxie said in appreciation.

"I've seen a lot of wild things in the woods, but this is one of the craziest." Suzy shook her head.

Heaving a rope lashed to several two by fours, Tyler hauled the wood up the tree, his corded muscles handling the load with ease.

"I don't know if I believe the malarkey regarding his nakedness making a statement," Roxie said good-naturedly. "With the gifts God gave him, I'm sure he's just itchin' for chances to take off his clothes."

A babble of excitement coursed through the crowd. A knot of onlookers parted, and a reporter, trailed by a cameraman, stalked up to the base of the tree.

After fifteen minutes of adjusting the lens, checking the angle of the light, sound checks, and a make-up retouching, the reporter began his monologue, "I'm here at Camp Baranhof, a few miles outside of Forks, to witness the protest of the possible sale of this pristine forest to either a logging company or developer intent on leveling it. The individuals around me have gathered to voice their objection that these shrinking woodlands will be one more casualty in the war against unimpeded progress. Tyler Hammond, a well-known voice for environmental conservation, has vowed to live in the old growth tree above us until the forest's future is confirmed to be in safe hands." The reporter gave a dramatic pause. "And he's going to do it all, without clothes."

"He won't have to do it alone." Without a single

stitch on her voluptuous body, Misha emerged from the forest. Her Marilyn Monroe stride wasn't marred one bit by the inevitable mud and water one attracted traveling through a rain forest. The cameraman swiveled to record her self-assured walk to the base of the tree.

Tyler flashed a wide, perfect grin from his perch above them, his teeth gleaming in the sun filtering through the canopy of his tree. "Misha, I'd be honored to have you join me."

"We'll stand for what's right, together. Can a girl get a hand up?"

Tyler kicked the rope at his feet, and it unraveled down the length of the tree. Cheers filled the glade at Misha's bold appearance, and the cameraman zoomed out to record her clinging to the rope as Tyler hauled her up the tree. Soon, she stood beside him on the platform, which must have been sturdier than it appeared to hold both of them. They clasped hands and thrust them in the air to joyful hollers.

"I must say, beautiful people getting naked and a full-blown party breaking out is high entertainment. I'm glad we made the trip down here." This rowdy group of environmentalists had produced an enormous grin on Roxie's face, and she swiveled her head in an attempt to catch every bit of the action.

The reporter left the base of Tyler and Misha's tree and began circulating, asking questions, and presenting his microphone for the answers.

"I don't want to leave this behind, but we better get back for lunchtime." Roxie sighed with both satisfaction and disappointment. "We're going to have some hungry guests soon."

Suzy grimaced at the reminder that they were working. They took one last look at the fun before turning together to head to camp. Crystal hadn't taken more than one step when a voice called out behind her. Spinning, she found a microphone shoved in her face.

"What precipitated your coming here today to protest Frederick Baranhof's possible decision to sell this old growth forest to a logging company?" The reporter stood close enough that Crystal could see the glistening of the pomade holding his immaculate salt and pepper hair in a modern pompadour.

"Oh, I'm not protesting."

"So, you agree with Mr. Baranhof? You think it's his right to dispose of his land how he chooses, no matter the consequences?"

Several faces behind the reporter darkened at his questioning, but their glares were centered on Crystal, not on the reporter or his leading questions.

"I didn't say—" Crystal protested, but Roxie stepped between the reporter and Crystal.

"Who do you think you are?" Lifting her head to look up at the man, Roxie poked the reporter in the sternum, hard enough to make him grunt. "You're putting words in other's mouths to make them agree with the story you've already written and are casting them as villains to be demonized."

The reporter transferred his focus to Roxie. "Then tell me, what are your feelings on Frederick Baranhof selling his property?"

Working herself into a righteous anger, she jabbed him in the chest again. "I wish he wasn't, and I told him so. I don't want anything to happen to this one-of-a-kind forest, and I don't want to lose my job. However, he's free to do what he wants. How would you like it if you couldn't sell your house because someone liked the rose bushes in front? Doesn't seem fair, does it?"

With a final piercing glare at the reporter, she wheeled and marched toward the camp, flanked by Suzy and Crystal.

"Thanks for coming to my rescue, Roxie. I was shocked when he surprised me with that microphone."

"You let the jerk have it," Suzy added with enthusiasm. "I wish I'd thought to tell him off."

"Thanks," Roxie said. "It makes me madder than a wet hen to see my friends picked on by bullies."

****

Back at camp, Roxie produced lunch from the refrigerator. Suzy and Crystal helped by carrying an impressive spread of sandwich makings and paper plates to a series of picnic tables overlooking the lake.

Suzy rang the dinner bell this time, and the tour group gathered for their midday meal. Crystal joined the throng and had completed the assembly of her roast beef sandwich when the now grating tone of Janice rose over the crowd. "I don't see any Dijon mustard. Does anyone see the Dijon?" After a chorus of negatives answered her question, she focused on Crystal, who had been trying to avoid her attention. "Will you check if Roxie has any?"

Fighting an unprofessional sigh, Crystal set down her paper plate and walked inside the log cabin. Roxie wasn't there, so she rooted around to see if she could find the missing condiment. She was on the verge of giving up and returning to lunch, when the image of Janice's sneer, and her threats of bad reviews, flashed in her mind. With a grimace, she called out, "Roxie?

Are you here?"

Just above a whisper, an answer came from one of the back rooms. "In here."

Venturing down the hallway, she peered in the first room. Roxie's coat was slung over a chair, but she wasn't there. Seeing another door open, she headed farther down the hallway and asked, "Where do you keep...?" The question died on her lips. Roxie stood with a massive chef's knife clutched in her hand over the still form of Frederic Baranhof. Blood stained the blade, and crimson pooled around the unmoving body.

Chapter Five

"Roxie! What happened?" Crystal fumbled for her phone.

Roxie turned, a dazed expression on her face. "I came in with his lunch, and he was just lying like this."

Crystal noted the plate of food atop the dresser. Her hand trembled so violently it was difficult to type the three digits, but she managed to dial.

"Nine-one-one, what is the nature of your emergency?"

"I'm at the log cabin at Camp Baranhof. It looks like Frederick Baranhof has been stabbed. I don't think he's alive."

Roxie stood mutely, her forlorn gaze fixated on the body of her friend and employer.

"We have an ambulance and police en route."

"Thank you." Crystal hung up before the operator could ask any follow-up questions. Timidly, Crystal crouched down to check his pulse, careful not to touch the oozing blood. Fumbling around his neck, she detected no response from his carotid artery.

"Roxie." Crystal stuffed the panic inside and managed to keep her voice gentle. "Did you find the knife by the body?"

"I did. It's my knife."

The hollow tones from the normally vivacious hostess caused Crystal to look at her face. The dazed expression was still present, and her skin was several shades paler than her normal dusky hue. Crystal coaxed her to return to the kitchen. The shocked chef followed her lead, gently setting the knife on the counter. Guiding her by the elbow, Crystal eased Roxie into one of the chairs at the breakfast table.

"Do you have any idea what happened?" Crystal sat across from her.

Tears trickled down Roxie's cheeks. "None. I laid out lunch with you and Suzy for the tour group. Afterward, I made Freddy's favorite, ham and Swiss on rye, but when I took it to him…" It was too much, and her deep breath morphed into a sob. Soon her whole body rocked back and forth as the reality of the situation sank in. Crystal put an arm around her and whispered it would be okay, the police would be here soon, and they would get to the bottom of it.

"Hey, what's taking so long? Janice is getting herself worked up out there." Suzy's voice wrenched Crystal from her own daze.

"Suzy, someone murdered Mr. Baranhof." Crystal's announcement wracked Roxie with another round of sobs.

"What? No. Are you serious?"

"Deadly serious." Crystal cringed at her unintentional and inappropriate pun. "I've already called the police." In the distance, sirens grew steadily louder.

"What's going on in here?" Janice strolled into the cabin. "Did you find the mustard?"

Suzy pointed an accusing finger at Janice, who took a hasty step away at the furious expression on the wilderness guide's face. "No one was aware of the possible sale of the property until we told you. You promised Crystal you would keep it secret, but you couldn't help yourself." Janice took another step back as Suzy approached.

"But—" Janice's protest was cut off by Suzy.

"But, what? 'Stormy Janice' of Twitter had to announce it to the world."

Janice flared up. "So what if I did?"

"And now, someone killed Mr. Baranhof over it."

Janice paled. "What do you mean?"

"Do you hear those sirens? They're coming here." Suzy was remorseless.

Janice spun and fled, flinging open the door and sprinting to her friends.

With the door left open from her abrupt departure, they had a clear view of the ambulance, police cruiser, and fire engine's arrival.

The paramedics were first inside. "Where's the victim?" Crystal pointed down the hall toward Frederick's room.

A pair of policemen followed, one towering like a professional basketball player, and the other shorter than Crystal but wide enough in the shoulders to turn sideways to pass through the front door. They began taking statements from everyone, beginning with Crystal and Roxie. They took turns describing the scene they had walked into before retreating from the flashing lights and urgent radio calls to come to terms with what they had just witnessed.

****

It was a solemn group Crystal and Suzy led home. Janice hadn't said a word the entire trip, but Crystal did see Suzy offer an apology on the ferry for accusing her of being the cause of Frederick's death. Crystal was happy her friend had taken the time for that. Janice was an obnoxious busybody but didn't deserve the guilt of a man's death on her conscience. Surprisingly, Janice hugged Suzy after the apology. Suzy patted Janice's back while making a what-do-I-do-now face at Crystal over the woman's shoulder. Crystal gave an encouraging nod and a thumbs up until Janice released Suzy.

The cathartic moment eased the tension enough to allow quiet conversation the rest of the ride to Seattle.

After dropping the college students off at their downtown hotel, Crystal was relieved to swap the van for her rust-spotted Honda at the Emerald City Outfitters store parking lot. The old car had been handed down from her parents when she left for the University of Washington and had a tendency to not start from time to time. Still, Crystal loved the old vehicle, if not its temperamental ways.

Driving the short distance to her condo on Capitol Hill, she contemplated sending a quick text to Conner. She could use his comforting presence but didn't feel up to going anywhere. She shot off a message before stepping into the elevator of her complex—*Want to come over tonight?*—

By the time she made it to her front door, his response chimed on her phone—*You're home, already? I'll get us a pizza.*—

—*You know just the right thing to say to a girl. See you soon.*— She finished with a heart and smiley emoji.

Entering her condo, she suffered a storm of meows from her ragdoll cat, Elf, voicing his protest to her several day absence.

"What's all this? I know Mrs. McReady always gives you plenty of food." Crystal bent down to stroke his head. In response, Elf sprinted to his eating area on the kitchen counter and circled, howling even louder.

"Didn't you miss me? I've been gone for days and what you want is the one thing you were given all along? Wet food?" Crystal approached her cat.

At the words, wet food, Elf purred and butted her arm.

"Fine, you win." She grabbed a fresh can of salmon pâté from her cupboard. As soon as she peeled the lid, Elf's eagerness got the better of him, and he swatted it from her hand. Murphy's Law took over, and the can landed upside down on the kitchen floor. Tsking, Crystal lifted it, and the entire contents plopped out. Elf sprung from his perch into the middle of the mess, stuffing as much as he could into his furry face.

"Did you behave this way for Mrs. McReady? She'll never watch you again." Crystal reached to keep him from gorging on the entire can, but her feisty pet let loose a feral growl.

Elf was short for the nickname her father had graced him with, Evil Little Feline. Contrary to the ragdoll nature of docility and sweet disposition, Elf wasn't afraid to back up his bark with a bite, or at least a swipe of his claws. Crystal left him to his impromptu victory feast and headed for the shower. Hopefully, he'd finish by the time she was done, and the remainder could be mopped up before Conner arrived.

She tossed her pack in her room, stripped off her clothes, still scented with smoke from the campfire, and ducked into the bathroom for a quick shower.

She was toweling off when Conner knocked.

Wrapping herself in her robe, she wended her way through her condo to let him in.

Opening the door, she gave him a warm kiss. "Am I ever happy to see you." Her words were not only for his six-foot rugged frame and tousled dishwater-blond hair, but for the fact he carried pizza from Pompeii's and a bottle of red wine. Pure heaven. "You must be angling for boyfriend of the year award."

With a big grin, he joined her inside. "The trick is, you have to pay attention to what your girl likes. Your kryptonite is the secret to my success." He sniffed and wrinkled his nose. "Why does it smell like fish?"

"Elf. Why else? He knocked his food over and wouldn't let me clean it up." She pointed at her impertinent cat, grooming his face with his paw in the middle of the feline crime scene.

"Did you, little guy?" Conner scooped up the cat and set him on the counter where he usually ate his meals. Responding with purrs, Elf began rubbing his face against Conner's arm.

"I don't know why my cat has such a crush on you. I've fed and sheltered the ingrate for five years and I still get scratched at least once a week."

Conner ran his hand through Elf's fur and shot Crystal a wink. "Elf has good taste." He rubbed one of Elf's ears, a place guaranteed to earn an attack. Nothing. Conner was showing off.

Giggling at his antics, Crystal retrieved a spray bottle of cleaner and a rag from under her sink. "While I clean this up, why don't you open up the bottle of wine. I need a glass after the last few days I've had."

As she cleaned up the remainder of Elf's meal, Conner popped the cork and laid out their food. By the time she was finished, a glass of red and a couple slices of pizza awaited her as she joined Conner at the table in her dining area.

"I couldn't believe your text messages." Conner took a bite of the pepperoni pizza, and Crystal grabbed her own slice. The best thing about Pompeii's was the deep-dish crust. Crisp on the outside, but soft and fluffy on the inside, with the barest hint of roasted garlic. "How are you doing? It couldn't have been easy walking into a murder scene."

"Surprisingly okay, but it is haunting after seeing a dead body for the first time. I don't know how you handle it when you volunteer with Search and Rescue."

"You get numb after a while. Finding people alive makes the tragic times worth it."

"I'm most worried about Roxie. He was her friend, and she's the one who found his body." Crystal sipped her wine.

"Me too. I texted her, but all she wrote is that she's 'fine'. I know she's not fine. Her entire world has flipped upside down."

"She cried constantly after his death. Suzy and I offered to take over the meals, but she insisted on cooking. We had to do it outside over camp stoves in the rain since the cabin was blocked with police tape, but she said a hostess has to persevere."

Conner snorted. "It's not like she's the captain of the *Titanic*. I think the world of Roxie, but she takes her job too seriously sometimes."

"She'll be in the city tomorrow after she finishes shutting down the camp. Do you want to visit her in the evening?"

"Tomorrow's Sunday, right? I'm free all day."

It was easy to lose track of the days when you worked the irregular shift of a wilderness guide, so Crystal was a little stunned to realize tomorrow was indeed Sunday. Remembering her conversation with Roxie about taking him to her family's weekly event, a wave of nervousness washed over her. She took a long sip of wine before gushing her words. "If you aren't busy, do you want to go to brunch tomorrow?"

"With your family? I'd love to." Conner acted casual, but he couldn't hold back a slight smile. He picked up his glass and clinked it against hers.

Relief flooded through Crystal, along with a decent mix of anxiety. Conner was a sensational guy, one she foresaw a future with, but hoped her family would consider him in the same light. She also pondered what Roxie had told her and came clean. "I think I owe you an apology. I should have asked you to come a long time ago but was too nervous. My family, in all their glory, can be a lot to handle."

He waved away her concern. "I'm the last person you need to apologize to when it comes to family. The first time you met any of mine was when I introduced you to my police officer cousin on the fake pretext that you were my girlfriend so we could work her for information, and you met my aunt and uncle just a few weeks ago." Conner topped off both of their glasses.

His aunt and uncle had raised Conner when his father left and his mother had become addicted to drugs. The delightful couple lived in Portland, Oregon, a three hour drive away, and had welcomed Crystal with open arms. Conner's cousin, Holly, worked for the Seattle Police Department, and the information Conner and she had weaseled from her helped Crystal solve the murder that had occurred at the mountain chalet the previous winter. The upside of deceiving Holly was Conner realizing how much he liked Crystal as a fake girlfriend, allowing him to muster up the courage to ask her out on a first date.

"Maybe we don't have the best track record of introducing each other to our families," Crystal admitted with a wry smile. "We'll start fixing that tomorrow."

****

Across the street from her parents' home sprawled a vast cemetery. Rather than detract from the Queen Anne neighborhood, it added a serene charm to the old Victorian houses. Crystal and Conner parked next to her mother's rhododendron bushes, honeybees darting in and out of the bright red and purple flowers that appeared this time of year. As they emerged from their car, the rumbling of lawnmowers and the scent of lawn clippings suffused the air.

Crystal grabbed Conner's hand and led him through the front door, calling out, "We're here." She had texted her parents the night before, telling them to set another place at the table.

Her mother, who usually hollered back, instead rushed to greet her at the door, followed by her father and their Yorkshire terrier, Bingo.

Her mother greeted him with a hug. "Hello, Conner. I'm so pleased you could join us."

"Welcome to our home." As soon as her mother let him go, her father shook Conner's hand.

Her parents were going a little over the top with the warm greetings, but they were excited with the prospect of her not dying alone with her cat.

Conner took the hug and handshake in stride, thanking them for inviting him into their home.

"Come in, come in. We're making blueberry pancakes this morning." Her mother led them to the kitchen. "Help yourself to some coffee or juice."

Crystal poured coffee for both Conner and herself, and they joined her parents at the table, the pancake preparation forgotten.

"Tell us about the first time you met," her mother urged.

"Through work," Conner said. "I'm also a guide at Emerald City Outfitters."

"You were with Crystal on her first snowshoe hike," her dad said. "You were on the cover of the paper when they reported the murder of Philip Calvert."

"That was me. I was part of the Search and Rescue effort."

"We're here." Her sister's voice carried to the kitchen as the front door opened. Everyone stood to greet the new arrivals, and as usual, her nephew, Joshua, raced ahead of everyone. He crashed into his grandfather's legs and wrapped them in a hug. Joshua transferred his leg hug to his grandmother, and then to his Aunt Crystal before halting in front of Conner.

"Who are you?" he asked with the bluntness of a three-year-old.

Laughing, Conner introduced himself as Crystal's boyfriend.

Crystal's sister, Heather, followed her son. "The mysterious Conner. I've heard so much about you, but until now you were like Bigfoot. A lot of rumors, maybe a blurry photo, but no reliable sightings."

Nick, Heather's husband, followed, carrying

Crystal's niece, Tabitha. "Don't let them tease you too much, Conner." Extending his free hand, he introduced himself. "They'll wear you out with questions, but they mean well."

At his pronouncement, a chorus of mock protests erupted from the family followed by good-natured laughs.

Having deemed him acceptable, Joshua thumped Conner in the thigh to get his attention. "Do you wanna play? I have blocks."

When Conner agreed, Nick unslung one of the various bags from his body and passed it to his son. Joshua led Conner to the adjacent living room and inverted the entire bag onto the floor.

Conner sat cross legged on the carpet as Joshua chattered away and showed him the best way to play blocks. Conner shot a glance at Crystal and winked as he began stacking pieces, only to have Joshua snatch them and show how they should have been put together.

The pancakes were hitting the iron skillet when Crystal's phone showed an incoming call from "Securas." Puzzled, she didn't pick up, but seconds later it rang again. Curious, she answered.

A robotic voice began speaking. "This is a call from the Washington Corrections Center for Women. Will you accept a call from…"

There was a pause before her friend's voice finished the recorded message, "Roxie."

The robot spoke again. "Press one to accept the call."

Crystal tapped one, a sensation of dread washing over her.

"Thank the Lord you answered, Crystal." It was

Roxie, but all trace of her southern accent had vanished.

The strain on the other end of the line made Crystal shoot out of her chair. "What's going on?" The chatter in the kitchen went silent at her serious tone.

"I was arrested this morning for Freddy's murder."

Chapter Six

"What? How?" Crystal couldn't believe it.

"It's a long story, but I have a few strikes against me. I wouldn't have bothered you with this, but I couldn't think of anyone else who could help."

"I'm glad you called. I'm at my parents with Conner right now. What do you need us to do?"

"I'm so happy to hear you took him to meet your family. How's it going?"

Crystal slapped her palm on her forehead. "Focus, Roxie. I'll tell you later."

"Right. I need you to get me a lawyer."

"Do you know any that you want me to contact?" Crystal had no idea how to get a lawyer for someone accused of murder. *Can lawyers be looked up on Yelp?*

"I don't know any, but I learned my lesson using a public defender a long time ago and am not going to make the same mistake again." Roxie's mysterious answer piqued her curiosity.

"Why did you need a public defender, Roxie?"

"The guard is giving me the wrap it up sign. I'm at the Purdy Women's Prison in Gig Harbor. Get me a lawyer, come visit me, and I'll tell you everything." The line went dead.

Crystal took her phone from her ear, dumbfounded.

Conner, hearing the serious tone, had stood to join her. When the line went dead, he asked, "What's going on?"

She filled him in while the rest of her family listened. Since they were all watching, she asked, "Do any of you know a good lawyer?"

"I know Mitch. I play poker with him on Friday nights," her father offered. "He does patent stuff, though."

"I don't think Mitch will be any help." Crystal brought her phone out to start searching the internet.

Conner interrupted her work. "We may not know any good criminal attorneys, but you know someone who does."

It took a moment, then the answer dawned on Crystal. "You mean Madeleine."

"Do you have her number?" Conner asked.

"I don't, but I know where she lives. We can pay her a visit."

"Doesn't she volunteer down at the mission on Sundays?"

"You're right. She does. I see her once in a while when I have time to help, usually when you're out of town. I bet she's volunteering there right now."

She faced her family to explain, but they already reflected understanding in their faces.

"Go help your friend, pumpkin," her dad said. "Conner, we hope to see you next week."

****

Conner parked in front of the shelter and they hopped out. Crystal began marching toward the front door past the line of homeless when a hand grabbed her arm.

"No cutting, lady. It's pizza day today, and if you didn't get here early enough, that's your problem, not mine." A scrawny fellow with a hunched posture glared at her with suspicion.

Conner seized the offensive hand holding her and eased it off. "Let's keep our hands to ourselves and keep this civil."

"J.P., let 'em be. She's a server, not a patron." The familiar lanky form of Joe appeared.

Crystal smiled at the grizzled face of her friend. "Joe, is Madeleine here today?"

"Sure is. She's in the kitchen."

"Thank goodness. How've you been?"

"Can't complain. The weather is starting to turn for the better, which helps my arthritis. Talked to your lady cop friend, Holly, last week, too. She tips me twenty bucks from time to time to keep tabs on things in the International District."

"That's great to hear. This is her cousin, Conner. Can you help us through the line? I need to talk to Madeleine."

"Can do. Not everyone is as protective of their pizza as J.P. here." He shot a scowling J.P. a pair of finger guns to show he was kidding.

Escorting them through the throng like an usher, Joe led them past the serving area to the kitchen. Sure enough, Crystal spotted Madeleine's dark hair with its streaks of gray among a group of volunteers, several of whom Crystal recognized.

"Madeleine, can I talk to you for a second?"

The former business owner turned philanthropist, flour on her nose from the dough she kneaded, looked up. "Crystal, so nice to see you. Here to help?"

Crystal waved goodbye to Joe, who was already halfway back to his place in line. Returning her attention to Madeleine, she shook her head. "Not today. I was hoping to ask a favor, if you don't mind."

"Sure thing. What can I do?" Crystal was pleased to smell no trace of alcohol on her breath. Six months ago, Madeleine had been in a constant drunken stupor, fighting depression both before and after her husband's death. Their paths crossed once in a while, and every time Madeleine's lucidity strengthened.

"I don't know if you remember my chef friend, Roxie. She's been arrested for a murder she didn't commit. I know you've worked with some of the best attorneys in Seattle, and I was hoping you might give me a name to call."

"You'll want Isabella Contreras. She represented Philip. You couldn't ask for a better defense attorney."

"This means so much to me. I'll look her up and give her a call."

"I can do better than that." Madeleine wiped the flour from her hands on the blue apron all volunteers wore, produced her phone from her pocket, and tapped a few buttons.

"Hello, Isabella."

There was a muted reply on the other end.

"I need your help, Izzy." There was a pause as Madeleine listened. "No, not for me, for a friend." Crystal strained to hear what was said but couldn't make it out. A look of displeasure crossed Madeleine's face. "I don't care. I have you on retainer, so make room in your schedule." Madeleine's face smoothed at the next reply. "Sounds great. Thanks."

Hanging up her phone, Madeleine focused on Crystal. "She'll meet with you and Roxie tomorrow afternoon at one. She'll call you later to get the details.

What's your number?"

Crystal told her and Madeleine typed it into a text for the lawyer.

"Madeleine, I don't know how to thank you. This is more than I could have asked."

Madeleine waved her hand to dismiss the thanks. "It's the least I can do. You solved the case involving my husband's murder, remember? Without you, I would have never had any closure. I've been able to start healing since that day."

The words touched Crystal. Helping Madeleine hadn't been her primary mission when she'd jumped into playing detective, but the fact she helped turn Madeleine's life around made Crystal even happier to have become involved. "What did you end up doing with your architectural firm?"

"I sold it to an up-and-coming architect who wanted her own firm. Since then, I've made myself busy finding ways to put my money to good use. I just started a new non-profit to help the homeless and have been spending more time here."

"I'm excited for you. Congratulations on the non-profit, and I'm happy you're doing better."

"Thanks, Crystal. I wish you luck with Roxie. If anyone can help her, it's going to be Isabella. She's a shark, but when she's on your side, that's a good thing."

Unexpectedly, Madeleine gave Crystal a hug. She broke the contact after a short moment, but the sentiment was heartfelt.

Crystal wished her goodbye and left with Conner.

"Is there still time to go back to your family's brunch?" Conner unlocked the vehicle and tugged open the creaking door.

"They'll be wrapping up. Let's go to your place for a bite, take Maggie for a walk, and wait for this lawyer to call."

****

It had taken over an hour of throwing a tennis ball into Lake Washington for Conner's Labrador retriever until Crystal's phone rang. The lawyer had made it clear Crystal was to join her the next afternoon at the prison since she wanted another perspective on the events that had transpired.

That was how Crystal found herself in Gig Harbor on a Monday afternoon. Luckily, she had the day off, but Conner couldn't make it since he was teaching a kayaking class. The quaint city was charming, named for the type of small boat used to explore the picturesque harbor centuries before. On the outskirts, though, was the ugly complex of the prison. Twenty-foot-high fences topped with razor wire surrounded several buildings reminiscent of army barracks, and inmates wandered aimlessly around the yard in light gray uniforms.

Parking in the visitor's section, she cast about for Isabella. A gleaming black Mercedes sped into the lot, tires squeaking on the asphalt as the driver spun the wheel to park next to Crystal's ancient Honda. A second later, a plump Hispanic woman, barely five feet tall and dressed in a black pantsuit was out of the car and striding toward Crystal. A black leather satchel with brass buckles was slung over one shoulder and a pair of Dolce & Gabbana sunglasses perched on her forehead.

"Isabella?" Crystal had been leaning against her car

73

but stood and straightened her posture. The approaching woman's impeccable attire and powerful stride made Crystal feel self-conscious about the dark blue jeans and white fleece she had thrown on this morning.

Her questioning tone earned a sharp nod. "I'm glad you're here. I don't have patience for those who don't respect my time." With an abrupt turn, Isabella was off in the direction of the gate. Crystal lurched after, but found it tough to keep up, even with the vertically-challenged lawyer wearing one-inch heels.

After walking through a metal detector and undergoing a pat-down, they were issued visitor's badges. A burly prison officer escorted them to a concrete room painted in a dull gray. Several cameras were mounted on the walls and pointed at the table and chairs in the center of the room. Isabella busied herself, producing a recorder, pen, and legal pad from her bag.

A few minutes later, a buzzer sounded, the door opened, and Roxie, dressed in the same drab outfit Crystal had spotted on the inmates in the yard, was escorted into the room by a guard.

"Bless you, Crystal." Roxie was out of place in this lifeless environment. Her usual *joie de vivre* and affected accent were absent, replaced by uncharacteristic worry.

Crystal gave a forced smile, trying to pretend like everything was going to be okay. "Of course I'm here to help. Are they treating you well?"

"Well enough, given the circumstances. I'm working in the kitchen, if you can believe it. The food isn't up to my usual standards because of the ingredients they give me, but a lot of the other inmates have complimented my cooking."

"You do realize this is the most expensive discussion regarding Roxie's culinary abilities you have ever had?" Isabella snapped her satchel shut. "We can discuss boys and braid each other's hair next, but it still costs four hundred dollars an hour."

"Wow." Crystal blinked several times at the amount. "That seems expensive."

"It is. I'm also very, very good."

"Well, let's not waste time." Roxie's eyes had flown wide at the number. "I don't want to be in here any longer than I have to be, and I don't have unlimited funds."

"I got the file from the prosecutor handling your case, and it seems the evidence against you is more than circumstantial," Isabella said in a no-nonsense tone. "The murder weapon was confirmed to be your knife, with your fingerprints. You were documented minutes before the death confronting a newsman and telling him on camera, 'I don't want anything to happen to this one-of-a-kind forest, and I don't want to lose my job.' "

Crystal opened her mouth to explain those words were taken out of context, but Isabella was relentless.

"No other suspects were spotted near the scene of the murder. Last, but certainly not least, you are listed in Frederick Baranhof's will, a very wealthy man. He bequeathed several prime properties and a sizable amount of money to you."

"He never told me that he'd put me in his will." The normally calm Roxie raised her voice in protest. A guard's head appeared in the window to check on the noise before turning away.

"That is your word only." Isabella held up one finger to forestall any further comments. "Now, you can see what I am up against. If I were the prosecutor, I would portray you as an angry, soon-to-be-ex-employee who killed her boss, hoping to cash in before losing her livelihood."

Crystal's heart sank at this unfair description.

Isabella's voice shifted from harsh to sickly-sweet. "However, I'm here to portray you as a traumatized victim who was horrified to discover her dear friend's body and handled the murder weapon in shock. You were surprised when learning of the inheritance and want nothing more than the world to return to the way it was."

"But that's what happened, honestly." Roxie's hands trembled where they lay on the table.

"I believe you," Isabella assured her. "My job is to make a jury believe you, too. I must say, this will be a challenge if the prosecutor is at all competent. Now, Crystal, what do you remember that might help?"

Crystal sat up straight. "Help in what way?"

"Either to exonerate Roxie or muddy the situation for the jury."

"Well, a lot of people were angry upon hearing Frederick was selling his property," Crystal mused. "There were the naked environmentalists at the front of the camp, the old logger, the reporter—"

"Don't forget the developers," Roxie cut in. "Frederick was also considering donating the property to the Nature Conservancy or the National Parks program. The lady meeting with him from Evergreen Resorts may have pretended to be civil, but she wasn't pleased when he didn't leap at her offer."

Isabella arched a brow at the mention of naked environmentalists but kept writing in her notebook at top speed. "This is what I need to know. As many other suspects as we can put into play, the better chance I have to cast reasonable doubt on the case." Isabella wrote a few more notes before looking up again. "Tell me what happened thirty-seven years ago."

Roxie blanched and studied the ceiling. "I don't see how that's relevant."

"Everything is relevant. What happened then is going to be used to smear your character now. I need to know details so I can spin the story correctly."

Roxie sighed. "I was twenty-three years old. I had received my American citizenship and was working in the Seattle theater scene. I had started to get myself a reputation, and my résumé was impressive enough to consider moving to New York to see if I could make it on Broadway. I wanted one last big role to cement my reputation before I left. When I scored the part of Sarah Brown in *Guys and Dolls*, I hit the town to celebrate with my friends. We drank more toasts than we should have, and instead of driving home, I slept it off in my car in the nightclub parking lot. Turns out, I crashed in the wrong car. The owner found me in the morning and called the police."

"And you were arrested and charged with grand theft auto and a DUI." Isabella glanced up from her notes.

Roxie nodded, looking sick to her stomach. "An officer woke me, tapping on the glass at five in the morning. They booked me and the owner pressed full charges."

"Why didn't you fight it?" Crystal was angry on behalf of her friend.

"The public defender convinced me to plead guilty.

I was naive and took his advice since it got me a reduced charge. I spent a month in jail and served six months of community service. However, I was forever branded a felon, and no one would hire me. All of the acting groups black-listed me."

"How did you meet Mr. Baranhof?" Isabella asked.

"I had managed to find a job cooking in a small cafe. One day, the hostess and server called in sick, so I was doing three jobs at once. Turns out, one of my tables was none other than Freddy. After the lunch service ended, I found him waiting outside on a bench. He was so impressed by my grace under pressure, not to mention my food, he offered me a job on the spot."

"That's how you started working for him," Crystal exclaimed.

"Not quite. I didn't accept right away. He returned to the restaurant three more times. The whole idea of cooking food in the wilderness as a business idea seemed ludicrous. I even told him I had a felony to spook him. He didn't care one whit. Finally, his persistence paid off and I agreed." A soft smile lit her face, the first happy expression Crystal had seen since walking into the depressing building. "Sometimes it's nice to be pursued."

Isabella glanced up from her scribbled notes. "This is what I need if I'm going to get you off on murder charges. When I'm standing in front of the jury, I need to paint a picture of what Frederick meant to you." Isabella steepled her fingers. "Now, how much of a budget do you have?"

"Budget? I don't really have any savings." Roxie inspected the lawyer with trepidation, worried what this meant.

Making a tsking noise, Isabella pondered, chewing on the end of her pen. She had been such a fierce presence, Crystal was relieved to see a human idiosyncrasy like this.

"So we have no money to work with. For the amount of time necessary to defend a murder case, my typical fees would amount to between thirty and fifty-thousand dollars. That doesn't cover the cost of P.I.'s to investigate the area, conduct interviews, and do some digging."

Roxie nodded her head in defeat. "I was afraid of that."

"However, I am going to make an exception for two reasons. One, Madeleine asked me to do this as a favor. Even though her philandering husband is dead, I made a fortune defending him, so I feel a personal debt. Second, you stand to inherit five hundred thousand dollars from the Baranhof estate, not to mention the properties. If I succeed in my defense, you will cover my full bill. We'll call this extra incentive for me to do my job properly."

"That's great." Roxie's face lit up at the news.

"But…" Isabella cut off.

"But what?"

"Private investigators don't work for promises."

Crystal piped up, "Do you think you can defend her without any extra evidence?" It didn't feel fair Crystal's friend could end up with a life sentence just because she didn't have any money.

Tapping her pen on the table, Isabella locked gazes with Crystal. "I will do my best, but it would help if I had someone funneling me information to generate enough reasonable doubt to convince a jury. If we only knew someone familiar with the area. Someone who has an idea where to start digging for clues. *Someone who has Roxie's best interest at heart…*"

Crystal stared at the two before comprehension dawned. "You mean me? I don't know how to be a private investigator."

Roxie, however, was thrilled with the idea. "Of course you do, Crystal. You solved Philip Calvert's murder. You questioned suspects, followed leads, and got a confession. You'll do great. I know it's a lot to ask, but I need your help." Roxie clasped her hands in supplication.

Panic seized Crystal. "It's not that I don't want to help. I'd do anything for you, Roxie, but I don't want my inexperience to be the reason you end up in jail for life."

Isabella interrupted. "It's not like she has a lot of options. You've sussed out one murderer. That's more than I can say for a lot of the professionals I hire."

Looking into Isabella's penetrating eyes and crumbling under Roxie's hopeful pleading, Crystal tamped down her fears and nodded. Her friend needed her, and Crystal would do her best to help.

Chapter Seven

Outside the prison gate, Isabella handed over her business card. "Call me when you find information that's worthwhile. I'll start building the case on this end, but anything useful you find can help direct what I'm doing."

"Any suggestions on where to start?" The scope of the task she had volunteered for was overwhelming, and the concern she had repressed for Roxie's sake threatened to crash over her like a tsunami.

The lawyer just shrugged. "Ask good questions, but be careful." Isabella shifted her sunglasses from the top of her head to her eyes. Without another word, she clicked her car fob, jumped in, and sped off at what Crystal deemed a reckless speed.

"Thanks for the tips." Crystal shared her sarcasm with the empty air. She sent a quick text to Conner.— *Want to go on a camping trip?*—

He responded in seconds.—*Always. Where are we going?*—

—*To the Olympics. We need to clear our schedule for the next few days to help Roxie.*—

By the time she had made it to her condo, Conner texted that he had taken care of organizing things with the other guides. Suzy had agreed to cover a beginning hiking course for Crystal, and Ethan took on a kayaking class for Conner. Ethan's leg was still healing, but he was starting to undertake less strenuous adventures.

Crystal still hadn't unpacked her camping gear from before, so all she did was swap out her dirty clothes for clean and call her cat-sitting neighbor to make sure Elf was cared for.

Conner joined her an hour later, and she recounted the meeting with Roxie and the lawyer. Crystal finished with a deep sigh. "So, in the end, I'll be returning to my role as a junior detective. I figured you would jump at the chance to help Roxie, so you get to go, too."

Despite her pessimism, Conner expressed excitement at their mission. "This will be the most unique camping trip I've ever been on. It's like a murder mystery party, but outdoors."

His usual grin and easy-going manner helped calm Crystal's worry, but the next words popped out before she could stop them. "Let's not forget the fact the murder, and murderer, are real, though."

His face fell. "That ups the stakes. Do you have any idea how to start investigating once we're there?"

"Not a clue. I thought we'd start by looking around the scene of the crime."

"Sounds good to me. I've got my gear in my car, and Maggie is off to doggie-daycare for a few nights. You ready?"

"All set."

"Then let's hit the road. If we hurry, we can catch the next ferry."

Crystal grabbed her pack from her room. Conner lifted it from her hands and swung it with effortless grace over one shoulder, leading the way to the front door.

Turning a suspicious glance on her mischievous

cat, Crystal warned, "Don't get into any trouble while I'm gone." Elf stretched out his paws and picked at the fabric of the couch, which was already showing signs of stress from his ministrations. Snorting at both her cat's behavior and Conner's ensuing chuckles, Crystal shut the front door and locked the deadbolt.

"I hope this isn't interrupting any plans you had," Crystal said.

"I was about to call to see if you wanted to look at a few houseboats with me, but we can go window shopping after we help Roxie."

"Wait one sec. You're ready to buy a houseboat? This has been your dream for years."

Conner punched the elevator button to take them to the street level.

"I didn't say I was ready to buy, but I am ready to start looking. I've got more saving to do, but I figured it would be a fun way to spend the day off together."

"This is huge." Crystal gave him a hug and a quick kiss. "You're almost there."

"Helping our friend is way more important than dreaming about my future home. Let's get Roxie out of the slammer."

****

Conner swung into the same parking spot the Forks Logging pick-up had once occupied. The Baranhof property was abandoned, yellow police tape still barricaded the cabin, and a notice had been tacked to the door.

Conner switched off the vehicle and Crystal jumped out to read the note. The Forks police seal was printed in the upper right-hand corner.

"What's it say?" Conner slung a pack over each

arm and hefted the cooler from the back of his rig.

"It says the cabin is the site of an active police investigation and it's a felony to trespass inside."

The melting ice sloshed in the cooler as he shrugged. "I can't imagine we could determine much from the actual murder scene. It's not like we have fingerprinting kits and whatever it is you use to analyze DNA."

"I guess not," Crystal grumbled. "We'll have to start looking around the local area and start asking questions. I suppose it's too much to hope the glamping beds are still set up."

A quick check showed that the structures that had once held warm blankets and soft beds still stood, but the comforts had been removed.

Taking in her sour expression, Conner couldn't help but tease her. "Well, Miss Wilderness Guide, we'll have to do without the luxury mattress and down comforter. Instead, you and I will have to survive on our wits, skills, and whatever can be carried in a mid-size sport utility vehicle. I'll set up the tent in the field over there. Why don't you check on the restrooms?"

Thankfully, nobody had locked the bathrooms. Checking the taps, Crystal was doubly-relieved to see running water. Sometimes, power and water were shut down at remote locations, but not this time. At least they didn't have to act like bears, and you-know-what in the woods. Even though she and Conner were getting more comfortable with each other by the day, she wasn't sure she was ready for that.

By the time she reemerged in the sunlight, the ever industrious Conner had the tent pitched and the rain fly unfolded.

"Did you leave anything for me?"

"The stove is still in the car. You want to set it up on the picnic table by the tent?"

Crystal grabbed the green Coleman two-burner and lugged it to where her last tour group had shared their meals.

She unpacked the kerosene fuel tank stored inside and fit it into the holder. By the time she was finished, Conner had set the cooler on the table and wrapped his arms around her from behind. "I unrolled the pads and sleeping bags. Looks like we're all moved in."

A worry crossed Crystal's mind. "This isn't trespassing is it? I was here earlier this week, but technically, we're not invited right now."

"I wouldn't sweat it too much. There are nudists living in trees and drum circles making a racket. Compared to that, we're two harmless campers who got confused and pitched their tent outside the park boundaries."

They had driven by the protester encampment when they arrived. Much of the action was hidden by the trees, but the packed helter-skelter impromptu parking alongside the entrance of the campground and side of the road had shown more environmentalists had joined the others. Their carefree lifestyle struck a pang of jealousy in Crystal. "Must be nice for them not to have any responsibilities."

"Seems they see this as their responsibility. I can't figure how they make ends meet, but it isn't like they're living the lifestyle of the rich and famous."

"Well, that's true. Most of them look like they haven't seen a shower for months."

A grin ghosted onto Conner's face. "That happens

to the best of us. I've been on excursions into the national forest for weeks on end. Bathing opportunities can be hard to come by in the mountains."

"You've done that?"

"Heck, yeah. Eventually, you can't stand it anymore and jump in the water. The memory of the cold makes it so I could never understand the appeal of the polar bear plunge on New Year's Day."

"But my last tour group swam in this lake." Crystal gestured at the body of water she had canoed in.

Conner snorted. "We're close to sea level here. I'm talking five thousand feet up or more. Alpine lakes are only a degree or two above freezing, even in the heat of summer."

Crystal enjoyed the distraction their banter offered but couldn't contain her anxiety any longer. "Conner, I have no idea where to start. Roxie needs our help and I'm at a total loss. I said I'd look around, but where do we begin?"

"Well, does the cabin only have the one entrance?"

"It has a sliding glass door in the back, overlooking part of the lake and woods. I'm sure the police taped it off, though."

Conner looked thoughtful. "You said that according to Isabella, nobody reported seeing anyone leave the cabin. I can tell from here the guest quarters have a direct line of sight to the front door. What I'm thinking is someone snuck in the sliding glass door and left the same way."

Crystal nodded at his reasoning. "Roxie liked to crack it to let in fresh air, so I doubt it was locked. There are trails leading up to it, so the killer could have approached from the forest."

"Let's explore and see if we can't discover where a killer may have come from."

They grabbed their packs, now lighter with only food, water, and the rest of the ten essentials for safe hiking: first aid, map, compass, sunscreen, flashlight, fire starter, knife, and extra clothing. Circling around the log cabin, they weren't surprised by more bright yellow caution tape crisscrossing the sliding door. The solemnity of what had occurred behind the flimsy barrier cast a pall as they marched toward the idyllic forest. They passed thorny salmonberry bushes stretching away from the woods in search of sunlight, the orange fruit a welcome sight this time of year. Conner paused to pluck several and hand them to Crystal. She popped them in her mouth, the tart and subtle flavor always a Northwest treat.

At the trailhead, they had an instant choice to make since the path split into two directions. Crystal took the lead, given she had recently hiked here. "I vote the one on the left, if you don't have any objections. They both crisscross multiple paths, so we've got some miles to cover."

"Left works for me."

With a sharp tug on her straps, Crystal cinched her pack tight and led them between two towering spruces flanking the start of the trail. The shadows of the massive evergreens dropped the temperature sharply, sending a shiver down her arms.

****

"That was unproductive," Crystal groused. Her wet clothes steamed faintly as rays of light stretched over the tops of the trees, but the sun was already beginning its descent.

"That was a pretty nasty rain storm that rolled through. Looks like more clouds coming in, too." Conner pointed at a patch of ominous black clouds miles away.

"Let's enjoy the weather break while it lasts and get some dinner in us before it hits."

"Don't let a little precipitation bother you."

"I know. I'm worried for Roxie is all. This feels hopeless." Crystal set her pack on the damp picnic table. "And I need a shower."

"Shower? You're roughing it. If you need to bathe at all, I'll show you how it's done." A mischievous sparkle kindled in her boyfriend's eyes. In one smooth motion, he tossed his rucksack beside hers, and tugged his shirt off. Before she could say anything, he'd shed one boot, followed by the other.

"Conner," she hissed. "What are you doing?"

"Bathing."

"We're in the middle of…of a forest."

"The word you were looking for is nowhere." His pants came off next.

"Are you freaking kidding me?"

"I explained this to you this morning. How do you think you get clean in the wilderness?"

"Showers are right over there." Crystal pointed at the bathroom she had checked earlier.

"Pfft. What's the fun in that?"

He tossed his boxers to the side and took off with a whoop toward the dock, his taut rear end daring her to join.

"What am I even doing," muttered Crystal.

Conner launched himself into the air and splashed into the lake. A fountain of water exploded upward as

Crystal struggled out of her clothes. "You coming, or are you chicken?" he taunted from the water.

"Hold your horses." Crystal managed to fling away the last of her clothes and took off toward the water, gingerly treading through the grass to avoid any rocks.

"Foxy." Conner gave a wolf whistle as her feet hit the rough wood of the dock, the surface giving better traction than she would have imagined. Hollow thumps echoed her footsteps as she hustled down the wooden walkway.

"I can't believe I'm doing this," Crystal yelled in a singsong voice. With as graceful a dive as she could manage, she plunged headfirst into the water next to Conner.

****

Pat. Pat. Pat. The first drops of the promised rain spattered the tent.

Her head resting on Conner's chest, she wiggled in closer to his warmth. The staccato beat of the precipitation became more insistent, building into a steady cacophony in a matter of minutes. The day had ended with a surprising amount of fun. A stab of guilt washed over her, since she'd had such a memorable time while her friend was stuck in prison.

To combat the self-reproach, she wracked her brain for ideas. If their exploration found nothing tomorrow, her next step would have to be tracking down the suspects and questioning them, without them knowing they were being interrogated. She pondered joining the hippies down the road, but they were a close-knit community. She wouldn't blend in with her fleece jacket and moisture wicking pants.

She tossed and turned, seeking an angle to

approach her suspects. The constant lullaby of the rain shower eased her to sleep, but her worries kept dragging her to consciousness. She lay on the edge of slumber, her brain not aware enough to provide any new insight, but alert enough to churn over the same problem, again and again.

****

At some point, she must have drifted off because when Crystal cracked her eyelids, the tent was filled with the warm glow of morning sun. Her nose informed her the sizzling and popping next to the tent meant that the coffee was brewed and bacon was crisping in a pan. A sharp thwack, and an eggshell split. Early-bird Conner began humming as he prepared breakfast.

Crystal stretched luxuriously. If this was roughing it, she didn't want to return to her so-called comfortable life. Despite her unpleasant night's sleep, the evening leading up to it had been memorable. Now, breakfast was being made by her dreamy boyfriend while she lay wrapped in a cozy sleeping bag. A girl could get used to this life.

"Are you awake? I can hear you rustling around." The sounds of Conner whisking followed. "Eggs and bacon will be ready in five minutes, sunshine."

"I'm up," she mumbled, sleep still tinging her voice. Eking one more inch from the stretch, she sighed and collapsed into herself. Bliss radiated from her heart. "This is going to be a great day. I can feel it in my bones."

****

They had been investigating the path on the right for almost an hour when they spotted daylight glinting in a clearing ahead. They approached and were greeted by a scene of devastation. The forest had been clearcut for the next quarter mile. In the distance, they could see where the trail continued on, but in between was a swath of rough wasteland. The lush underbrush and the ever-present moss were trampled and browning in the sun without the canopy overhead to provide protection from the rays. Ragged splinters stuck up from stumps that had once been majestic conifers. A job trailer sat in the middle of the clearing next to a dingy yellow bulldozer, and several hulking pieces of equipment littered the scene, awaiting their crew's return to begin deforesting anew.

"Is this the same logging company that met with Baranhof?" Conner squinted at the job trailer.

"I don't know. The name was Forks Logging, but I don't see identification on anything."

"Let's look around."

They crept into the clearcut. Limbs had been shorn from the timber and left to lie, making the footing treacherous. Occasionally, Crystal or Conner's boot would shoot through the debris into a hole, and once, Crystal ended up on her rear as they picked their way toward the work shack.

After a tedious and occasionally painful slog, they made it to the firm footing of the roadway. Gravel had been spread in the mud, giving them a stable place to walk. Circling around the bulldozer revealed no logo or company name on either side.

Two steel steps with jagged tread led to the door of the trailer. A small window coated in oil and dirt was adjacent to the entrance. Crystal caught Conner's eye and flicked her gaze toward the steps. After glancing at the empty tableau around them, he gave a small nod.

Despite her best effort to channel her inner ninja, the hanging stainless steel stairs creaked when she mounted them. Peering through the filth on the window, Crystal could make out a chair, a desk with some papers, and a coffee pot atop a small filing cabinet.

"Anything?" Conner whispered from below. A quick glance showed him preoccupied with watching the road.

"Nothing useful. I don't see anybody, though, so I'll try the door." Crystal twisted the stainless-steel knob, but it wouldn't budge. "Locked. I'll try the window."

Stretching a hand from the top stair she gave a tug on the bottom of the sash. Grudgingly, the window shifted upward an inch. Crystal shoved her fingertips underneath and managed to force it open the entire way. "I think I can fit through it." Crystal heard the skepticism in her own voice.

"I can help." Conner clumped his way up the steps.

Crystal poked her head in. "Let me peek inside to see how to…"

Crystal never got a chance to complete the sentence as she received unexpected assistance when Conner planted his palms on her backside and gave a powerful shove.

She toppled onto the desk with what she hoped was a ladylike grunt. The words she muttered were definitely not, though.

"You're in." Her helper's exultation carried through the window.

Grumbling, she placed her palms on the desk and drew her dangling feet the rest of the way through the small opening.

"Unlock it from the inside."

Clambering off the desk, Crystal managed to get her feet on the ground. "Yeah. Yeah. I'm coming." She twisted the lock and opened the door.

Conner joined her inside and hit a light switch on the wall, brightening the gloomy room.

"How does it have power?" Crystal didn't remember any power lines running to the shed.

"It'll have a battery. These are meant to be dropped in remote locations like this. Usually, they have enough juice to power a computer, a few lights, and that coffee pot for a couple of weeks."

The sludge at the bottom of the pot earned a disgusted look from Crystal, and she resolved to ignore it. The smell of stale coffee, dust, and something she couldn't place made her nose wrinkle. Conner stretched past her and slid the top drawer open on the desk. A can of chewing tobacco, the source of the unknown odor, sat atop a purchase order, detailing the cost for the delivery of diesel fuel. The name, Forks Logging Company, graced the top of the document, along with the silhouette logo of a towering tree.

"Well, that answers that." Crystal shoved the can of tobacco aside and tapped the name. "They have a good route to the cabin from their job site. If they killed Frederick Baranhof, it wouldn't have been hard to follow the trail, do the deed, and hoof it back here. Furthermore, if they've worked this forest for generations, I'm guessing they know these woods better than they know the back of their hand. The loggers must have known this trail was here and where it led."

"But why would killing Baranhof give them an advantage when it comes to getting the land?" Conner mused.

"No idea. Maybe one of these drawers has the answers."

Conner opened the second drawer, but it contained a collection of office supplies. He was opening a third when he froze, his brow furrowed.

"What is it?" The look on Conner's face worried her.

"Do you hear something?" He cocked his head to one side.

They stood still, Crystal holding the purchase order clutched in her hand. The unmistakable sound of tires on gravel filled the air, and it was getting louder.

"Crappity, crap, crap. We gotta get out of here." Crystal jammed the paper in the drawer it had come from and slammed it shut.

Conner was already moving. Snatching her hand, he tugged her toward the door. He flung it open and it rebounded off the wall. He caught it with his boot and kicked it open.

"I see a red pick-up coming. Not sure if they've seen us, though." They clanged down the metal steps, Crystal tripping on Conner's heels. They darted for the opposite side of the trailer to avoid being spotted by anyone in the closing truck.

"Careful," Conner hissed. They approached the edge of the maintained area. The path ahead was strewn with logging debris, and from the long trek they had taken to the trailer, they were aware of how hazardous it was. Plunging in, they picked their way ahead as fast as possible, struggling through roots, brambles, and hidden holes toward the safety of the forest's edge a hundred yards away.

Behind them, the rumble of the truck's diesel engine grew. Not focusing on the treacherous path in front of her, she risked a quick glance backward. The truck halted next to the job trailer. The door creaked open and Crystal stumbled over a blackberry vine, the beastly bush sliding up her leg and raking her shin with thorns. Seizing her arm, Conner steadied her. The sound of the truck door slamming urged them on.

"Hey! What the hell are you doing on my property?" The furious, raspy bellow startled them into redoubling their pace.

Another ill-advised glance showed Crystal they were almost to the tree line. "Keep going. We're almost there."

An ominous metallic click caught her attention, followed by another. A gunshot blasted through the serene wilderness and Conner fell, gasping and swearing.

Chapter Eight

"Conner!" Crystal whirled to see him writhing on the ground. "Where are you hit?"

"My knee," he hissed between clenched teeth. Both of his hands gripped his left knee and he rolled to his side, moaning.

Panic seized control of her body, and Crystal grabbed under Conner's armpits and attempted to lift him to his feet. He hissed in pain, but with her help, he levered himself up onto his right leg. With a tentative step, he put his left foot forward, which immediately crumbled, forcing him to the ground.

The ominous snapping of sticks heralded trouble, and Crystal glanced up, recognizing the scowling face of the logger who had spat at Frederick Baranhof's feet several days before. He brandished a long rifle before him, but the muzzle was pointed at the sky. He sauntered forward, his natural instinct avoiding the discarded limbs and tangling vines that had caused them so much trouble.

The fire surging in her veins urged Crystal to sprint away as fast as her feet would take her, but she wouldn't abandon Conner. She snatched a branch from beneath her feet and stepped between him and their attacker. "Don't come any closer." Her voice shook, but at least she managed to force the words past the lump in her throat.

The logger stopped ten paces from her. He furrowed his brow and tugged at his salt and pepper beard. Crystal's frantic brain latched on to the fact that his stocky build and rough canvas jacket made him look as if one of the stumps littering the clearing had attacked them.

"Not shot." Conner gasped on the ground behind her.

"Are you going to hit me with your stick?" The logger slung the rifle over his shoulder. "Just so you know, getting knocked upside the head with that itty-bitty branch is another day in the office for me. Won't do much of anything to this thick old skull."

Crystal, never taking her attention from the stout man, spoke to Conner, "What do you mean, not shot?"

"He didn't shoot me. I fell."

"He didn't shoot you?"

Conner's words held a touch less strain. "No. The gunshot startled me. I turned, saw him pointing his gun in the air, but didn't see the root under my foot. I went down when I twisted my knee."

"Course I pointed it away from you. I meant to scare you, not kill you." The vindicated shooter harrumphed. "You think I go around plugging trespassers? I'm not a savage." With a throat-clearing rasp, he spit to the side.

Dropping her branch, Crystal knelt next to Conner, who sat up and winced. "Why did you even fire your gun? Couldn't you have watched us run away without scaring us even more?"

That earned her a stern glare. "When I see someone breaking and entering into my job headquarters, I take it damn seriously. I don't want trespassers feeling welcome to come and go as they please."

Slinging Conner's arm around her neck, she gave the best smooth heave she could manage. With the assistance of his good leg and her help, he was on his feet again. Well, foot anyway.

"It's a clear-cut. Unless I'm planning on hot wiring a bulldozer, I don't know what harm I could do you haven't already done." Crystal glared at him from her hunched stance under Conner's arm.

The bearded stump squinted at her, studying. "You don't have a clue, do you?"

"Don't think she does," Conner said. "I do, though. Studied forestry in college."

Crystal didn't care for being discussed as if she weren't there. "What don't I understand?"

The logger studied Conner in turn and nodded. Closing the gap between them he held the rifle out to Crystal's free hand. She recoiled from the weapon.

"Just take the gun, miss. I'll help this lad to the job shack. I'm a fair bit stronger than you."

Crystal closed her hands around the wooden stock of the gun with a tentative grasp, pointing it at the ground.

The man cautioned her as he stepped to Conner's other side. "Point the barrel at the sky. Don't want to accidentally blow any toes off."

The logger sidled next to Conner, whose weight came off Crystal as he leaned on their attacker-turned-rescuer. He was the perfect height for Conner, with neither slouching into the other, the man's wide, stocky legs compensating for the unsteady path ahead of them.

It took almost fifteen minutes, but they managed to get Conner to the trailer. Using the hand rails, he navigated the metal steps into the makeshift building by swinging himself. He crash landed on the chair she had sat in earlier when they rooted through the desk.

The logger stomped up the steps to join them.

"Lass, there's a first aid kit in the bathroom. Why don't you grab it."

Mounted on the wall, the unmistakable red cross made it easy to spot. She grabbed the metal box from its bracket and carried it to the desk.

With a practiced flick of his thumb, the old logger opened the case. Wordlessly, he handed an aspirin bottle to Conner, who dry swallowed two, grimacing as he choked them down.

"Why don't you get the lad some water from the tap in the bathroom to wash those all the way down, and make me a pot of coffee while I have a look at his knee?"

Crystal found a stack of waxed Dixie cups beside the sink, filled one, and handed it to Conner, who slugged the whole thing in one gulp.

"What's your name?" Crystal asked, grabbing the coffee pot and heading to the sink.

"Emerson," he growled. Grunts, growls, and rasps were his preferred method of communication, but he wasn't shooting at them anymore, so Crystal could put up with his rough edges.

Fine green fuzz lined the top of the remaining coffee. "There's mold in the carafe."

"Hasn't killed me, yet. Rinse it out and start a fresh pot."

Crystal shrugged. She wasn't going to join him for a cup, so it was up to Emerson's constitution to fight whatever pathogens made their home in his coffee.

After several thorough rinses, she filled the pot and returned to the work area to see Conner's knee deftly wrapped in an ace bandage, Emerson gone, and the door swinging open. He returned a minute later, passing an ice pack to Conner.

"Missus puts one every day in my lunchbox to keep my food cold. Put it on your knee." Emerson leaned against the desk. "Now, we're as comfortable as we're going to be. Why don't you tell me what you're doing here?" The hiss and sputter of the coffee maker was followed by the refreshing scent of fresh coffee.

Glancing at Conner, who gave her a weary nod, Crystal told the truth.

"After Frederick Baranhof was killed, our friend Roxie was arrested for the murder. If you knew her, you would know that isn't even a remote possibility."

"Isn't she the nice southern lady who made me a sandwich?"

Crystal nodded.

"Why did Big and Little Tony arrest her? I always suspected their mamas drank when they were pregnant, but, geez, your friend is who they came up with? She doesn't seem the murdering type."

"The reason we're here is because you were one of our suspects. We found a trail leading to this clearing from the property, and we kinda broke in to see if it was your trailer." Her cheeks burned at the embarrassing admission.

"Kinda broke in, huh? Well, I get standing up for a friend, but forgive my lack of support, since it's my property you're trespassing on."

"Trust me. I understand if you're angry with us, but I didn't see what harm we could have done, even if we meant to. There was no reason to come at us with guns blazing."

Emerson headed toward the coffee pot. "Son, you studied forestry like me. Maybe you can explain to your sweetheart what mischief can happen out here." He grabbed a coffee mug from next to the carafe. Inspecting it with a squint, Emerson gave a quick puff of breath to clear whatever offending dust he'd seen and poured a cup from the still percolating maker, evoking a hiss from the machine as coffee dribbled onto the burner.

"Eco-terrorism is a real thing." Conner's voice sounded stronger. The pain killers and ice must have been helping. "The protest outside the camp is pretty tame, but there has been much worse done to protect trees."

"Terrible things," Emerson muttered as he produced a small flask from inside a pocket. With a few twists, he poured a healthy splash of amber liquid into his beverage. Noting Crystal watching his addition, he gave a toothy grin. "Kills those bacteria you were worried 'bout."

Conner continued explaining, "Some of the things you can think of might be obvious. Sabotaging equipment or burning this job shed. However, the most insidious thing might be spiking."

"Spiking?"

"They'll take long iron spikes and hammer them deep into the trees so the bark masks the head. As you can imagine, it can be deadly to hit one of those with a chainsaw or when it passes through a lumber mill."

Emerson took a healthy slurp of his Irish coffee. "My own son lost his leg hitting one of those damned things. His saw-blade ripped to shreds and tore into his thigh. Docs managed to save him, but he has a titanium replacement. That injury forced him out of the family business. He manages a gas station now."

"I'm beginning to see why you wanted to frighten us off." Crystal had no idea this sort of vandalism occurred.

"Yeah, well, with those tree huggers protesting outside of Baranhof's property, I'm taking the safe, rather than sorry, route. I sent my boys to work on some different acreage until the hippies clear outta town to keep the tension down. If any of those idiots got it in their heads to lie in front of a bulldozer, tie themselves to a tree, or some such nonsense, they could get hurt if we're working out here. I check on the property several times a day to see if any of them have been prowling around."

"Have you spotted anyone so far?" Crystal asked.

"Not until you."

"Emerson, after I saw you meet with Mr. Baranhof, you were the first on my suspect list. You were so angry with him."

"I'm not proud of my actions, but in truth, I was hopping mad. Ever since the restriction of logging due to the spotted owl protection, the amount of land we have access to has dwindled. Entire generations of families have been laid off. Do you know what happens to an area when you take away its economic base? Poverty and drugs. It's tough watching all I've known, and held dear, crumble. When I heard old Baranhof might be selling off his prime piece of timberland, I figured it was a long-shot, but I threw my hat in the ring."

"But Baranhof was a well known conservationist. What made you even try?"

"A drowning person will grasp at any lifeline. When he turned me down cold, I wasn't surprised, but I knew I'd failed the entire logging community, families I've known for decades. Kinda pissed me off, and I might have vented my spleen at ole F.B."

Crystal hung her head in frustration, staring at her mud-spattered boots. "If you didn't do it, who did?"

It was a rhetorical question, but Emerson answered after he slugged down the last of his drink with a satisfied sigh. "There are several folks I can think of. The developer in the meeting with me, Kinsey Laughlin. Baranhof gave her a 'probably no' after her sales pitch. She was more polite than me 'bout the rejection. She and her brother Grant are angling to make this area the new resort for all of the money in Seattle."

Seattle's renaissance, driven by tech companies, had sent salaries through the roof. As the first generation of the tech-made millionaires aged, they had begun to look for vacation homes to create memories with their growing families.

"Do you think she has as much riding on this as you?" Crystal hoped he'd divulge if Kinsey had enough motive to see Frederick dead.

"I don't think so, but it's a matter of perspective. I'm worried for my family and the community's way of life. They're trying to close a deal for a potential multimillion-dollar resort. The stresses are real for both of us."

Conner interrupted. "If Kinsey purchased the land, she'd want it cleared for construction. Wouldn't she hire Forks Logging Company?"

Emerson gave a dubious frown. "Aside from it looking like neither of us is going to get the property, it would be up in the air whether we'd get the logging work. The new owners would probably put it out to bid, and we may or may not win."

Crystal steered the conversation back toward the suspect list. "Is there anyone else you can think of?"

"I didn't close up shop and come out here to check on my property for nothin'. There are dozens of demonstrators smoking pot and singing songs in the woods. They seem ridiculous, but maybe they're not as harmless as they appear. If one of them got angry or righteous enough, they might have killed Baranhof if they figured it would stop a sale of the land to either me or the developers."

"How would I even investigate them?" Crystal mused.

"Not easily, that's for sure." Emerson slid open the drawer of the desk and opened his tin of chewing tobacco. He grabbed a pinch and stuck it behind his lip. "The protesters all seem to know each other, so if they've circled the wagons, it's going to be tough."

Conner tried extending his knee while holding the ice pack in place, and winced. "I won't be tromping around in the woods for a few days."

Emerson gave a sympathetic chuckle. "Try weeks, son. I can see the swelling from here. I've been around enough twisted knees to know how long you'll be out of action."

"Well, it's time to test out how bad it is. I'll find a branch for a crutch, and then Crystal and I've got to get going before dark sets in since my leg will be slowing us down."

Emerson snorted at the idea. "Don't be stupid. I'll drive you."

"You would drive us even after we trespassed like this?" Crystal's stress of the return trip was replaced with relief for his kind offer. With Conner in this much pain, she didn't know if she had the stamina to support him the entire hike to their campsite.

"Course I would. You two aren't all bad. Just trying to help a friend, and I can see why you'd suspect me. Hell, I'd suspect me if I saw what you had. Besides, I've got a soul. I'm not going to watch you hobble your sorry selves off my property and worry all night if you made it."

He proffered a calloused hand to Conner, who hefted himself up with the assistance. Clenching in anticipation of a jolt of agony, Conner eased his wounded leg to the ground. His foot met the dingy floor, and the stress that etched his face eased as he tested the knee.

"Feels much better. Not ready to summit any mountains, but I can get along."

His first step vindicated his words, but his second gave truth that not all systems were one hundred percent. He hissed in discomfort and shifted his weight to the good leg.

Crystal slung her arm under his, trying to help. By the time she assisted him from the trailer, Emerson had produced an axe out of the tarnished tool chest mounted behind the cab of his truck. The old logger stomped behind a slash pile of limbs.

Crystal kept some of her attention on his actions as she navigated Conner to the truck. They'd had a nice chat, but she kept her wits. If someone you had recently considered a murder suspect had an axe in their hand, you don't pretend everything is hunky-dory. That was simple common sense.

A few whacks emanated from the other side, and leaves rustled as the whole pile shook. Emerson reappeared, axe still clutched in one hand, and a forked limb almost six feet in length in the other. He had crafted a crutch.

The scent of his chewing tobacco and coffee arrived before he did. Without a word he planted the butt of the makeshift support next to Conner to size it up. With another of his trademark grunts, he flipped the crutch on its side, bracing it against a log. A few swift axe blows at opposite forty-five-degree angles sent chips flying, and the aroma of fresh cut wood competed with Emerson's powerful scents. With a final swing, the last several inches fell free and the resized crutch was handed over to her limping boyfriend.

Conner wedged the limb under his armpit and nodded his thanks. "You've got a knack for this. Perfect length."

Emerson's axe banged and rattled as he tossed it into his steel tool chest. "Not the first time I've helped someone out of the forest with a bum leg. Let's get you to where you're staying."

With the assistance of a few shoves from Crystal, Conner manage to wiggle his way to the center of the bench in the old truck. The dashboard radio was of the antiquated pushbutton variety with a red line indicating the station. A moth had maneuvered its way into the radio display and perished, now exhibited like an entomology showcase. The gun rack in the window held two slots, one populated with a rifle, the other empty. The vehicle smelled of dirt and oil, reminding Crystal of her father after a day of working on the family's cars.

Through the grimy windshield, Crystal kept an eye on the woodsman as he reentered the mobile office. He shut the window she'd climbed through and returned bearing the rifle he had fired in an effort to scare them off. He fetched keys from his pocket and locked the office door. His heavy boots rang down the metal stairs and he headed in their direction, jabbing another wad of tobacco in his lower lip.

The driver's door gave a half-creak, half-groan as it swung open. Emerson unslung his rifle, guided it into the rack, and spit on the ground in one smooth motion.

Crystal flinched at the rifle handled in such a casual fashion. She hadn't grown up around guns and trusted them like you would a wild beast. It was best to avoid them, and if you did stumble across one, hope they didn't kill you. Her anxiety increased as he passed the bullet clip to her and asked if she would put it in the glove box.

The truck roared to life, and Emerson drove around the circle dozed for logging trucks to haul loads out. As they bounced and swayed down the potholed road, the seat's springs squeaked in response, and they were serenaded by an old country song on the radio encouraging mamas to not let their babies grow up to be cowboys.

"What's your next move?" Emerson broke the silence.

His question interrupted the reverie she had fallen into. "I don't have one, yet. I'm pondering how to approach the developer and protesters."

"Don't you mean we?" Conner asked.

Crystal gave him a side-eyed look. "No way, mister. You're going back to town, getting your knee looked at, and resting. I'll call Olivia to drive my car here so I can get around. She always wanted to try camping and doesn't work until this weekend."

Conner opened his mouth to protest.

"Forget it, son." Emerson rolled down his window and spit. "Not only is she running the show, she's right regarding the leg. You may have done worse than twist it, and you need to have the docs look at it as soon as possible."

Conner closed his mouth and pulled a stubborn face. Crystal slid her hand into his larger one and squeezed to take the sting from the situation.

They slowed at the end of the gravel road when it intersected the highway, and Crystal told him where to go. After a rolling stop to check for traffic, Emerson took a right toward their campground.

A few drops of rain spattered the windshield, and instead of the slow buildup they had experienced so far in the rain forest, a powerful deluge roared in, drowning out the radio.

Growling, Emerson flipped the windshield wipers to full speed.

A short while later, he turned off the highway. Crystal recognized a couple of the vans parked at the entrance of the property, but the protesters had retreated to the shelter of their vehicles and tents under Mother Nature's onslaught.

"Thank goodness," Emerson muttered. "Last time they threw a banana at me when I left. Would have hated to see what they had in store this time."

They rattled the rest of the way down the road and Emerson parked next to Conner's red four-by-four. The rain continued to thunder down atop the cab of the truck.

Emerson faced them. "Good luck clearing your friend's name. I'm headed home. The missus will be wondering where I got off to."

With many thanks, Crystal clambered out and assisted Conner, who dragged his crutch with him.

In moments, they were soaked. Grabbing their packs from the cab, they swung the door shut with another creaking bang. Emerson gave them a salute that they could barely make out through the streaming rain and backed out of the parking spot. His tail lights flashed off and he drove away from the campground.

"That was an unexpected day." Conner planted his crutch in the mud and pivoted toward where they had pitched their tent.

Frustration gnawed at her. "We're no closer to finding the murderer, and now you're hurt. I'll get you something to eat, but you're to head straight home to rest. I'll be okay camping alone for the night."

Conner stopped abruptly, peering at the field. "It's a good thing you never had aspirations to be a fortuneteller."

"What do you mean?" Crystal followed his stare, confused. *Where was the tent?* Then, she saw it.

"When you woke up this morning, you predicted that it was going to be a great day." Conner scowled at the tumult that had once been their campsite. "It seems you aren't staying here tonight."

Crystal could only nod. Even through the

rainstorm, the lingering acrid odor of the tent still stung her senses, now a heap of burned plastic. A metallic zipper from one of their sleeping bags gleamed in the jumbled mess. The cooler had been tossed on the conflagration and sat to the side half melted.

"I have to quit jinxing myself."

Chapter Nine

Surveying the brown room, Crystal supposed it could be worse. The chestnut curtains almost matched the deeper umber carpeting. However, the ochre comforter was all wrong, clashing with the russet walls. No, the Forks Motor Inn was not an interior decorator's masterpiece, but it was affordable, dry, and not so filthy as to make her want to don a hazmat suit. The rumble of a semi on the neighboring highway was punctuated by its jake brakes hammering as it slowed through town.

"Peachy." Crystal tossed her bag on the bed. Conner had driven her to the front door and waited until she had secured a room. He'd tried to help her carry her belongings, but she'd teased him about being overly chivalrous with his hurt knee. He left her with the remainder of their gear and headed home. By a stroke of luck, the injured knee was his left and he was able to drive away with only a wince or two.

After a hot shower, Crystal unpacked her meager belongings. Two changes of clothes, four dehydrated meals meant to be boiled in a pouch, and one bag of trail mix, not even the good kind with chocolate candy in it. A fit of health-minded guilt had made her choose the variety with dried cranberries, and, at this moment, she regretted the decision with all of her heart.

The room lacked the typical motel amenities like a

microwave, so without a way to heat her food, she opted to open her trail mix and filled a cup from the tap.

Slouching in the tawny chair, she shoved a few handfuls of the healthy mix in her mouth and washed it down with a highly chlorinated swig of motel water.

"This is what sadness tastes like." Crystal voiced her displeasure out loud, zipped the bag closed, abandoned her water, and crawled under the blankets.

The sound of another semi slowing through town prompted her to squeeze a pillow over her head. She made herself as comfortable as possible with just her nose poking out. Having learned her lesson, she chose not to predict the next day would be better.

****

Hard knuckles rapping on the door snapped her awake.

"Crystal! Get up. I know you're in there. It's Suzy."

"And me." The second, bubbly voice belonged to none other than her best friend Olivia.

"What are you two doing here? Do you even know each other?" Crystal regretted the grouchy words as soon as they left her mouth, but she'd been up all night counting tractor trailers.

"Conner called us and said you might need some help getting Roxie out of the slammer." Suzy sounded peeved, propelling Crystal out of bed and to the front door. A cranky Suzy was worse than a toothache for ruining a day.

Unbolting and opening the door revealed her friends' silhouettes against the morning sun. They nudged past her into the room, tossing their bags on the bed. Suzy wore a rumpled pair of cargo pants and a long sleeve T-shirt from Yosemite. "Whaddya got to eat?" She flopped into the lone chair in the room.

"Do you have any coffee?" Olivia gave a hopeful look, the bags under her eyes seconding the request. In contrast to Suzy's no-nonsense outfit, Olivia wore a patterned, blue, full-length sundress with a jean jacket thrown over it to ward off the morning's chill.

"Breakfast is this." Crystal brandished the remainder of the trail mix. "There isn't a coffee maker."

"Do they have a continental breakfast? We've been driving since four o'clock this morning." The red rims to Suzy's normally bright eyes told Crystal this had been a rough morning for her night owl co-worker.

"I doubt it. It's a dump if you hadn't noticed, but we can check." Crystal led her weary friends across the sparsely populated parking lot to the lobby.

A bell chimed as she swung open the door.

A teenager with a patchy mustache greeted them at the front desk with a suspicious glare. "Can I help you?" His name tag read Tad.

"You got breakfast in this crap hole, Tad?" Suzy tapped the counter impatiently.

"Round the corner, but it's only for paying guests."

"We are guests." Crystal edged in beside Suzy.

This elicited a further scrutinizing stare. "Fine. One muffin each and no refills on the coffee."

"You're a walking, talking five-star review, Tad." Suzy took off in the indicated direction, leading them through a doorway to an adjacent room. A dozen sad muffins, several days past their prime judging by the stale edges, sat on a plastic platter atop a dingy tablecloth. The aroma of burnt coffee caused Crystal's nose to wrinkle, and she suspected it had been on the burner all night. Rorschach coffee blots sat amidst small piles of spilled powdered creamer and sugar. A three quarters filled cup amidst the mess showed someone had abandoned drinking the sludge after a sip or two.

Taking a tentative nibble on the edge of a bran muffin, Crystal spit the bite into a napkin and confirmed it had long since passed its expiration date.

"Matches the coffee." Olivia tilted a cup to show off the concentrated liquid.

After taking a look at their reactions, Suzy shook her head. "Leave it. We're outta here." They bustled by a smirking Tad, who glanced up from the check-in computer, where he was busy playing a game of solitaire.

Olivia typed on her phone, using some sort of sixth sense to step around obstacles in her path. "There's a place a half mile down the road, Mother Earth Café.

"Get in the car," Suzy grumbled. "If I don't eat something soon, I'm going to get cranky."

Not wanting to see what happened if Suzy got even more upset, they clambered in her Subaru and drove the short distance. During the drive, Crystal told her friends what had happened the day before and explained the need to investigate both the developer and the eco-protesters.

Nestled amidst towering redwood cedars, Mother Earth Café was an old clapboard home converted into a bistro. Straight out of the Wild West, the old-timey building was capped with weathered cedar shingles and a generous bed of moss.

The delectable smell of sweet baked goods complemented the alluring scent of coffee. When the door swung open, the hiss of an espresso maker filled the air.

"Now we're talking." Crystal could feel the pressure building in her head from lack of caffeine and her stomach joined in with a muted rumble.

"About time," Suzy added.

Inside the toasty building, a board above the barista's head displayed the menu. Patrons grouped together, their outfits a mishmash of styles. Several patchouli-scented people bedecked in tie-dye shirts and dresses gathered at one table, while hikers sat at another, their fleece pullovers and hiking boots matching Crystal's own. Still others were dressed in work attire, their faces set in the resigned expression of people bracing to begin a nine to five.

"Why is ham and egg in quotation marks on the breakfast sandwich?" Suzy asked.

"It's because we're a vegetarian cafe." With a practiced twist, the woman behind the counter removed the coffee portafilter from the machine and banged the grounds out in a stainless-steel container. "The ham is made of soy, and the egg is a tofu substitute."

"What about the cheese?" Crystal ventured.

"It's real cheese, but we substitute cashew cheese if you're vegan." With a twirl of her full length skirt the barista spun and grabbed more beans from the counter behind her.

"I'll take one vegan breakfast sandwich," Olivia announced at a volume that was too loud by half, even for the bustling cafe, "with a soy latte." Crystal shot a side-eyed glance at her friend. Olivia had never shown any proclivity toward vegetarianism before.

Olivia gave a short shushing motion to the

unspoken question along with a quick, be-quiet-I'll-tell-you-later glare.

The distracted worker gave an approving nod. "And for the rest of you?"

"I'll take the same, but can I have my latte with regular milk?" Crystal had never tasted fake cheese before, but when in Rome.

"Of course."

"Can I have a shot of double espresso and can I substitute real ham and egg on my sandwich?" Suzy didn't look pleased with the prospect of her meal.

The barista stopped working the machine to spare a disapproving look for Suzy. "We can do real eggs if you must, but not ham. Those are animals, ma'am. Living beings like you and me."

Suzy's mouth opened for what was bound to be a sharp retort when Olivia cut in. "Don't you even care, Suzy? I've been trying to get through to you for years, and this is how narrow your view is?" Her raised voice caught the attention of the crowd, and many refocused their attention from their coffee and breakfast to see what the fuss was.

Suzy focused her ire on Olivia, but Crystal gave Suzy a swift kick in the shin. The two of them hadn't known each other for that long. Suzy saw past her own irritation, and her scowl switched to confusion.

"Uh, fine. Make it three ham and egg breakfast sandwiches." Suzy put a dose of scorn in her tone when she said ham and egg. Olivia motioned to a table next to a gas fireplace, with gentle flames dancing among polished pieces of crushed emerald glass.

They sat, Crystal and Suzy both casting questioning glances in Olivia's direction.

"I've got a plan, but you two need to play along." Olivia spoke in a hushed tone, clearly not meant to be overheard by the couple sitting at the next table.

"What are you plotting?" Crystal furrowed her brow. Olivia was an excitable human being and tended to act first and think later.

Olivia leaned forward and whispered, "Now, you explained you have several leads to run down, right?" Olivia gave a questioning look to Crystal.

"Yes."

"One of those leads is this group of granola types, right?"

"Extra crunchy granola types." Crystal didn't see where Olivia was going with this.

Olivia nodded vigorously. "You think they may have had something to do with Frederick Baranhof's death. So, how will it go over when you ask them if they murdered him?"

Suzy snorted. "Pretty damned bad."

"That's right. Shhh." They quieted as the barista delivered their breakfast. She gave Olivia a smile but set down Suzy's food with more force than necessary. She fetched their coffee from the coffee bar before disappearing back behind the counter.

Olivia waited until the server retreated far enough away to not overhear. "I'm going to infiltrate the protesters."

"That's crazy." Crystal wasn't positive she'd heard right.

"I like it." Suzy gave a light smack on the table with the palm of her hand. "Shows guts."

"I don't care how much guts it shows," Crystal hissed at both of them. "I'm worried how safe it is."

Olivia dismissed her concern with a wave. "I'll be fine. Let's face it, Crystal. No one else can do this. You don't give off that radical vibe and Suzy is, well, Suzy."

Suzy gave a sage nod. "I thrive in the outdoors, but I'm not a tree hugger. I don't play nice with those hippie, dippy types."

"This is crazy."

"As crazy as breaking into a logging company's job site?" Olivia flashed a roguish grin. "Conner told us everything. Don't worry. I'll be careful. I'm sure after a couple of days I'll be able to figure out if anything fishy is going on."

"You think you can uncover their darkest secrets in a couple of days?"

"I'm very lovable." Olivia batted her eyelashes. "Now, to make this happen, you need to meet me at the hotel room after I leave the coffee shop. But first, Suzy needs to throw her sandwich at me. I need to make a scene to establish some cred."

"Why would she do that?" Crystal frowned at the insane suggestion.

"Anything to help." Suzy stood, seized her meal, and flipped it at Olivia's chest.

Olivia sprang to her feet, turning over the chair she sat on. "I've had enough of you two! It's like you don't even understand the crisis our planet is suffering. I'm getting my stuff and hitchhiking home."

The ambient noises in the coffee shop silenced as the patrons tracked Olivia storming from the café. After a quick glance at each other, Crystal and Suzy hustled after.

Olivia strode out of the parking lot toward the hotel, almost a quarter mile away. Suzy and Crystal piled into the car and drove alongside her.

"Get in the car, Olivia," Crystal called out of the window.

Olivia gave a dismissive wave. "Get out of here before you spoil everything."

Suzy took the cue and stepped on the gas. A short squeal of tires on pavement only added to the scene they were putting on. A few minutes later, Olivia met them at the motel. "Ok, I can't stay long. I'll text you when I can to let you know what I find out."

"How is this going to get you in with them?" Crystal asked.

"At least six of those customers had to be protesters. Where else in Forks are a bunch of nature worshipping hippies going to eat other than the Mother Earth Café? I'm going there with my bag, breaking the ice by asking for a lift to Seattle, and see if I can't fast talk my way into joining their protest."

"Commune," Suzy added. "New Age types live in communes."

"Is that relevant?" Crystal didn't like splitting up without a well-thought out plan.

"It is since I'm joining one. You start looking into the developer." Olivia grabbed her phone and stormed out in mock fury.

"Crud. I still haven't had breakfast," Suzy grumbled.

****

Crystal sipped her scalding coffee, staring into the distance as Suzy put away her fourth sausage at the roadside diner they had found. *How was she to gain access to these developers?*

"Hey, isn't this the place?" Suzy said through a

mouthful of food, holding up the menu to show Crystal.

"Evergreen Resorts. That's the place." Advertisements made up the back page, and Evergreen Resorts had paid for top billing. The upper half was an artist's rendering of a luxury cabin in the woods overlooking a lake, with the slogan, "Life is meant to be lived," written in a whimsical font.

The advertisement made Crystal's wandering mind seize upon an idea. "How are you at forging documents?"

Suzy swallowed her last bite. "Never done it, but sounds like fun. What do you need?"

"A press ID."

****

Crystal held her phone side-by-side to her face. "Does she look like me?"

Suzy, sitting in the motel room's recliner, glanced up from her phone. "Kinda. She's older and in worse shape than you."

"That's cool of you to say, but she's the only Seattle Times reporter I come close to resembling, so it'll have to do. Her name is Brenda Carlson. Can you have that added?"

Suzy tapped on her phone.

"Can I see what you have so far?"

Suzy looked up from where she had been working on her phone the last half hour. "Me? I don't have diddly. I put my roommate on it. She's a coder for a tech company so she's good with computers."

Crystal didn't know how to respond. She'd assumed Suzy had dove into the project the way her attention was locked in. "What have you been doing this whole time?"

"Playing Candy Completion." She spun her phone around to show a screen populated with bright sweets in a grid.

Crystal repressed a grin. Suzy was turning out to not be much of a planner. Crystal warned her companion to be quiet and dialed the number to Evergreen Resorts.

A bubbly, cheerful voice greeted them, the sort that had cornered the market on answering phones for companies. "Evergreen Resorts, where life is meant to be lived. How may I direct your call?"

"Hello, this is Brenda Carlson from the Seattle Times. I'm calling to speak to Kinsey Laughlin regarding the resort and its amenities for our upcoming summer travel section." Crystal's cover story earned an enthusiastic thumbs up from her companion.

"One moment please."

Light jazz filled her ear until the other end of the line picked up. "Can I help you?" the voice answered in clipped tones.

"Hello, Ms. Laughlin. My name is Brenda Carlson. I'm a reporter for the Seattle Times. I'm in Forks doing a summer travel article for the paper. I would like to include your resort in both the 'Places to Stay' and 'Things to Do' sections. If you could spare an hour or two of your time, I wanted to meet and discuss your existing property and what business plans you have for the future."

"I have a busy schedule and don't do much marketing anymore."

"It's free advertising to half a million readers. Surely, you don't want to pass up the opportunity."

A deep sigh followed. "I suppose not. Can you

come tomorrow morning? I believe I can carve out some time."

"Tomorrow morning works for me. What's a good time for you?"

"Eleven o'clock. I'll leave your name with security at the gate."

Crystal clicked off her phone and looked up to see Suzy staring.

"You're good." Suzy gave a slow nod in awe.

"It's all in being prepared. Next stop is clothes shopping. I look like a camper, not a reporter, and the nearest place to remedy that is Port Angeles. Are you up for driving me?"

"I thought you'd never ask. I'm bored sitting here."

****

Crystal examined her outfit in the hotel mirror. The gray pant suit was too monochromatic for her taste, but it was much more appropriate for what she imagined a reporter would wear. They had even found an old camera fitted with a large lens in a thrift shop to strap around Suzy. It didn't take pictures anymore, but it made the right clicking noises when you pushed the buttons. Suzy still had her customary cargo pants, long sleeve tee, and fleece vest, but with the camera, she resembled every stereotypical photographer Crystal had ever seen in a movie, so they called her outfit good. During their shopping spree, Suzy's computer-savvy friend had photoshopped official looking press credentials, which they printed at a local library, and now hung from black lanyards dangling around their necks.

"Did you get a text from Olivia?" Suzy asked around a mouthful of granola bar.

"Not yet. I'm getting worried. If one or more of them are murderers, she walked into a nest of snakes. She's smarter than she lets on, but one slip and my best friend goes the way of Frederick."

"Says a person ready to walk into a fake meeting, impersonating a reporter, to speak to another potential murderer."

"I'm not interested in logic, Suzy."

"Hey, I'm putting this in perspective. We're all taking risks, Crystal. Roxie is a friend to all of us guides, and Olivia is your friend. We're all looking out for both her and one another."

Crystal gave a glance at the normally hardened Suzy waxing philosophical. It was obvious Olivia wasn't the only one who hid brains behind a carefree attitude.

However, the reminder of what they were up to twisted Crystal's stomach, making her regret the greasy hash browns and fried eggs she'd had at the diner earlier this morning.

"Can we go, photographer Ava DeSoto?"

Suzy had made up her name, rather than use one of the photographers listed on the paper's website. Her exceedingly firm stance was that if she were working under an alias, it needed to sound cool. She slipped the camera strap over her neck and clapped Crystal on the back. "If you're anywhere near as good as you were on the phone, we'll be fine. Do you know what you're going to ask?"

Crystal tamped down her frazzled nerves as she led Suzy out into a gorgeous sunny morning. "Pretty much. I composed the questions in my head and wrote them down in this official looking notebook in case I forget anything." Crystal waggled the object in question in her left hand.

They piled into Suzy's car and drove toward Evergreen Resorts, twenty minutes away. The road was the typical two lane highway, always seemingly in danger of being overgrown by the lush vegetation along the route, but as they approached their destination, the road surface transitioned from rough, and in need of a paint job, to fresh, smooth asphalt, the tar on the edges still gleaming. Oversized signs cautioned them to slow down to thirty miles per hour.

Turning a bend, they spotted a stylish sign welcoming them to Evergreen Resorts. Newly constructed homes flanked either side of the highway, the grass in the yards starting to sprout. On the western slope, several hundred yards away, the Pacific Ocean stretched to eternity, waves crashing down on the typical slate gray and rock-strewn Washington coast. The homes were distributed to maximize the number of water views. They waited at a crosswalk for a young couple pushing a stroller on a sidewalk, a black and white Boston terrier trotting beside them on a leash.

Suzy took a left into the eastern section of the community. Crystal pointed to a sign proclaiming management and sales, and Suzy headed in that direction. They wove through a charming commercial district consisting of a small grocery store, ice cream shop, wine shop, and a pair of restaurants. Unattended children were flocking in and out of the ice cream store with monstrous cones piled three scoops high. Tables outside of the wine shop were crowded with guests who, despite the early hour, were enjoying vino, nibbling on cheese plates, and breaking into gales of laughter inspired by generous amounts of chardonnay before noon.

They wove around the meandering road, passing idyllic cottages punctuated by small parks filled with more excited children, a nature walk trailing into a stand of trees, and a dog park filled with cavorting pooches who raced after one another with as much abandon as the kids in the parks.

"This is a regular *Truman Show* sort of place, isn't it?" Suzy regarded the neat rows of bungalows with skepticism. For someone who thrived on camping in one-person tents in the middle of the woods, the crowds and noise put her ill at ease.

"Whatever they're selling, people are buying. Look how crowded it is." Every open space had a person taking advantage of the area. "I wonder where they all come from?"

"Beats me. Hey, a *For Sale* sign."

"Stop the car." Crystal hopped out as Suzy obliged, and grabbed a flyer tucked into a protected compartment underneath the realty sign.

She returned to the car and read it aloud for her friend's sake, "Three-bedroom, two bathroom, gorgeously appointed bungalow in the Garden District of Evergreen Resorts. Six hundred thousand, plus HOA dues."

"That sounds pricey for a bungalow in the middle of nowhere."

"I guess they're worth what buyers are willing to pay, and based on how crowded it is, they are willing to pay this." Crystal flapped the leaflet. "It goes to show, the property Frederick Baranhof died for was worth way more money than we can imagine if Evergreen

Resorts got their hands on it. How much could they charge for lakeside homes on his property?"

Suzy eased the car forward toward their destination. "I'd guess millions for the lakeshore properties. That doesn't include the rest of the land."

"Maybe enough money to murder a man."

Ahead lay a security gate. A bored-looking guard sat on a stool inside a shack, reading a Stephen King sized novel. Suzy rolled down her window.

He lazily swiveled his head. "Name and business?"

Crystal gave her fake name and mentioned her appointment with Kinsey Laughlin.

He glanced at the computer screen, pecked at the keyboard a few times, and nodded in satisfaction. He tapped a button under his workstation, and with a buzz, the gate swung open. "Ask at the front desk. They'll help you out." He returned to his book.

Suzy parked her car in a visitor spot and they climbed out.

"Ready?" Suzy muttered.

Crystal tugged her outfit into place. "Ready." Before her thundering heart gave out, Crystal strode toward the entrance. A burbling fountain and manicured garden greeted her, helping calm her nerves. Suzy's car beeped when she pressed the key remote and her footsteps closed in behind Crystal as she hurried to catch up. The name of the resort was etched into the front window, and inside she could see a secretary talking on a headset. As she tugged open the door, the conversation became audible.

"Mr. Laughlin and Ms. Laughlin aren't available for comment right now. They are currently in a meeting. I can take a message if you would like, and whichever one is available will return your call at their earliest convenience."

Crystal, trailed by Suzy, sidled up to the desk. The secretary held up a finger and mouthed, "One sec."

"Well, sir, I don't care how many times you've called. They will speak with you when they have a free moment. They are important individuals and have full..." She stopped speaking and focused on Crystal and Suzy. "They hung up," she said in way of explanation. "What can I do for you?"

"I am Brenda Carlson, and this is my photographer, Ava DeSoto. We have an appointment with Ms. Laughlin." Crystal gestured at Suzy when she announced her pseudonym.

"I see you're with the paper. I'm surprised she consented to an interview."

"Why's that?"

The receptionist peered over her eyeglasses. Studying the two of them, she mulled over her answer. "No reason. Please follow the hall to meeting room four. I'll let her know you've arrived."

Suzy set off toward the indicated direction. Crystal was torn between working her over to clarify that cryptic answer or following her friend. The phone rang, and the secretary accepted the call in an instant, pretending Crystal didn't exist.

Giving up, Crystal left but strained to listen to the fading conversation of the phone call being redirected as she trailed after Suzy.

Suzy turned into a room several doors down and Crystal joined her seconds later, only to see her colleague's cell phone in her hand as she navigated the sea of chairs.

"This isn't the time for more Candy Completion." For an avid outdoors woman, Suzy's phone addiction was surprising. Maybe she needed to double down on her usage to catch up from all the times she was out of range.

"I'll play later. Right now I'm looking up this company from a news perspective. The secretary gave the impression reporters aren't welcome at Evergreen Resorts."

"Good point. Find anything?"

"Not yet. Reception is terrible." She lifted her phone into the air, circled the room, and stared at the screen.

Crystal fished out her phone and tapped on the Internet icon. Hers wasn't responding any better, and soon they were both shuffling around each other.

"Got something." Suzy squinted at her phone held at arm's length. "Customers enraged over the mounting costs at Evergreen Resorts. Click for whole story." Suzy tapped her screen.

"And?"

"Loading. This sucks."

"Hurry up." Crystal's nerves were unraveling at lightning speed.

"Crystal, unless you have a cell tower in your pocket, you telling me to hurry isn't going to download this any faster."

"Ixnay on the Crystal. Here, I'm Brenda," Crystal hissed.

Suzy winced at the correction and muttered a curse word. This plan was such a disaster, it was a virtual burning plane crashing into a volcano.

"Hello," an all-business voice announced from the

doorway.

They both wheeled to see a tall woman standing in the doorway. Her knee length skirt and matching black blazer were tailored to her frame and screamed to the world this was someone to be taken seriously. Her raven hair was styled in asymmetric cuts, crossing above her left brow in what must have taken her at least thirty minutes to style in the morning.

"Do you have Wi-Fi?" Suzy waggled her phone.

"We do, but the password is lowercase this, uppercase that." She gave a dismissive wave before extending her hand to Crystal. "I'm Kinsey Laughlin, one of the owners of the property."

Crystal shook it. "I'm Brenda. This is Ava." Kinsey shook Suzy's hand in turn and gestured for them to sit.

"I thought this meeting was between us, Brenda." The woman gave Suzy a disapproving frown.

"Ava is here for photos to accompany the article. She isn't a reporter, and trust me when I say, you wouldn't care for any pictures of your resort if I took them." Suzy held up her camera and gave an unconvincing grin.

Kinsey's frown was replaced with a tight smile that didn't reach her eyes. "You said this will be featured in the summer travel section of the paper. Nothing more?"

Kinsey's suspicion intrigued Crystal. What did the owner of a resort have to hide from the newspaper? Crystal gave a reassuring nod, though. "That's what our assignment is. I've been to Hurricane Ridge, the Hall of Mosses, Point of the Arches, and Shi Shi Beach, but tourists want to know about more than sights in a first-rate travel guide. They need to know where to eat, shop, and stay. I wanted to feature your resort since it provides all three, and I can tell from the drive in, our readers can do that in style here."

Kinsey leaned back in her chair. "We do indeed provide that. Evergreen Resorts is the brainchild of my father and seeks to cater to the rising demand for vacation homes for the new upper middle class in Seattle."

"Your father?"

"Ed Laughlin. He started this fifteen years ago. His vision was a standalone community where guests come to unwind, relax, and forget the stresses of long work weeks."

Crystal remembered she was a reporter, clicked the button on her pen, and began dashing words on her steno pad. Kinsey stared after the delayed start, and Crystal could swear she heard a small sigh.

"Does your father still manage the resort?" Crystal kept writing without glancing up.

"He retired last year due to health concerns, leaving my brother and myself to oversee the company. Is this relevant?"

"It's part of the color needed for a good story." Crystal scribbled more notes and gave herself a mental pat on the back for her quick answer. Given Kinsey's clear impatience with the interview, Crystal jumped straight into the heart of her question. "Do you have plans to expand in the future? There is only one *For Sale* sign, so demand seems high."

Kinsey gave a long-suffering sigh. "Look, I'm extremely busy, so here's what we're going to do. I'm going to direct our receptionist to give you a copy of our brochures. Furthermore, I'm going to put you up in our guest suite for the night with vouchers for any restaurant you would like."

Crystal's eyebrows shot up in surprise. "That's kind of you."

Suzy snorted. "Sweet. The place we're staying is a real dump."

"This isn't generosity." Kinsey folded her hands in front of her and leaned forward. "Take your time. Look around. Enjoy, and see everyone having a good time. Include everything in the article. Maybe it will make up for the hit job your paper did on us earlier this year." Kinsey's nostrils flared with rage.

Crystal shrank from the unexpected ire. "Ummm... okay. Maybe this will help."

"It better. You're lucky we didn't sue your paper for slander. Good day." She shot up from her chair, gave a final scathing glance, and stormed from the room. Her heels clicked down the hall, until they were eventually masked by the closing of the gently swinging door.

"Huh. Wild." Suzy stared at the door with a perplexed expression.

"You can say that again. Let's scram."

Crystal grabbed her pad and they retreated to the receptionist, who eyed their approach with an astonished expression. "You two are something. My boss sounded like she was chewing gravel, but I'm to give you access to our VIP bungalow with a free dinner voucher. I'm not sure I've ever seen her so mad and generous at the same time."

"That's us. Lovable pains-in-the-butt." Crystal gave a weak smile, but her mind raced. *What had just happened?*

Chapter Ten

Crystal dropped the key on the credenza and her bag on the slate floor of the entryway. "This place is something."

Suzy whistled in appreciation when she entered the foyer, tossing her pack next to Crystal's. "Glad we checked out of the motel. Let's hang here until we're done investigating."

Ahead, floor to ceiling windows at the far end of the room overlooked the crashing waves of the ocean. Crystal paused, admiring the view.

"This place is swaaaaan-ky." Behind her, Suzy clicked something, and light jazz piped in from speakers set into the ceiling. Suzy tapped the buttons several more times and stopped when rock music began blaring.

A quick exploration revealed three bedrooms, a powder room, and a high-end bathroom with dual sinks set in a black granite countertop.

"What's in the fridge?" Suzy raised her voice over the music. Not waiting for an answer, she sidestepped Crystal into the kitchen. Stainless steel appliances gleamed amidst more black granite, but inside the refrigerator were empty shelves and barren drawers.

"Kinsey told us we'd get a free voucher for a restaurant of our choosing. I guess they want us to experience what this place has to offer." Crystal picked up a stack of papers from the countertop between her and Suzy. "Here we go. Dinner and breakfast courtesy of Evergreen Resorts."

"Does it include booze?" Suzy gave a pleading glance at the piece of paper in Crystal's hand. "I need a drink after that interview with Kinsey."

"It doesn't say it *doesn't* cover alcohol." Crystal had reservations about going out for drinks with Suzy when they were here trying to get to the bottom of who committed the murder of Frederick Baranhof. On the other hand, she was in the middle of enduring several of the most stressful days of her life. "Let's go."

"I vote for the wine bar we passed on the way in. That'll kick things off nicely."

The restaurant was a short distance from their new accommodations, so they strolled down the sidewalk, passing joggers and families headed in the opposite direction toward the beach.

The bar itself was packed. They squeezed into a table with two women appearing to be around sixty years old, who offered to share when they spotted Crystal and Suzy hovering near the entrance. An empty wine bottle and glasses sat in front of them and their cheeks sported a healthy glow.

Suzy waved down a waitress and pointed at the empty bottle on the table. "We'll have one of these." The waitress nodded and asked if they wanted anything else. After a quick glance at the menu, Suzy added a buffalo chicken wrap, while Crystal opted for a Cobb salad.

Their two table mates lit up as chocolate tortes and flutes of champagne were placed in front of them.

"Do you two own one of the homes at the resort or

are you guests?" Crystal asked.

"We're owners," the one across from Crystal answered. Her bright red hair was not quite a natural occurring shade, and the dirty blonde roots indicated that it was time for another bottle of color.

"We're sisters, who wanted to get a vacation spot for our families." This woman matched her sibling's natural hair color. Now that they mentioned their relation, the resemblance in their facial features was obvious, their large crooked noses hard not to notice. They simultaneously cut the points from their tortes and chased the bites with healthy swigs of champagne.

"How do you like Evergreen Resorts?" Kinsey's odd behavior had tipped her off that strange things were going on, and maybe these two could enlighten her.

"It's charming here, and we adore the home we bought. They keep the property in perfect condition and always have an event or two scheduled for entertainment."

The redhead picked up where her sister left off. "But if you are thinking of buying, watch out for the homeowners dues. We bought ten years ago and they've more than quadrupled."

The blonde sister scowled at the mention of the dues. "They say costs keep going up every year." She picked up her champagne and bobbed it up and down to emphasize her point. "But how does it go up so much in such a short amount of time? This isn't due to inflation, it's highway robbery. We complained, but our contract states it can go up anytime based on market costs."

"It's all excuses to get more money out of us." Red took over for her sister, tilting her nearly empty champagne flute to point it at Crystal. "Either they're terrible at calculating costs, or they baited and switched us."

"What's a bait and switch?" Suzy leaned forward to hear.

"Where they offer you a deal too good to be true, and then switch it to something you didn't want." Crystal jumped in and answered Suzy's question.

The sisters clinked glasses. "That's us, baited and switched. We love the resort and so do our families, but this place is getting expensive. We've considered selling, but no one wants to buy anymore with the monthly dues so high."

The waitress returned with the bottle of wine. She presented the label to Suzy, who stared blankly. "What?"

"That looks perfect." Crystal took over.

The waitress gave a relieved sigh when Crystal answered. She nodded, unfolded a small knife from the wooden body of a corkscrew, and trimmed the foil. Their table guests tittered at Suzy's ignorance of wine protocol.

Next, the waitress deftly put the corkscrew into action, and with practiced ease, withdrew the cork with a satisfying pop. A few quick twists freed it from the corkscrew, and she passed it to Crystal.

Crystal took the proffered cork and gave a delicate sniff. The earthy odor contrasted with the deep, rich note of the wine. She wasn't positive what would constitute a bad bottle, but she did know her role. She gave what she hoped was a knowledgeable nod to the waitress, while Suzy stared at the whole process with skepticism.

A delicate splash was poured into one of the two

ample glasses and passed to Crystal. She completed the ritual by swirling the glass and taking a small sip. The freshly opened wine had a peppery spike that mellowed into the cherry and plum flavors the label promised. After a perfunctory pause, she nodded to the watching waitress again.

"Excellent," the waitress spoke for the first time since returning. She poured two full glasses, set the bottle on the table, and left.

The blonde sister piped up, "Pay attention to your friend, and you'll be an aficionado in next to no time."

The two sisters gathered their oversized purses and took their leave.

"How did you learn so much about wine?" Suzy slugged down a healthy swig of the merlot.

"I don't know a whole lot. Look at the label, sniff the cork, nod, sip, then nod again. Then they fill your glass and leave you alone."

"Naw, you totally knew what you were doing."

"I know it's to tell if the wine is what you ordered and if it's corked, but I've either never been served a bad bottle of wine or have no idea what corked wine smells or tastes like."

"You pulled that off like a boss." Suzy lowered her voice as the waitress breezed past.

"You mean it? Because I feel like a fake when I do it."

"Fooled me. Maybe not the princess of the wine ceremony who served us, but I bought it."

"If I'm fooling you, I'm fooling others. Bluffing my way through life seems to be my superpower. First, I'm attempting to be a private detective, which led me to fake being a reporter, and now I'm a wine connoisseur." Crystal sighed and slumped in her seat. "All I want to do is be a wilderness guide. Is that too much to ask, universe?" Crystal tilted back in her chair and covered her eyes with her palms. After a moment of lamentation, she leaned forward and blinked to clear her vision. Suzy had returned to looking at her phone. Crystal stared for a second until her cohort glanced up.

"I thought you were done. Did you want to vent some more?" Suzy put her phone on the table, flipping it upside down to demonstrate her commitment to the conversation.

Crystal drew in a breath before letting it out in an extended exhale. "No. I think I'll check in on Conner and Olivia. Go back to your Twitter."

"Facebook, actually."

Crystal took a small sip of her wine, drew her own phone from her pocket, and logged onto the bistro's internet.

—*How's the knee? Did you get it looked at?*— Guilt at not texting Conner earlier gnawed at her, so she stuck several heart emojis to show how much she cared. It had been over twenty-four hours since she'd last seen him, and he'd been embarking on a five-hour drive home with his knee in bandages.

Olivia was next.—*Have you made any headway with the protesters?*—

She clicked off her phone and glanced up to see Suzy's zombified expression as she flicked her phone's screen, presumably scrolling through social media.

At least Crystal had wine to keep her company. After the last few days, a glass or two would help soothe the raw edges of her nerves. She took a sip and stared into the distance, savoring the hearty red.

Her phone buzzed, and the screen alerted her to Conner's reply.

—*Sprained the knee, but not bad. Got some ibuprofen and a brace for a week or two. Quite the party going on here.*—

—*Haha. I'm happy you didn't sprain your sense of humor. Hope you're not bored sitting around recovering.*—

—*Not bored. Sam came over and kept me company.*—

—*Glad to hear it.*— It was a good thing Conner had someone to help entertain him. He wasn't the type who could waste days watching television.

—*I have something we need to talk about when you get home.*—

Crystal frowned at her phone, not liking the ominous ring of the last text.—*Just tell me.*—

—*This needs to be done in person.*—

—*I'll be home as soon as I can. We'll talk then.*—

When she glanced up, Suzy was watching her. "What's up?"

"I'm finished looking at Facebook. It's all old news from here on out. How's Conner?"

"How did you know I was texting him?"

"Because I read it upside down. Besides, who else would you text?"

"Olivia, but she hasn't answered."

"What's up with Conner's knee?"

"Sprained, but not too bad. His search and rescue friend, Sam, popped in to cheer him up."

Suzy took another healthy swig of wine. "Not Sam. Samantha. She worked as a guide with us for a couple of years."

"Samantha? Who's Samantha? How do you know?" Conner was the most trustworthy man she'd ever dated, but that didn't mean she was thrilled with him hanging out with ex-coworkers named Samantha.

"Saw it on Facebook, just now. Nice girl. Being a wilderness guide wasn't her thing, so she left to do something else. Sales, I think."

The acid of jealousy started to eat at Crystal's stomach, and she couldn't control her impulse to check out this interloper. "Can I see her?"

"Sure." With a few vigorous flicks on her phone's screen, Suzy located the post in question, and handed the device to Crystal.

Crystal grabbed the offered phone, mind burning with curiosity. The image on the screen was a nightmare come to life. Luxurious crimson hair framed a heart shaped face with lightly freckled skin. Sparkling emerald orbs twinkled with the laugh captured by the camera, and a delicate arm was thrown around the neck of Crystal's boyfriend, who stood with an idiotic grin on his face.

Chapter Eleven

"What are they doing?" The arctic chill from her voice caught the typically oblivious Suzy off-guard, who widened her eyes in sudden realization.

"Uh, I don't know. It says, 'Having fun at the lake' in the caption."

"What's Conner doing walking around the lake with some redhead when his knee is in a brace?" Crystal couldn't take a deep breath. Maybe wine would help clear the lump in her throat. She grabbed her drink and drained it with a tilt of her head. She plunked her empty glass down in the middle of the table.

Suzy watched Crystal with concern. "Are you okay?"

"I'm fine. Fine. Conner's a great guy. He wouldn't cheat on me with some bimbo."

"Actually, you'd like her. She's hilarious, and tons of fun. Once, we decided—"

"You're terrible at this." Crystal cut her friend off mid-sentence. "I need to know she's annoying, and has an obnoxious laugh, because Conner texted me he has news he needs to tell me in person."

"Oh, that's not good." Suzy poured them both more wine.

The waitress returned with their food and placed it on the table. The scents would have ordinarily caused Crystal to salivate, but the creamy dressing from the salad twisted her stomach.

"Excuse me, can we get another?" Crystal tapped the half full bottle.

The waitress gave a judgmental look but nodded and left.

"Why did she quit working with you guys?" Crystal needed to know everything about this situation.

Suzy took a bite from her wrap. "She told me she could make more in sales than as a wilderness guide. Since you know what we make, that's pretty plausible." Suzy fiddled with her napkin and kept looking down.

"But you think it was for a different reason." Crystal could read Suzy's guilty face like an open book. She wasn't sharing everything she knew.

"Yeah. She might have quit because of me."

Crystal pursed her lips and nodded. Suzy's nature could rub a person raw faster than sandpaper when you got on her bad side. "What did you do to make her leave?"

Suzy sat up in her seat and adopted an innocent expression. "Nothing bad, I swear. She's awesome." Crystal's face must have been darkening into a fierce thunderhead because Suzy threw her hands up. "Fine. I'll tell you. I heard a rumor around the store she had a crush on another guide. I told Ethan, so he asked her out. Turns out, her sights were set on Conner."

Crystal's jaw fell as she unpacked everything in that sentence. "You've got to be kidding. She's been pining after Conner?"

"Maybe. It's been a while since we worked together, and we don't talk anymore. She told me it was unrelated, but she quit the week after Ethan asked her out."

"What made Ethan think he was the one she liked?"

Suzy snorted. "Ethan's overblown sense of self-confidence makes him believe everyone has the hots for him, so when he heard she was interested in a co-worker, he went for it. I'm not surprised, because anyone would give their right arm for a chance to date Samantha."

Slapping her palm over her face, Crystal gave a drawn-out groan. "This is *not* helping." She rested her forehead in her hand and squeezed her eyes shut. "Can we get out of here?"

"Uh, yeah." Suzy waved at the waitress returning with their second bottle. "Can you put all of this in to-go boxes?" Suzy handed over their voucher.

Setting down the bottle of wine, the server took the paper and left. While she was gone, awkward silence reigned over the table. Crystal wanted nothing more than to break the tension, but her brain was trying to process too many negative emotions to make chit-chat. Anger at Conner for spending time with Samantha, jealousy at their joyful expressions, hope that it was all a big misunderstanding, and crushed that the best relationship she had ever experienced might be over. She blinked back tears, grabbed the unopened bottle of wine, and stood.

"Ma'am?" The waitress had returned with the boxes but blocked her from leaving. "Alcohol isn't allowed to leave the premises."

Crystal was twenty-seven. She wasn't a ma'am. Knowing her anger had flared to irrationalism, but also not caring, Crystal leveled an impassive stare. Then, with deliberate steps, she circled around the blockading waitress, heading for the door with the bottle clutched in her hand.

"Ma'am." The server's voice called out in indignation.

"Don't worry, I'll go get her." Suzy grabbed the first bottle and dashed after Crystal, who was heading out the door. "Darn it. One sec." Suzy disappeared from Crystal's view as the restaurant door swung shut, but returned a moment later, backing out of the door and juggling the wine bottle and to-go boxes in one hand, her buffalo chicken wrap in the other.

A quick couple of steps brought her even with Crystal's listless pace.

"Are you going to be okay?" Suzy took an enormous bite of her food, but never took her concerned gaze from Crystal.

"Probably not until I find out what Conner has to tell me and we spring Roxie out of jail. I can't believe he's going to break up with me in the middle of this."

"You don't know that." Suzy's words, even around a mouthful, had the higher pitched version one uses when trying to convince someone, even when the facts are stacking up in opposition.

Crystal brushed at her tears and blinked a few times. "I've got to compartmentalize. I'm here to clear Roxie's name. I'm going to forget Conner for now, and this wine is going to help."

****

The dry, gritty sensation in Crystal's throat was followed by bewilderment. Where the heck was she? A few rapid blinks didn't do anything to clear her vision, but she spotted a glass of water on the table beside her. The sight of the liquid made her acutely aware of the

Sahara Desert having taken up residence in her mouth. She maneuvered the glass with a trembling hand, but, after some mental geometry, concluded she couldn't drink from her prone position without pouring the brimming glass over her face.

An awkward twist managed to get her upright with only a dribble of water on her shirt for the effort. The first tentative sip of the lukewarm liquid was heaven, easing the scratchiness of her throat and helping clear her cottonmouth.

"Back from the dead. I see you found the water I left you." Suzy strolled into the room, already dressed in her standard fleece and jeans. This fleece was a deep red, but in every other way the exact same as the blue one she had sported the previous day.

"Thank you." Crystal's typical timbre had a rasp to it. "What time is it?"

"Nine. Time to get going."

"Where?"

"We have another meeting with Kinsey this morning. Her assistant called an hour ago. She said Kinsey really, really wanted to talk."

"Why the urgency?"

"No freakin' clue."

Crystal took a long gulp and set down the glass. She rolled into a seated position, checked her phone, and confirmed the time. Her head gave a few warning thumps, but the pain eased after a minute. "Why am I on the couch?"

"You get stubborn after a bottle of wine. You wouldn't go to your bedroom, so I set a glass of water next to you and left you alone. Last I saw, you were texting someone."

"Oh, no." It rushed back, and she snatched up her phone to check the damage. "One, two, three…yikes, six total times."

"Six what?" Suzy dropped into the black leather recliner opposite Crystal and flung a leg over the arm.

"I told Conner I loved him six times last night. What's wrong with me?"

"Did he say he loved you?"

"Once. He asked if we'd been drinking and said he loved me, but only once."

"That's something." Suzy gave an encouraging nod.

"More concerning is not receiving a response from Olivia." Crystal gnawed on her thumbnail as she stared at her last outgoing text, willing a response.

"We deliberated that last night. You can't expect her to safely send messages with watching eyes all around."

"Not even once? Even when she goes to the bathroom?"

Suzy gave a snort. "There aren't any bathrooms in the woods, only his and her trees. Besides, we know service is spotty in this area."

"I'm getting concerned. She's too trusting, and I'm worried she's going to be discovered by the murderer."

"We discussed this last night, too. Don't you remember anything? Our main suspect is Kinsey, or at least she ordered someone to do it. After talking to those two ladies last night at the wine bar, things seem unsavory here."

Crystal stared out the enormous windows at the misty rain rolling in, masking the view of the waves. "If they're exponentially increasing rates on all of the current tenants, is it because Evergreen Resorts is desperate for money or because they're raising capital for expansion, such as buying and developing Frederick Baranhof's property?"

"We're not going to figure it out sitting here. Go get cleaned up and then you can pick Kinsey's brain for clues."

Crystal downed the last of her water and forced herself to stand. Nausea twinged her stomach once she was on her feet. "I'm starving, but I also don't want food."

"I bought a loaf of bread along with some other stuff at the convenience store last night while you were texting and guzzling vino. I'll make you some toast."

"You're a lifesaver."

Suzy gave a wry grin. "I'm nice like that."

Crystal staggered to the bathroom, hopeful a shower would restore her energy. The charcoal slate floor, the expansive tub, and the rainfall shower head made her feel like she was at a resort, which she supposed she was.

After puzzling out the dials to prevent being scorched or frozen, she stepped under the cascading water. She helped herself to the revitalizing shampoo, conditioner, and body wash in the shower nook. She left the enclosure smelling like lavender, and almost feeling human. Even considering everything she had just learned concerning Evergreen Resorts, this opulent bathroom tempted her to buy a vacation home.

She dried herself off and, with her meeting closing in, twisted her hair into a ponytail. Jeans, a long sleeve shirt, and a puffy white vest to keep the chill off the wet morning were more appropriate for a wilderness guide than a reporter, but Crystal hadn't banked on continuing that role for more than a single interview.

The smell of browning toast wafted into her room, luring her out. She owed Suzy for nursing her through the worst of her hangover. As Crystal entered the kitchen, her coworker turned caretaker smeared butter on her breakfast. Crystal sat on a barstool and took the proffered food. "Thanks, Suzy. Just what the doctor ordered." Crystal took a large bite off the corner, the crunch loud in the quiet home.

Suzy snorted, loaded two more pieces into the toaster, and shoved the lever down. "If you're nice to me, I'll share my secret buttered toast recipe with you. Passed down from generation to generation." Crystal cracked a smile at Suzy's levity, appreciating her efforts to lighten the stress of the previous night.

"Can I show you my coffee recipe in return?" Crystal hopped up and found a coffee maker on the counter. After a series of button taps, she and Suzy were brainstorming how to get information from Kinsey while sipping their morning caffeine.

"I think we should employ the shock and awe technique and ask her if she had anything to do with Frederick Baranhof's death. Once we make that accusation, I bet she falls all over herself trying to make excuses and come up with alibis." Suzy's fist thumped on the countertop to drive her point home.

"That plan doesn't get us anywhere. Looking guilty isn't enough to get Kinsey arrested and Roxie set free. We need her to reveal something we can use to prove her guilty or at least exonerate Roxie."

"How do we do that?"

"No idea." Crystal dropped her chin into the palms

of her hands and let out a deep exhale. They fell into silence, thinking. The tick of a clock mounted in the dining area reminded them they needed a plan and didn't have all day to come up with one. After a minute, Suzy opened her mouth as if to speak. Crystal leaned forward, hopeful her friend had a suggestion, but she clamped her mouth shut without any words.

A sharp rap on the front door broke Crystal's concentration, and she sat up straight. Exchanging a quick glance of surprise, they stood and headed to the entryway.

Crystal unlocked the door and was greeted by a glowering Kinsey, flanked by the policemen she recognized from when they had taped off the murder scene at the campground. The one on Crystal's left towered over everyone, almost a foot higher than Conner's six feet. His long arms were crossed over his chest, and he studied the scene intently.

The policeman on the right was shorter than Crystal, but made up for it with his impressive width, looking like nothing other than a fireplug, if fireplugs scowled and squinted at the world with distrust.

"Kinsey, I didn't think we were meeting until later." Crystal tried for collected, but the police presence edged her toward panic. This wasn't going to end well.

"What's with the cops?" Suzy squeezed in next to Crystal in the doorframe.

"The cops are here because I spoke to your boss at the newspaper. According to him, you aren't assigned to do a travel piece on the Olympic Peninsula. As a matter of fact, you were supposed to be in the office putting the final touches on a story about Hawaii."

Kinsey stabbed a finger at Crystal. "Then he transferred me to Brenda Carlson, who explained she was in the office working. All this means that you aren't who you say you are. So, who are you, and what are you doing pretending to be a travel reporter?"

"Why don't you mind your own business?" Suzy, always ready to mix it up, thrust her chin out and returned Kinsey's glare with interest.

Kinsey didn't relent. "This is literally my business. You are staying in a model home we use to advertise to prospective homeowners. It doesn't get any more 'my business' than this." The typically collected Kinsey finally lost her temper as she berated them.

"Do we have to answer her?" Suzy directed her question at the officers. Crystal spotted the corner of Suzy's mouth turn up when Kinsey's eyes bulged.

The taller cop shook his head, speaking with a slow, methodic voice. "No miss, you do not. But it would help us all feel better if you explained yourselves. Regardless, you do need to leave the premises if Ms. Laughlin says you are no longer welcome." His deep, rumbling voice was soft, easing the tension after Kinsey and Suzy's heated exchange.

"Or, we'll arrest you for trespassing." The shorter deputy's voice had a little too much eagerness for Crystal's comfort.

"Fine, we'll go. Give us a few moments to get our stuff." Crystal held up her palms in an attempt to calm the situation.

Kinsey piped up. "I don't trust them. My personal assistant will catalog the home to check they didn't steal anything."

"Is that necessary?" Crystal glowered at the

implied insult.

"You little…" Kinsey spluttered. "For what it's worth, I'm glad your boyfriend dumped you."

Crystal's jaw dropped at the cruel statement. *How did this woman even know about Conner?*

A sparkle in Kinsey's eye betrayed that she knew she'd hit home. "Eunice, get in here and make sure these two squatters didn't rob us blind."

From behind the towering officer, a young woman with supermodel features bustled in, dressed in a form fitting charcoal pantsuit and clutching an electronic tablet. Her blonde hair was slicked back tight to her scalp and gathered in a low bun behind her neck. She did her best to look stern as she strode through the house, tapping the display.

"We didn't take anything." Crystal's voice shook with anger. The accusations and cutting words regarding Conner were a rug burn on her frayed soul.

"Who knows what you two are up to?" Kinsey folded her arms across her chest, clamped her mouth shut, but never broke the glare she directed at Crystal.

"Don't I know you?" Suzy's voice broke the impromptu staring match. Her friend studied the tablet-tapping girl with an intense stare.

Lifting her head from her work, the young lady locked gazes with Crystal's fellow guide. Crimson bled into the woman's cheeks and she refocused on her work. "I've never met you before."

"Are you sure?" Suzy stared at her, frowning.

"Positive." After one last click of her nail on the tablet, the blushing object of Suzy's inspection switched off the device. "Everything's here."

"So you aren't thieves, only trespassers," Kinsey

snapped.

"Pardon me." The towering officer interrupted. "You informed us you invited these two to stay in this home. She is not trespassing, and your assistant confirmed nothing has been stolen. No crimes have been committed at this point."

"They lied about who they are." Kinsey's belligerent voice rose in anger.

The bulky cop nodded. "She did, but maybe you should have a better screening practice before you put guests up for the night."

The property manager's voice dropped, and a chill began pulsing from her. "My company raises more tax money for this city than you've seen in decades. I pay your salary and this is how I'm treated?"

"Now, Kinsey." The tall officer's slow voice commanded attention. "I know you're not suggesting we skirt the law because you give us money."

Crystal watched the unfolding scene with a small sense of satisfaction. The headstrong Kinsey had met her match, and she deflated at the suggestion of bribery. "Of course not, Tony."

These two must be the Big and Little Tony, the cops Emerson had referred to.

Big Tony shifted his attention to Crystal. "And you are no longer welcome here. If we catch you on Evergreen Resorts property, you will be arrested and Miss Laughlin will have the right to press charges. Do I make myself clear?"

The self-satisfied smile easing its way onto Crystal's face collapsed. There was so much more to unearth here, but the officer's stern words dragged a meek, "Yes, sir," from her.

"Well, then. Why don't you gather your stuff, and we'll let these fine folks get back to work."

Crystal nodded and spun to see Suzy still studying the assistant. "C'mon. Time to go." Crystal seized her friend's bicep and gave a tug. Suzy snapped out of her reverie and came to life.

They shoved clothes and food into their bags and were ready to go in minutes. Kinsey radiated disdain as they walked to Suzy's car.

Parked behind the police charger was a black Mercedes sedan, polished to a high gleam. An older, bald man in a tailored black suit leaned against the trunk. The assistant stood next to him, clutching the tablet to her chest. The frowning man stared at the two guides toting their bags, but his eyes were hidden behind wraparound mirrored sunglasses.

"Who's that guy?" Suzy nudged Crystal in the ribs with her elbow. As they returned his stare, he snapped something out of the corner of his mouth at the assistant. A look of profound fury crossed the young woman's face, but she bit her tongue.

"How the heck should I know?" His ominous stare and bulging arms were plucking at Crystal's already fragile courage. She yanked open Suzy's car door and tossed her bag in the backseat. Suzy flung hers on top and the two of them climbed in the car.

Suzy twisted her head to reverse out of the parking spot when a sharp knuckle tap on the window caused them to jump. Big Tony was crouched and peering in. Suzy fumbled for a second before hitting the descend switch on the window.

The officer spoke in his calm voice. "I'm not sure what's going on here, but my purpose is to keep the peace. Based on the fact the entire Laughlin clan has gathered to chase you out of their community means you two are into some mischief. Why don't you head out of town and let this feud lie?"

"Thanks for the advice." Suzy powered the window up.

The cop straightened and left to join his partner at their vehicle.

"Well, we aren't going to leave Roxie to rot in prison to keep them from being miffed." Waves of righteous anger washed away the fear induced by the glowering Kinsey and the cryptic warning from a small-town cop more interested in quiet than justice.

"I knew there was a reason we were friends." Suzy broke into a wide smile. "What's the plan?"

"Back to the depressing Forks Motor Inn. Time to come up with a strategy."

Chapter Twelve

Crystal and Suzy flung their bags on the brown comforter. The patrol car had followed them from the property until they arrived at the Forks Motor Inn. If there were any doubts in the cops' minds as to whether they were going to head out of town, they were now aware that the two wilderness guides weren't planning on leaving soon.

"There are three things we learned from our morning run-in with the police." Crystal flashed three fingers in the air.

"I always wanted a run-in with the law." Suzy hadn't lost her smile. "Shows we're pushing boundaries. Makes me feel like a badass."

"You climb mountains for a living and don't feel like a badass already?"

"Different kind of badass."

Crystal pursed her lips. "True. Anyway, since the officer called them the Laughlin clan, the first thing we learned is the bald guy must be Kinsey's brother, Grant." Crystal folded her first digit down. "Second, two do not constitute a clan. The girl who checked if we'd stolen anything must be related. I could swear we've seen her before, but I can't place her."

"Maybe she was getting a coffee at Mother Earth Café."

"Yeah, I suppose so."

Crystal folded down another finger. "Third, Kinsey must have a camera or a listening device in the room we stayed in." She dropped her last finger.

"Seriously?"

Crystal nodded. "She told me she was glad Conner dumped me." A lump lodged in her throat at the words, but she forced the next few out. "I'm positive the waitress didn't overhear us last night, so Kinsey must have been eavesdropping. I imagine it's how she found out I was pretending to be a reporter."

"Why would she do that?"

"I'm sure to figure out who's interested in buying, who's not, who needs to be cajoled, and who is willing to pay. I imagine it's pure gold to listen in on private conversations of couples on the fence when you're trying to close deals."

"That's messed up. What does it prove, though?"

"It proves we're dealing with unscrupulous human beings."

"How much do you think she knows about our murder investigation?"

Crystal shrugged. "Whatever we spoke aloud in that house, we need to assume she knows."

Suzy's phone chimed and she glanced down. "Aw, hell."

"What's up?"

"Ethan's wondering where I'm at. I'm supposed to meet him at Emerald City Outfitters to escort a group to the coast."

"When?"

"Five minutes ago." Suzy began typing and muttering, "Meet me in Forks."

"Is it along the way for him?"

"Luckily, yes. We're going to Ruby Beach and hiking up the coast to Point of the Arches. We'll camp on the Makah Reservation for a night, before heading home."

"Have you got your gear?"

"It's in my trunk. I'll leave my keys with you and jump in the van when he gets here. Looks like you'll be on your own for a little while. Whatcha got planned?"

"I might try and tail Kinsey, but I'm not sure what that'll prove. Still, it's not like I have other leads and it's obvious they're hiding something."

"Just be safe."

"That's what Conner always says." Crystal's heart squeezed in pain. He was hiding secrets, too.

"I'm sure there's an innocent reason he didn't tell you." Suzy's expression was filled with concern, but her words held no conviction behind them. "I know you'll save Roxie, too."

Rather than reassuring her, Suzy's words caused the weight of the world to nestle behind Crystal's neck. Save her friend from a murder charge, avoid some maniac who had burned her tent down, dodge the cops in this small town intent on keeping tabs on her, all while ignoring the fact that the man she adored was sending up red signal flares in their relationship. Her head dipped with the stress.

Suzy attempted an upbeat, motivational speech. "You got this. I'll be back tomorrow afternoon, so try not to get into too much trouble. You know what'll help? I'll buy us lunch."

****

Ethan arrived with a carload of hikers and a wry grin for Suzy. The fiery mountain climber did her best to look sheepish, but the expression was so foreign on Suzy's face, it had caused Ethan to break out into a full belly laugh. The troop had flooded the diner as Crystal finished off a Reuben sandwich.

She sipped a vanilla shake amid the smell of deep fat fryers and sizzling food, enjoying Ethan teasing Suzy about forgetting her job. After his ribbing stopped producing any effect, he changed the topic to his recovery. "Doc says my broken leg is fine. I've got some more physical therapy, and I'm not to put too much strain on it, but other than that I'm good to go."

"Not too much strain? Carrying an overnight pack on an eight-mile round trip hike along a rocky shore isn't what I would call taking it easy." Suzy shot a skeptical look at their recovering colleague.

"That's why you get to carry all of the heavy gear. I was going to make you do it since you bailed on me, but I'll play the sympathy card instead. Besides, it's all hands on deck. With Crystal looking into Roxie's case and Conner laid up for a couple of weeks, even Amelia is making a few treks out. We all want to see Roxie cleared, so we're happy to help." Ethan ran his hands through his thick mop of dark, curly hair. "Did I tell you that I visited her two days ago?"

"How's she holding up?"

"Not too bad. When she dishes out the food in the service line, she told me she makes a joke. She asks if they would like to dine-in or break-out. If they laugh, she figures they're okay. If they ignore her, she ignores them. If they glare, she stays out of their way." Ethan cracked a slight smile. "I was happy to see she was keeping her sense of humor, but I could tell she was worried. Our Roxie isn't made for prison life."

"I wish we were making some sort of headway." Crystal's meal settled like a stone in her gut. "So far, we've been shot at, our tent torched, the cops called on us, and I've lost track of my friend Olivia."

Ethan sat up. "Isn't Olivia the cute girl who's always hanging out with you? You can't lose her before I get a chance to ask her out."

Suzy snorted. "Maybe we should check if she's safe first, then you might get the guts to ask the poor girl out. Heaven help her if she agrees."

Ethan adopted a wry grin. "You wound me. I have nothing but honorable intentions."

"C'mon, Romeo. You flash those dimples at all the girls and two weeks later you're crying that you feel smothered. Keep away from Olivia. She's good people."

Ethan rested his hand over his heart in mock hurt before he collapsed into good natured laughter. "Fine. Fine. I'll save it for the single ladies on the tours. He cast a glance at two women from the group sharing a basket of fries. One ignored Ethan, but the other returned his glance with a small, satisfied smile.

Suzy snorted. "Finish your meal, champ. We've got miles to travel and Crystal has a murder to solve."

After two quick bites to polish off his hamburger, Ethan called out to the dining room, "Five more minutes and the van leaves with or without you."

****

Crystal waved at her departing friends, the dust stirred up from the van leaving the parking lot causing her to cough. The talk about Olivia had vaulted the anxiety for her friend's safety to the forefront of her brain. She sat on the rear bumper of Suzy's hatchback and squinted at her phone. Tilting her body to block the interfering rays of sun, she tapped her screen. Tendrils of fear constricted around her as she ventured a message.

—*How are you doing?*—

Her text should be innocuous enough that a chance person who saw her screen wouldn't suspect anything. Crystal bit her lip, praying for a reply to ease her worry. After a minute of silence, Crystal couldn't help it. She dialed Olivia's number. Intense relief blossomed at her missing friend's voice but dissipated when she recognized the recording.

"Hi. This is Olivia. I'm doing cool stuff right now and can't talk. Leave me a message."

Crystal jabbed at the red hang-up symbol. It was time to do a drive-by and see if she could spot her missing bestie. She dug out Suzy's keys and clambered in. She scooted the seat back a smidge and tweaked the mirrors.

As she drove toward the Baranhof property, she pondered her options. She didn't know where else to dig if Olivia found nothing. Her only other option was to tail the Laughlins around town and see if they did anything suspicious, but that bet was a long shot at best. Still, no stone would be left unturned if it meant freeing Roxie.

As she neared the protesters' site outside the fateful campground, she focused on the gathering next to the group of vans lining the entrance. Several men and women were sitting on camp chairs around an impromptu fire ring of round river rocks.

Crystal drove down the road to the Baranhof cabin. The grind of gravel underneath the Subaru's tires alerted a slender blonde tying a rope to a bucket underneath Tyler's hemlock. Crystal's spirit lightened for the first time in days, but when the woman spun at the noise of the car's passing, it was a stranger squinting in suspicion and not her best friend.

With effort, Crystal tamped down the panic clawing at her. Olivia must be in one of the tents or out for a stroll on the property's trails. *I'll wait half an hour and drive out. Olivia will for sure be there.* Parking in the same spot she had when she and Conner camped here, she got out of the car.

To distract herself from worrying, she walked to the crisped remains of the campsite. Despite several rainfalls dampening the scent, she wrinkled her nose at the odor of burnt plastic still permeating the area. At first, Crystal suspected animals had pawed through the charred lump of tent, sleeping bags, and cooler because it had been spread out. However, some of the debris littered the picnic table, making it clear that a human had searched the remnants of her and Conner's hiking equipment. Inspecting it closer, she could tell the items were separated into individual lumps of melted plastic. Whoever did this had been thorough.

An inquisitive chipmunk approached where she sat on the picnic table. It tested the air with several nose twitches and clambered up a fir tree, chittering in annoyance at her intrusion of its home.

"Fine." Crystal threw her hands up. "I get it. Do something or get moving." At her outburst, the chipmunk fell silent and raced several branches higher.

Checking her phone, the time showed twenty-one minutes had passed and zero replies to her text message. Close enough. Crystal jumped in the car and headed out. As she approached the encampment, she again slowed to a crawl.

The protesters ignored her. Four of them were erecting a sign by the road, but none were Olivia. As she headed to town, she glanced in the rearview mirror at the sign. "Protect Mother Earth, or she won't protect you." *Is that what happened to Frederick Baranhof? And Olivia? Were they not protected?*

****

Sitting in a drab room in a two-star motel wasn't going to save Roxie and sure as heck wasn't getting Crystal home any faster. Crystal's first order of business was to get a caffeine fix, and then stake-out Evergreen Resorts to spy on Kinsey. Tailing a suspect had helped her solve Philip Calvert's murder several months earlier. Maybe lightning would strike twice.

Before heading out of town, she swung into Mother Earth Café for an almond milk latte as well as one of the vegan chocolate muffins she had seen her first time there. She loved the comforting aroma of roasted coffee beans and got in the line behind a rail thin woman with curly, mousy hair studying the menu. A minute ticked by, and the barista behind the counter began tapping her fingers in impatience.

Her deep contemplation of the cafe's menu completed, the lady spoke. "Is your yogurt normal yogurt or something weird?"

A sigh slipped past Crystal's teeth before a sense of propriety caused her to bite her tongue. The lady glanced in annoyance, but Crystal studied her phone's screen like it was the source of her exasperation, and not the extra sixty seconds of life that had been wasted.

"It's coconut yogurt. It tastes the same as dairy

yogurt." Crystal had to hand it to the barista. She mustered a marvelously polite voice despite the impatience etched on her face.

"Eww. Gross. I suppose I'll take your last bran muffin instead." The whiny, nasal tones were nails digging into the tattered remnants of Crystal's patience.

"That's chocolate."

"I was hoping for bran, but I suppose it'll have to do."

She was taking the last chocolate muffin, and she didn't even want it? Before her brain could intercede, Crystal heaved another very audible, very exasperated sigh.

The shock on the barista's face told Crystal she had overstepped a social boundary, a moment before the indecisive muffin hijacker spun to confront her.

It was as if a spiritual vision of Crystal witnessed the scene from above, judging. With a giddy swoop, the consciousness flew into Crystal and the ludicrousness of her action struck her.

She had sighed at a complete stranger for ordering the last muffin in a coffee shop's display case. No ideas to defuse the situation sprang to mind, so Crystal sprinted from the café to the safety of the car. Banging her head against the steering wheel, she admitted the stress of this entire ordeal might be getting the best of her. After one last thump, she rested her forehead on the wheel, drew in a deep full breath, and blew out a slow, measured exhale.

"And some crazy girl yelled at me for taking the last muffin before running out of the coffee shop. No idea why. She must be on drugs." The lady's voice rose and fell as she walked behind Crystal's car, her phone to her ear.

Crystal eased out of the parking spot, overhearing half of the conversation. She hadn't said a word to the woman, much less yelled at her.

"She's peeling out of the parking lot right now. I can't believe there's some druggie loose in our community. I'm calling Tony." *Peeled out?* Crystal hadn't even stepped on the accelerator.

This was karma coming to bite her for getting frustrated at a complete stranger. Now, the town's lawmen had another reason to want her gone. Still, for one split second, the release of stress had helped her feel a tad better about everything going south in her life. However, the joy was washed away by the shame of not being able to control herself.

The roller coaster of emotions continued when she felt her anger rise after the accusation of being a drug addict. The lady was obnoxious to the point of rudeness and probably deserved a dose of confrontation by a stressed-out random stranger.

Satisfied with the justification of her actions, Crystal forwent her coffee and drove to the entrance of Evergreen Resorts. She turned onto the gravel shoulder of the two-lane highway and positioned her car to get a good view in case her suspects exited the complex.

Crystal tilted her seat and settled in. She meant to relax, but circular thoughts spun around her head. Olivia, missing. Conner, breaking up with her. Roxie, in jail for a crime she didn't commit. Her eyelid jumped. Olivia. Conner. Roxie. Tic. Olivia. Conner. Roxie. Tic. Crystal scrubbed the back of her hand over the rebellious twitch, but it persisted. Fed up, she rubbed her eyes and blinked them open. As the spots cleared, a familiar, immaculate black sedan approached from the resort.

The shining head of Grant Laughlin in the driver's seat caught her attention. His focus, however, was on the girl beside him, the one who had catalogued the house this morning, Eunice. They halted at the stop sign, and rather than drive, Grant twisted toward his passenger. Red-faced, he wagged a meaty finger, shouting his frustration. Eunice crossed her arms and stared out the side window, ignoring the tirade. A sheen of sweat glinted on Grant's forehead and he gave up any pretense of driving to give full attention to his bellowing.

With a quick whirl, the fuming assistant spun and slapped Grant with an open hand across his cheek.

The blow, even with her shoulder put into the effort, barely rocked his head. With a patient turn, he was face to face with the subject of his ire. He opened his mouth, but her hand shot out once more. He intercepted the strike, squeezing the captured wrist. Her mouth opened in a cry of pain, and she attempted to tug her arm free.

A logging truck, loaded with timber, cruised down the highway, passing between Crystal and the drama she was watching unfold. After it passed, the two combatants had settled down to glare at one other. A minivan stopped behind her quarry and honked its horn at the idling car.

Whatever was going on between these two, Crystal wanted to get to the bottom of it. Weird things were happening in this development, and this wild disagreement intrigued her. It may have nothing to do with Roxie, but it was the only lead Crystal had. As they merged onto the highway, Crystal started her car to follow.

Flashing lights in her mirror and the single whoop of a siren caught her attention. Crystal swore in frustration. The black sedan disappeared around a corner, the towering trees ensuring she had lost them for good. In her side view mirror, the long legs of big Tony led the way for the rest of his lanky frame as he exited the police cruiser parked behind her. His footsteps approached with the slow beat of a church bell.

Crystal's mind raced. What had she done to cause the police to want to talk to her again? Had the annoying woman from the coffee shop called to complain and they took her seriously? She was going to give big Tony a piece of her mind.

The tap of his knuckles on the window snapped her internal tirade. She punched the window button and it whirred down.

"Why are you still here, miss?"

"It's America. I'm allowed to be here." Crystal's ire bubbled and was being expressed as sass. A small part of her brain not overwrought with stress attempted to yank the reins on her mouth, but in her current mood, reason didn't stand a chance of taking control.

"Let's keep this on topic and civil." The officer remained calm, but there was an unmistakable undercurrent of vexation. "What are you doing here? Parked outside of private property you have been expressly forbidden to enter, watching two of the preeminent citizens of our community? Are you stalking them?"

"Of course not, I'm waiting to meet a friend here."

It was the best lie she could dredge out of her mind. She made a mental note to work on her ability to come up with falsehoods under duress. The need for that skill cropped up way more than a wilderness guide should ever expect.

"Uh-huh." The cop peered over his sunglasses. "Your meeting place is the gravel turn out between milepost thirty-two and thirty-three and not the coffee shop you left twenty minutes ago?"

"How did you know I was there?" *Were they following her around? Didn't they have anything better to do in this town?*

Big Tony heaved a sigh. "I saw your car in the lot when I was doing my rounds. A red station wagon with a ski rack and a bumper sticker telling me to 'go climb a mountain' is a bit noticeable. For crying out loud, I followed your car as you drove away from the resort this morning. Now tell me, what are you doing here?"

"Meeting a friend." Wow. Her brain had taken a siesta and kept spitting out the same answer.

"Fine. If you want to stick with that, tell me why you started to leave when I showed up?"

"My friend texted me to meet her somewhere else."

"Well, that makes sense." The cop put on an affable grin. "You're free to go." Crystal spirits rose with the words. "*If* you show me the text. Otherwise, I'm going to take you down to the station and we'll sort this out." And with that, her heart stopped beating.

"I don't have a text from my friend." The return of the lump in her throat caused the words to come out in a hoarse whisper.

"I didn't think so." Big Tony sighed in disappointment. "Why don't you get in the cruiser. I'll have your car towed to the impound lot, and we'll settle what's going on between you and the citizens of Forks."

"Okay." The fight fled from Crystal. Her break had come and gone, and now she was getting hauled off by the police. How could she save Roxie, rescue Olivia, and patch things up with Conner if she were arrested?

A strange feeling of relief chased the stress away. She didn't have to worry if she were in jail. She could wait until she was released—whenever that was—and tell everyone she'd been incarcerated because she'd pressed too hard. Hopefully, Mrs. McReady would take care of Elf until Crystal was freed. No one else would adopt her nightmare cat if she were locked up for an extended time.

She walked from her car to the Dodge Charger in a daze. The officer cuffed her, recited her Miranda rights, and guided her head through the door. Steel mesh loomed before her, reinforcing the depth of trouble she'd found herself in.

Past the barrier, Crystal stared at a radio with a green light and a shotgun locked in place beside the center console. Her arresting officer circled around the vehicle and folded himself into his seat. He grabbed the radio handset and depressed the button.

"Officer Maldinado. Code four."

An obnoxious, nasal female voice responded with an acknowledgment. "Copy, officer Maldinado. What is your situation?"

"I'm returning to the station, Dottie. Can I get impound to pick up a red Subaru Outback outside of Evergreen Resorts? License plate, alpha-tango-juliet-six-one-three."

"I'll notify them. See you in a bit."

The cop set the handset down in the holster of the radio and made a U-turn onto the highway.

****

A single bite had been taken from the top of the chocolate muffin. The bite had been deep, and she could tell how moist the cake was inside, making her mouth water. How could everyone in this one-horse town have her favorite treat, but she couldn't get her hands on one to save her life? The tip of her nose itched and she lifted one shoulder, tilting her head to get at it, but only succeeded in scrubbing her cheek when the handcuffs restrained her.

The small Forks police station didn't look much larger than her dentist's office and possessed the same amount of charm. All it was missing was the sound of a drill to complete the ambiance. Officer Maldinado had looped her cuffs through the slats of a steel chair and re-clasped them before telling her someone would be with her in a moment, as if this was a fine dining restaurant, and he the *maître d'*.

A door shut behind her, and the squeak of sneakers on concrete approached. The steps ceased, and the sound of paper shuffling was followed by a snort. Crystal wanted to muster the effort to turn and inspect her guest, but all she could manage was attempting a few deep breaths.

"I should have known you'd end up here." The piercing tones were a pick straight to Crystal's brain, making her head throb. "Coming off your high from this morning, I bet." Her nemesis from the coffee shop circled around her with more shoe squeaking, further compounding Crystal's burgeoning migraine.

"I'm not on drugs." Crystal mounted all the conviction she could manage, but her words weren't acknowledged.

The woman dropped into a chair on the opposite side of the counter, tapping her ballpoint pen. "Uh, huh." The sarcastic tone coupled with the obnoxious voice kindled the fire in Crystal's abdomen, but she fought the urge to lay into her annoying adversary. Ceasing tapping, the police secretary applied the pen to the paper in front of her, mumbling, "Better put you down for the drug panel, to be safe. Can't have you endangering the children of the community." With a sickening smile, she deigned to meet Crystal's weary eyes. "Now, do you have a home, or do you sleep in your car, sweetie?"

Crystal nearly choked on the venom in her mouth but managed a controlled, "I have a home. It's the same address as on the license the officer took."

"I don't seem to have that here. I'll put you down as transient." Crystal's tormentor jotted more notes on the paperwork in front of her.

It was a good thing she was locked to her chair, because the urge to throttle the woman would have landed Crystal in a lot more trouble than she was already in. Still, her jaw clenched until her molars ached, and the words left unsaid formed a painful knot in her chest. Instead, with the patience of a saint, she managed to ask, "How long am I going to be here?"

"It *was* until we processed you. However, since you're under suspicion of drugs, we'll need to wait for the tox screen from the blood sample we'll be taking. That only takes a couple of days, a week at most. I'd expedite it, but our budget is strained this quarter." Glee lit the nasty woman's face as she poured out her sickly sweet jabs. The secretary lifted a garbage can from under her desk, and not breaking eye contact with Crystal, swept the unfinished muffin into the garbage. "I thought it was going to be better than this."

Crystal's hand jerked to a halt, the cruel metal cuffs biting into her wrists as she instinctively lunged. The petty acts meant to taunt Crystal had finally elicited a reaction. Whether she meant to clobber the nasty lady, rescue the muffin, or snap her restraints, she didn't know.

"Tsk, tsk. Might do you some good to say no to drugs." With a loud scrape, the police secretary shoved back her chair, humming "zip-a-dee-doo-dah" as she left. After several interminable minutes, she returned. "The nurse will be here shortly to take your blood sample."

"What about my phone call?" Crystal wanted to call Roxie's lawyer, the best bet to get her out of this mess.

"Of course. Of course." The police secretary lifted the handset of the phone on her desk. "What number would you like for me to dial?"

"I don't know the number. It's on my cell phone. Can I have it to make my call?"

"Oooh, I'm so sorry, but it has to be on a monitored line. I can't do that."

"Fine. Let me look it up and then you can dial from your phone." Crystal let out a huge sigh. It was either that or start screaming.

"I would, but you see, I'm too busy to check out your phone from evidence, look up the number of your drug dealer, and see if he can bail you out. There is so much to do around the office." With a sweep of her hand, she gestured at the empty and silent workspace.

The front door opened and an older Asian nurse in baby blue scrubs walked in, clutching a small red box. "Knock, knock. How are you, Dottie?"

"Fine, Amy. Thanks for walking over. Can you take a sample for the lab? Standard drug panel, please."

"Are you sure? She doesn't look like she's high." The nurse studied Crystal with clinical detachment.

"Just do your job, Amy." With a harrumph, despicable Dottie left the room.

Amy sat in a chair next to Crystal. "Don't mind her. She sometimes lets her power get in the way of good judgment."

"Tough not to be upset, when she has my life in her hands." Bitterness flowed from Crystal.

"I know. But it will all work out. Trust me." The nurse set down the blood collection tray on the table and lifted the top off. Inside sat a collection of syringes, vials, and alcohol. With a deft and practiced motion she rolled up Crystal's sleeve, wrapped a rubber strap around her upper arm and had a blood sample drawn in under a minute. "There. That wasn't so bad, was it?"

Crystal ground her teeth with the frustration of it all. "It isn't the pain of having blood drawn that's the bad part. It's the humiliation of it all. I can't believe I've been arrested and tested for drugs."

"That's Dottie's petty ways. I know you're not on drugs. Your health is perfect and your vision is clear. She's making your life miserable for some reason."

"We might have had a run in at the coffee shop earlier today."

Amy grimaced, her wrinkles crinkling in

sympathy. "Dottie is a vindictive sort. If you're on her bad side, she'll get even any way she can."

"Tell me something I don't know."

With a kind look, the nurse gathered her things and stood to leave. Big Tony held the door for her as he returned to the station, a white fast food bag clutched in one hand and a large soda in the other. Grease soaked through one side of the sack and the smell of French fries reached Crystal's nose. He set the food and drink on the countertop in front of her.

"Now, if I unlock you, you'll behave yourself when I walk you to the holding cell, right?" He fixed Crystal with a steely stare until she nodded. He returned the gesture and removed the cuffs.

"Grab your meal and head down the hall to the left."

Crystal had grown tired of fast food at this point, but at least she was getting dinner. She picked up her meal and walked toward the indicated hallway, reveling in the freedom from the restraints.

The officer followed behind her. "Cell on the right." His sharp words caused Crystal to jump, and she headed to the right. There was only one other cell down the hall on the left, but the door was ajar, so it appeared she had a private suite.

A stone bench stuck out from the right side of the wall, covered with a scratchy looking army-green, wool blanket. A sink and toilet were off to her left, the entirety of her creature comforts.

The sound of the cell door hinges squealing halted with a metallic clang. The officer jangled his keys as he sorted through them. Finding the correct one, he inserted it into the lock. With a quick twist, the bolt thudded into place.

"Dottie didn't let me make my call." If she could speak to Isabella, she'd be out of here in no time.

"I'll talk to her." The officer's distracted tone didn't give Crystal a whole lot of hope that prioritizing the call was big on his to-do list. With a final tug on the door to ensure it was locked, he left Crystal alone with her food.

"I guess this is an unhappy meal." She grimaced at the food and her poor attempt at humor. She wished her family, Suzy, and most of all Conner were there to share her joke. They would roll their eyes but chuckle at the silly pun. Instead, all she got was silence.

Her growing hunger evaporated, and now, left alone to her thoughts, her appetite fled. She took a few sips of the cola, but the acid from the drink paired with her own churning stomach cause her to dump the rest and fill the cup with water.

The scent of grease exacerbated the beginnings of nausea, and she set the fast food on the sink to get it as far away as possible, before lying down. The stone bench was as uncomfortable as promised, cold and hard. The blanket, however, was even worse than it appeared, the rough fibers irritating her skin through her clothes. Squirming got the worst of the discomfort under control, and she took up a position staring at the ceiling. Her nausea receded, but her headache returned to its residence in her frontal lobe.

That's when her worries crept in. How was she to save Roxie from inside a jail cell? Would anyone notice her missing? Her sister and parents would wonder where she was next Sunday when she didn't show up for brunch, but with her new job as a wilderness guide, her erratic work schedule caused her to miss the family get-togethers from time to time. Conner might be relieved to not see her for a while if he planned to break up, ecstatic to delay the unhappy chore. He could bide his time by frolicking with his new girlfriend Samantha.

However, Suzy would notice her car was missing. She'd look into the situation when she returned to town, tomorrow. If she started at the police station, it shouldn't take her long to solve the mystery of Crystal's disappearance.

The fear that kept crashing over all others was Olivia. Crystal had dragged her happy-go-lucky friend into something not concerning her. Now, she was missing after investigating an enclave of what could be eco-terrorist murderers. Spikes of adrenaline competed with her stomach acid to erode her being from within.

The spiderwebbed cracks in the plastered ceiling offered no answers to her growing list of worries. She willed tears to come, anything to ease the tension clenching her entire body, but her vision remained dry. Part of her soul had become numb, and as the world abandoned her to a lonesome jail cell, she couldn't help but give up caring.

Chapter Thirteen

"You can't throw an innocent girl in a cell and leave her to rot with no charges," the gruff voice barked.

The words snapped Crystal awake to the sight of the same ceiling she had stared at for hours. Sometime during the night she must have drifted off. *Was it morning?* There were no windows, and the lack of natural light made it hard to judge how long she'd been there.

Officer Maldinado's slow, pedantic voice answered. "Calm down. We can detain suspicious people for up to twenty-four hours, but honestly, I didn't know she'd be here all night. She was supposed to cool down for a couple of hours in the cell to scare her, and then be released to her own devices. I'd hoped she would skedaddle to the city and leave the good people of our town alone."

That answered that question. Crystal swung her legs off the bench and stood. The cricks in her back and neck confirmed she'd been lying down for a lengthy time.

"So you're either cruel or incompetent. What in the seven hells is going on in this station?"

"Don't go crossing a line you don't want to cross, Emerson."

Emerson the logger? What was he doing here?

"Or what? You going to arrest me, too? Throw me in jail? Not tell anyone I'm locked up? Are you the Gestapo?" Her advocate's voice kept growing in volume the more he verbally sparred with Big Tony.

"I do what I need to keep Forks safe. My number one priority is to serve and protect the citizens, and this girl is harassing the respectable members of the Laughlin family." Something was off regarding the officer's sanctimonious defense, but she couldn't piece it together with cobwebs still befuddling her brain. Emerson could, though.

"Your job, if you must know, is to serve and protect all, not just the citizens living here. I know you think Kinsey and Grant crap sunshine, but I can't help thinking it has something to do with the tax money their development has injected into the community. You sure enjoy speeding around in the new Dodge Charger patrol car you got this year."

Crystal rolled her head side to side, and a few alarming pops issued from her neck vertebrae as they realigned. While she appreciated Emerson's help, she wished he'd broached the subject of her freedom with a touch more tact.

"Are you suggesting I've been bribed to abuse my power?"

"I didn't suggest anything."

"Well, all right then." Big Tony's mollified tone didn't last.

"I just came out and said you're a Laughlin stooge."

"You bitter ol' son of a—"

"Hello!" Crystal didn't want them to forget her in their quarrel. Besides, it didn't seem to be breaking in her favor. If she left them to their arguing, the best she might hope for was Emerson's companionship in the cell opposite her, at the rate he was going.

"Well, are you gonna let her out or stand there with your night stick in your hand?" Emerson couldn't leave well enough alone. Even though she wasn't witness to the scene, Crystal was positive the officer must have leveled a fierce glare, because the abrupt silence was palpable. Not a single noise invaded the calm for several thudding heartbeats.

The jingle of the keys broke the tension, and the slap of hard-soled shoes approached. The looming form of Officer Tony's nearly seven feet came into view between her bars.

"Am I free to go?"

"You are. Looks like your file was tagged for a drug screen, delaying your release. I'm not sure how that happened."

"It was Dottie who put me down for a drug screen. That bitter shrew did it because she has it in for me."

Big Tony's visage hardened, and his nostrils flared wide. "Why would my wife do that, huh? She's a fine Christian woman with nothing but love in her heart."

Well, crap. Maybe she should have left the negotiations to the fiery old logger. At least he'd only personally attacked the cop and not his wife.

Big Tony stood like a brick wall in the cell doorway, blockading her escape. His face grew blotchy as he stared down at Crystal, taking short, huffing breaths, until Emerson shouted from the lobby.

"What's the hold up? I ain't got all day."

After a forced, drawn-out exhale through clenched teeth, the officer spun on his heel. "Follow me, ma'am.

Let's get your stuff and get you outta my hair."

Crystal followed the lumbering giant to the lobby. A grinning Emerson stood waiting, eyes alight with mischief. The old logger tugged on his suspenders and gave a wink to Crystal, deepening her jailer's scowl.

"Don't push it," the cop growled before leaving the two alone. He returned with a black plastic bin. From it, he extracted Crystal's wallet, keys, and phone, handing each to her and making a tick mark on a sheet of paper stored in the box with her belongings. "The car you were driving is in the impound lot behind the station. The vehicle is not registered in your name, so we left a message with the owner to ensure it hasn't been stolen. Now, I suggest you leave town and head home."

"Now, wait one minute," Emerson butted in. "It's up to her where and when she goes. This isn't the Wild West, and you can't run her out on a rail."

"That's why I suggested it to her, you old coot. If she wants to stay in town, that's her business, but if she's caught harassing anyone else, I'm hauling her here for another timeout."

"And I'll be right behind, asking what the hell is wrong with you. Unless this young lady breaks a law—and annoying you isn't one of them—I suggest you let her lead her life how she wants."

Tony threw his hands up in frustration. "Just get out of my station. Both of you."

With a snaggletooth grin to celebrate his victory, Emerson nodded to Crystal and the two of them departed the police station. The rumble of a semi passing on the highway made it impossible to speak. As it sped away, Crystal gave the old lumberjack a grateful smile. "Thank you for coming to help me. You don't know what this means to me." She blinked away tears. "I felt like everyone had abandoned me."

He gave her an awkward pat on the arm. "That's the point of why they did it. They were isolating you to make you feel alone."

"How did you even know I was in jail?"

"Easy. My wife told me." Crystal gave him a quizzical look. "My wife is Amy, the nurse who took your blood. She told me what happened over breakfast this morning. I hate to let bullies have their way, so I thought I'd come down and raise some hell before my second cup of coffee. Besides, I've taken a liking to you and Conner. You seem like good sorts."

"I'm so happy you came to the station. The jail cell made me think all kinds of crazy things."

"Well, you're free now. Can that lad of yours come and pick you up with his bum knee?" The elation of feeling like someone was on her side crumbled as she imagined Conner.

Emerson read her face wrong. "Is his knee in that bad of shape? Hell's bells, I won't ever forgive myself for scaring him enough to take that tumble."

"He'll be okay, in time. It sounds like a couple of weeks and he'll be out of the brace. Thanks for worrying though."

"Why don't you come over to my place? I'll call ahead to Amy and have her whip something up. You can tell us how the sleuthing is going."

"I can't impose on you any further."

"Nonsense." He cut her protest off. He pulled his phone out and tapped a few buttons.

Amy's voice answered, "Did you get her out?"

"Course I did. Can you whip up another serving of

breakfast for her, and a little more for me? Arguing with cops is hungry business."

His wife's pleased assent issued from the phone's speaker, and he hung up.

"It's settled. You're coming over."

****

Of course, Emerson and his wife lived in a log cabin. After a winding drive up a steep slope, the classic home greeted them with its nostalgic charm. The crisscrossed logs were hewn at the joints to stack two stories high. Small panes of glass marked rooms on the top story, but a large picture window on the bottom floor promised panoramic views of the forest stretching below. Adirondack and rocking chairs were scattered pell-mell on the front porch, and the crumbling remains of a jungle gym graced the side of the yard in a patch of overgrown grass.

"Home, sweet home. Built this with my own two hands when Amy and I got married forty years ago. Barely got it finished in time for the arrival of our first son. Raised all four kids here." Emerson beamed with pride as he took in his residence. "We've taken care of our home, and it's taken care of us."

"Your place looks like a painting."

"That's kind of you." His grin widened with pleasure at her compliment. "Living rustic doesn't appeal to everyone, but for us, it has been a fairytale dream come true."

As they got out of the vehicle, motion caught her attention, and Crystal swiveled her head to the side of the house. A recently completed split rail fence, the scent of the cedar filling the air, encircled a garden laid out in neat rows. Three deer strolled inside the fence, nibbling on whatever caught their fancy.

"Aww, hell. They're eating my wife's strawberries." Emerson clapped his hands together with several sharp cracks. "Hey! Get outta there."

One of the deer lifted its head and stared at the noise. After a twitch of its black tail and a flick of its ears, it returned to its tasty snack.

"My new fence doesn't seem to have done the trick." Taking slow steps toward the animals, Emerson rode to the defense of his wife's fruit. When he passed a certain magical point, the herd of deer lifted their heads. "Go on. Git. You have a whole forest to eat, and you keep coming here. Are strawberry plants truly that good?" He took another step closer, and the deer began nervously stepping away. As one, they spun and walked in the opposite direction. With graceful leaps, they cleared the three-foot fence with room to spare and began trotting toward the tree line, a short distance away. Within seconds, they disappeared from sight.

The front door flew open, and Amy stepped onto the porch. "What are you carrying on about out here?"

"Flopsy, Mopsy, and Cottontail were in your strawberries."

"You named your deer?" Crystal found it hard to imagine a gun toting, classic woodsman like Emerson naming the woodland critters pestering his property.

Amy focused on Crystal standing by the vehicles. "I'm glad you got out. And, yes, Emerson named these three. They've been coming here for years and they eat anything we plant, but he loves them anyway."

"I'm right here, darling." Emerson pointed at the ground. "You're ruining my tough guy image."

His wife snorted. "Sure, sure." Turning her

attention to Crystal she gestured toward the front door. "Come in, come in. I have breakfast ready for you. How do you take your coffee?"

"A little cream and sugar. You don't have to do this, though."

"Nonsense. We love company." She led the way, with Crystal and Emerson trailing after.

The cabin was as cozy inside as it promised from the outside. The walls were logs but cut to create a flat surface inside. The gaps in between were packed with a gray material, creating a layered effect, not unlike a cake. The ceiling of the great room stretched to the second story. On the left, the adjacent living room had a ring of couches and recliners with quilts draped over their backs, inviting one to cover up if the weather got chilly. The kitchen and dining room were to the right of the entry way, where the delectable scent of baking emanated.

Her nose must have twitched because Amy answered her unspoken question. "It's strawberry shortcake. I have to buy the berries from the grocery store because of our friends outside, but I made the shortcake earlier this morning. I also whipped the cream myself. Interested?"

"I would love some. I didn't eat last night." At Amy's shocked expression, Crystal explained. "They gave me something to eat, but I didn't have much of an appetite."

"Well, I'm glad to hear they brought you food, at least. Our cops are intent on keeping our little town sleepy, but I never imagined they were cruel." Amy made her way across the large room to the kitchen. Without even glancing backward, she called out,

"Boots off, Emerson. I just swept."

Grumbling, her husband stopped in his tracks and bent over to unlace his boots. Sure enough, a trail of mud extended behind him. Crystal followed suit, but her hostess spoke up. "No need for you to take off your shoes. You're fine. He, on the other hand, spends his days tromping around the woods."

"I'm usually in the woods, too. I'm a wilderness guide." Crystal stripped off her boots to be polite and padded over to the kitchen. She sidled up to the island to watch Amy work.

Three plates with generous wedges of shortcake were laid out. Amy opened the fridge and retrieved two bowls. Snapping the fridge door closed with her hip, she set them on the counter.

A now bootless Emerson busied himself behind his wife. Taking three coffee mugs from the rack they hung on, he laid them in a row.

"Trespassing on your husband's job-site wasn't the most auspicious meeting, but once he realized we weren't there to cause mischief, he warmed up."

Amy ladled strawberries over each piece of cake. "We both know sometimes everyone needs a hand in life, and the fact you were trying to help someone makes all the difference."

Emerson added a measure of cream and sugar to each cup. "It's why we're here for you. You're trying to right wrongs and others are gonna get in your way. A little assistance once in a while shows you're not alone."

Emotion constricted Crystal's throat as Amy scooped a generous dollop of whipped cream onto each dish and Emerson poured coffee in the cups. The kindness of these two virtual strangers was restoring her hope. She blinked to clear her vision before they noticed. "I can't thank you enough."

Amy glanced up, giving her a sympathetic smile, but Emerson prattled on without a clue. "Don't thank me too much. Putting Big Tony in his place was the most fun I've had in years. I remember when he was a pimply teenager I caught joyriding in his mama's minivan in the woods. I found him in a mud-bog. Four-wheeling, he called it. He cried so hard, he blew snot bubbles. Ha!" Emerson sat with a thud on the stool at the counter. "I towed him out and sent him on his way, but he didn't bother to wash the mud off. From what I heard, his ma took one look and grounded him for a month."

Amy snorted. "I can't believe he ended up a policeman. He was a little hellion if his mother is to be believed. Now he does whatever those Laughlins tell him, meek as a lamb."

Crystal's mind roiled at her words. Was he crooked enough to kill Frederick Baranhof, arrest Roxie for the crime, and chase Crystal out of town to protect his overlords? It made a lot of sense. It was suspicious how Roxie had been arrested with no other suspects scrutinized. *How did one investigate a crooked cop?*

"Aren't you hungry dear? Can I fix you something else?"

Her attention refocused on Amy, who studied her with a worried expression.

"No, I love strawberry shortcake." To prove it, Crystal lifted a precarious bite with her fork and shoved it in her mouth.

"How do you like it?" Emerson asked as soon as

she took the bite.

Crystal chewed for all she was worth to answer when Amy swatted her husband's arm. "Stop that." Amy favored Crystal with a wry grin. "He loves to ask as soon as guests take mouthfuls. He thinks it's hilarious."

"You spoil all my fun." The woodsman scraped the bottom of his plate with his fork. Crumbs of shortcake decorated his beard, testimony to the speed of his eating.

Crystal managed to swallow and answer. "It's delicious. The strawberries are plump and juicy, and the shortcake crumbles and melts with buttery, sugary goodness. The whipped cream is rich and frothy, better than any I have ever tasted. I have to know how you made this."

"I bought the cream from Dixon's dairy farm, added a dash of vanilla, a sprinkling of powdered sugar, and whipped it." She pointed at a stand mixer on her countertop. "Nothing to it."

Now that she'd tasted the strawberry shortcake, Crystal polished off the rest of her serving with a speed that would have done Emerson proud. Amy could run a memorable bed and breakfast with her log home and baking acumen. Conner would love it if she surprised him with a romantic getaway to a destination like this. Her fanciful thoughts fled when her brain reasserted control. *Were she and Conner still a couple?*

"It looks like we're losing you again, dear." Amy propped her chin in her hand, gazing at Crystal. "Anything you want to share?"

"I don't want to worry you and Emerson with my problems. You've both done so much for me."

"Nonsense. I'll pour us more coffee and you can tell us everything. Maybe we can help."

They made their way into the living room, sitting on recliners, facing one another. A quilt composed of the star pattern in varying earth tones decorated the back of her seat. Crystal had never quilted, but she was sure her mother and Amy could talk on the craft for hours.

Sipping her coffee, Crystal explained everything since the murder happened. They ate up the gossip regarding the Laughlins and their shady business dealings but grew concerned for Olivia as the tale unfolded.

"So you're telling me you haven't heard from your friend for several days, after she inserted herself into a nest of possible murderers?" Amy's jaw hung open after the summary.

Crystal's stomach gave a queasy turn. "I can't stop worrying about her."

"You were right not to go in after her." Emerson had lost the mischievous glint and adopted the angry tone he'd used when catching her trespassing on his property. "You might end up dead, I mean in trouble, like her." He corrected himself when Crystal's eyes shot open at his words.

"It's not that I'm afraid to look for her. At first, I wanted to give her space so she could blend in while I investigated Kinsey on the Evergreen Resorts property. Then, I got arrested. Now, I'm here. Worried sick."

Emerson frowned as he stared out the window. "I'd go, but those crazed hippies know me on sight. It'll get ugly quick if they spot one hair of my beard. I'd tell you to call the authorities, but they aren't your biggest fans, are they?"

Crystal had settled on her course of action, though. "My other friend, Suzy, is going to be in town when she finishes her hike today. We'll rescue Olivia as soon as she gets here." Suzy would love nothing more than walking into the camp and demanding answers.

"You think your friend and you have enough nerve to face down an entire encampment?"

Courage overflowed Crystal. "Oh, most definitely."

Chapter Fourteen

Crystal and Suzy waved at the disappearing vehicle as Ethan tooted his horn and drove away from the Forks Motor Inn.

"Did you have a good hike?"

Suzy unslung her pack, and, holding it by a strap, rolled her shoulders. "You kidding? I love trips on the coast, and the Point of the Arches was awe-inspiring."

Crystal had seen photos of the rugged rocky outcroppings jutting into the ocean. It was a four-mile hike in, and the vista was a popular place to catch a sunset for the ages and to explore the tide pools. As the name hinted, grand rocky arches were carved out of the stone where it met the ocean.

"Did you find anything to help Roxie?" Suzy asked.

"It's a funny story. You'll appreciate it when I tell you." Crystal hoisted the backpack from her friend's hand, who gave a grateful nod. Crystal was surprised by the heft. "Geez, Ethan did make you carry all of the gear."

"Yep. Tent, stove, water, food. I think he carried his pillow and sleeping bag, but at least he's walking again."

Crystal started in the direction of their room.

"Crystal? Where's my car?" Suzy studied the parking lot, squinting at trucks and sedans as if by some miracle they would transform into her Outback.

"That's part of the funny story. Don't worry. It's safe. As a matter of fact, I can't think of a safer place for it to be." Crystal fished the key from her pocket, unlocked the motel room, and tossed Suzy's bag on the bed.

"Where's that?" Suzy tilted her head left and right, neck popping with each motion.

"The police impound lot. I got arrested. An officer left you a message on your phone, but I guess you haven't listened to it yet."

Suzy stopped in her tracks and stared at Crystal. Her whole face scrunched tight, as if in pain. It took another moment before she spoke in slow, measured tones. "I distinctly remember telling you to stay out of trouble."

Emerson and Amy's help, as well as Suzy's reappearance, fueled Crystal's mood with a wild energy. For the first time in days, her spirit felt light, and the tragedies of yesterday took on the beginnings of humor with the support of friends. "Really? I kinda sucked at that. Wish I'd listened. Do you want to go get your car? We have to walk, but it's only a mile away. Then we're going to rescue Olivia."

"You still haven't heard from her?"

"No, I haven't, and I'm worried. Emerson and Amy are worried, too."

"Isn't Emerson the old logger? And who the heck is Amy?" Suzy grabbed a water bottle from her pack and gave it a shake. Satisfied the sloshing meant the bottle was full enough, Suzy followed after a bustling Crystal.

The act of doing something useful had replenished

the bounce in Crystal's step. For the first time since breaking into the Forks Logging Company trailer, there was the promise of simple, straightforward action. The worry for Olivia gnawed at her, and the desire to see her friend's smiling face drove her to set a quick pace out of the motel parking lot toward the police station. Suzy was up for the speed-walk, not even fazed by the fact she'd hiked miles earlier in the morning.

On the way, Crystal described how events had unfolded since she'd been left to her own devices. Describing her arrest elicited the expected muttered expletives and threats from Suzy, but the details of Emerson's argument with Officer Big Tony Maldinado produced a toothy grin. "I'm beginning to like this guy. He sounds like my sort of person. I wish I'd been there to see it."

"If you'd been there, you would have been in the cell next to me, and not too keen on the experience." Crystal's new optimism hadn't spread to remembering her night in jail with any fondness.

A car whizzed past as they began hoofing it alongside the highway. Suzy threw a companionable arm over Crystal's shoulder. "It still would have been worth it. We could have whiled away the time playing harmonica and digging tunnels together."

"We wouldn't have made much headway in the concrete floor, but I appreciate your enthusiasm."

A loud honk made them jump, and a guy bellowed a rude comment from the cab of a pick-up truck as he swerved around them. Suzy shouted an expletive laden sentence at him, suggesting an improbable thing he could do to himself. A moment later, her voice was back to normal. "Is the impound lot behind the station?"

Crystal squinted in the distance. "Yep. I think I can see your Subaru."

"Let's get it and then save Olivia's bacon." Suzy broke into a dog trot and Crystal matched the pace to the entrance of the station.

With a hard yank, Suzy flung the door open. Crystal's least favorite person, the chocolate muffin pilfering Dottie, sat behind the counter, filing her nails. A phone rang next to her. Ignoring it, she favored Suzy and Crystal with an intense glare.

Through a tightlipped frown, Dottie growled, "What do you two want? Did your pimp send you down here to reclaim your stolen car?" The barb made the corners of her mouth turn up at her own cleverness.

Suzy took several steps to close the distance and leaned on the desk into Dottie's personal space. The confronted police secretary retracted and scooted her chair away. "Do you know what's going to get you in the end? It won't be karma, kismet, or any other holistic mumbo jumbo. It's the fact that one day you'll realize your life has been wasted using your petty power to make the world a worse place."

Splotches of red suffused her cheeks at Suzy's rant. "Well, I never."

Mid-splutter, Suzy spoke over her. "Just get me the paperwork for my car."

"If you think I'm going to—" She didn't get a chance to finish as the front door swung open and the square figure of little Tony ambled into the station.

Taking in the scene, he must have picked up on the energy in the room. "Is there something I can do for you ladies?" He circled the far end of the counter and stepped between Dottie and Suzy, his fists settling on his hips as he studied the two.

"We're here to pick up my friend's car." As much as Crystal enjoyed Suzy bringing Dottie the tormentor low, she was eager to get on the road to find Olivia.

"Dottie, why don't you get the form, take their payment, and then I'll escort them to the impound yard."

The authority lent by his uniform quelled any protests from Dottie. She couldn't help herself, and shot venomous looks at Suzy and Crystal, but gathered the necessary paperwork.

Slapping the forms down, Dottie spoke through clenched teeth. "Sign here, fill out this section, and I'll need a photocopy of your driver's license." The paperwork was filled out in tense silence, and they settled up under the scrutiny of the watching officer. As soon as Dottie thrust Suzy's license back at her after making a copy, the policeman spoke up. "Excellent. Let's get you outta here. Dottie, the keys."

With a contemptuous snort, the headache-inducing woman spun on her heel and disappeared behind a set of shelves. A few thunks and slams carried into the reception area.

Suzy began rolling her eyes at the noise, but when the officer leveled a glare in her direction, she tilted her head and studied the ceiling like the sprinkler system was the most interesting thing in the world.

A few more thumps, and Dottie returned with a black plastic tray. Sliding around inside were the car keys. Suzy snatched them and nodded at Crystal. "Let's make like a banana and split. It's time to save our friend."

****

Suzy's fire must have been stoked because she drove like a maniac to the encampment. She slid to a stop next to a van painted with psychedelic colors straight out of the sixties.

Two men who had been lounging in camp chairs sprung up. A gangly twenty-something swept long, unkempt hair from his eyes. A scraggly, ragged goatee graced his face in uneven patches, giving him the unfortunate appearance of being afflicted with mange. His tie-dye shirt and surfer trunks made him look even more ridiculous, but his deep scowl and clenched fists betrayed his hostile intent. The other guardian, looking like a truant from high school, and unable to grow any serious facial hair if his young life depended on it, jumped up and sprinted into the woods, hollering names at the top of his lungs.

Advancing on Crystal and Suzy as they got out of the car, the remaining person blocked the path leading to the encampment with a raised palm. "Who are you and what do you think you're doing?"

Channeling her emotions, Crystal released her boiling fear and anger. "Who I am is none of your business. Get out of my way." She took a few steps in his direction.

Stunned by Crystal's aggressive words and approach, he retreated a step, forgetting the camp chair behind him. He stumbled when it hit the back of his knees and sat down hard. With a soft creak, the chair collapsed to the ground, trapping the hostile hippie in a tangle of aluminum and webbing. Growling, he thrashed in an attempt to disentangle himself from the cage formed around his rear-end.

Suzy's snickers were cut short when shouts erupted

from the trees. A flood of people tumbled out of the woods to investigate the commotion. As they neared the scene, they began to talk amongst themselves.

"What did they do to Jasper?" A dark-haired girl with a glinting nose ring pointed at the trapped man on the ground.

"They attacked him," a burly protestor with swinging dreadlocks answered.

"I saw her with the logger." The same blonde she had mistaken for Olivia yesterday gestured at Crystal.

"They must be here to cut down the trees." A girl, sporting more bracelets than Crystal could count, quickened her pace.

Three women and two men marched toward the scene, trailed by the lookout who had fled upon Crystal and Suzy's arrival. Dressed in a hodgepodge of sundresses, tie-dye, and flannel, the group approached.

Several feet away, they halted in a loose semicircle. Kneeling in the dirt, one of the women helped Jasper escape from the collapsed chair. As soon as he was extracted, he jumped up, glaring pure hatred. "They shoved me when I stood up to them and laughed when I hurt myself."

A snort escaped Crystal's mouth at his words, and she flung her hand across her lips to hide her smile at the outrageous accusation. Jasper pointed, his righteous anger rising. "See, she's still laughing. Do you find my pain funny?"

Suzy placed a calming palm up and spoke in a much slower and softer tone than her usual no-nonsense pattern of speech. "Now, let's calm down. We're all friends here." Her words relaxed the tense stances and distrusting faces of the gang before them. "Jasper is an idiot who fell into his own chair and is now lashing out due to his wounded pride."

Crystal dropped her head an inch. She should have known better than to trust Suzy's peacemaking skills. As expected, Jasper spat vitriol, but when Crystal looked up, there were smirks sneaking onto the faces of the others. The dreadlocked man disguised his amusement with a fake cough, but his eyes twinkled.

When Jasper paused to take a breath, Crystal jumped in. "Have any of you seen my friend, Olivia?"

One of the women cocked her head and leaned forward at Crystal's question. "Who?"

"Olivia. She's been living with you for several days now."

Her question elicited an answer from Jasper. "There's no Olivia in the camp. Now, why don't you get in your car and scram."

Panic began eating at Crystal's stomach. "What do you mean, Olivia's not with you? She joined your protest, recently. I'm sure you've seen her around."

The nose-ring girl ran her hand over the short spikes of her black hair and elaborated, "I haven't met an Olivia. People pass in and out of the camp pretty often, but I've been here since the beginning and I've met everyone."

Jasper wasn't done being a righteous jerk. "Maybe you should check with your logger friend and see if he knows where she is."

His accusation, and the mention of Emerson, earned a renewed round of dirty looks from the others, who had begun to fall into sympathetic stances. Spines straightened as they considered Crystal in the light of her friendship with a deforesting monster.

Crystal threw her hands up in exasperation. "Do I look like a logger? I'm a wilderness guide." She traced an invisible circle around Suzy and herself. "We're wilderness guides. I'm not a logger. I'm not a reporter. I'm not a private investigator, drug user, or hooker. I'm someone who shows others the outdoors and how to enjoy themselves safely. Right now, though, I'm worried my best friend is in serious trouble."

At her rambling list of jobs, the faces before her fell into puzzled expressions, but Crystal didn't care.

Spiky-hair piped up. "I wish we could help, but no one by that name has ever been in our camp." Their continued denial was too much for Crystal. She shoved past Jasper, who raised a hand to grab her. Suzy seized his wrist, but the obnoxious man attempted to muscle past the hold. Suzy clamped down with the grip strength earned from a lifetime of rock climbing. Jasper's eyes widened and he opened his mouth to protest, but the exasperated looks from his compatriots caused him to clench his jaw tight.

Crystal blew by him and stormed down the trail leading toward the camp. Passing between several trees, she stepped out of the bright sun and into the shadowing boughs of the towering forest.

After the glare of the sun and the adrenaline of the heated exchange, the cool air from the shade raised goosebumps on her arms. Blinking to adjust to the gloom, Crystal took in the encampment.

The undergrowth had been trampled flat, causing Crystal to frown at the sight. The temperate rain forest ecosystem was delicate, and not only were the well-meaning protesters destroying the underbrush, but the foot traffic was hard on the root system of the century old trees, contributing to soil erosion and destabilizing the massive evergreens. In their zeal to protect the forest, the group was oblivious to the damage they themselves were causing.

Tents sprawled in haphazard fashion throughout the area and a ring of smooth river rocks surrounded a central fire pit. No flames were visible, but a small tendril of smoke crept upward into the canopy from the gray ash and black coals. Wet clothes were slung over an impromptu clothesline tied between two trees. Off to the side, a couple slept curled together in a hammock, swaying whenever one of them shifted to get more comfortable.

Small paths trailed from the makeshift campground. Having guided several camping trips the last few months, Crystal theorized they led to a source of water and restrooms. However, there were many more routes than could be explained by the necessities. A quick count showed at least six or seven shooting off in different directions.

Crystal cupped her hands around her mouth and bellowed, "Olivia! Where are you?" After a brief pause, with only silence for an answer, Crystal shouted again. "Olivia!"

"Hello, down there." Crystal glanced upward into the canopy, squinting past the one ray of sunshine sneaking through the trees. As her vision cleared, she could make out a set of chiseled pecs and abdominals leaning over the railing of what had become a rather impressive tree fort built fifty feet up. A completed wooden platform now encircled the trunk and a basic roof provided cover from the elements.

"Are you still up there with no clothes?" Crystal

couldn't think of anything else to say. The absurdity of his actions in the face of her friend missing were infuriating her to no end.

"Until I know this forest is in safe hands, I'm not leaving my post."

"I don't care." Crystal's exasperation was thrown at him with everything she could muster. "I only want to find my friend."

"Olivia?"

"Yes." Relief flooded her. "Do you know where she is?"

"I don't know her at all, but I heard you calling her name. I don't think anybody named Olivia has passed through."

"That's what everyone keeps saying, but I know she came here."

The rest of the group, led by Suzy, joined them in the clearing.

"Hey, hey, looks like the gang's all here." Tyler's lips twitched at the crowd flooding the base of his tree.

"Sorry, Tyler." Nose-ring girl's voice dropped to a low, husky tone and she glanced up at him from under her lashes. "They're looking for their friend, but none of us know her." She flashed a shy smile.

Crystal thought the girl was acting ridiculous given the seriousness of the situation, until she caught herself staring at Tyler as well. *Did he have twelve abdominals? Can the human body have that many?*

"You want us to get rid of 'em?" Jasper sounded like a thug from a comic book. His absurd goatee quivered in anticipation of Tyler's approval to remove them from the premises.

Tyler shook his head. "That wouldn't be hospitable

of us. They're a little worried, is all."

"A little worried? My friend is missing and there's a murderer on the loose. She could be dead in the woods, and you aren't helping me."

"See, I told you." Jasper shook his head in mock consternation. "They're hysterical. Besides, they've been seen with the logger who wants to chop this all down."

Tyler frowned at the accusation. "Is this true? Do you work for the Forks Logging Company?"

"Yes, we're loggers. I left my chainsaw in my other pants, though." Crystal spoke in her best you-are-a-freakin'-idiot tone of voice. "Are you going to tell me where my friend is, or do I need to call the cops?"

Tyler gave a condescending smile. "You don't think we've dealt with them? We're actually situated on a strip of public land, and not the Baranhof property. We filed for, and received, a permit to exercise our first amendment right to assemble. They check on us from time to time, but as long as we don't make a fuss in their town, they leave us alone."

"I don't care about your protest. I just want to make sure my friend is safe." Crystal's blood was beginning to simmer at being balked by a self-righteous, sanctimonious, naked tree-hugger.

"What if we don't tell you anything?" Jasper sidled behind several of his friends, using them as human shields against Crystal and Suzy.

Suzy piped up. "Then I'll file a complaint citing your lack of proper sanitation and the fact you're living in an unpermitted and dangerous structure. Looking around, I'm also going to take a wild stab and guess there might be some illegal drugs in your possession."

She gestured at the snoring couple in the hammock, who hadn't budged despite the shouting in the glade.

"Huh. Good points." Tyler nodded in approval at her list of threats. "I still don't know what we can do to help. No one knows of an Olivia."

"She's my height, long blonde hair, bright blue eyes, and snorts when she laughs."

Tyler's face lit up. "That sounds like Anastasia. Does she go by that name, too? Has a Russian accent?"

"What? No."

Tyler shrugged. "She's the only one who matches your description."

"Where is Anastasia, then? If you don't tell me, I'm going to chop down this tree with my bare hands." A remnant of Crystal's mind suggested she was being unreasonable to people trying to be helpful, but that voice was squashed by the terror and fear overriding her emotions.

"Whoa. Slow down, Ms. Bunyan. She likes to go for walks in the woods. It looks like it's going to rain soon, so I'd expect her any minute. Grab a chair and make yourself comfortable." Tyler left the railing and disappeared from view.

Turning, Crystal confronted the group surrounding Suzy and her. Now the show was over, most were dispersing. They all had sympathetic faces with the exception of a glowering Jasper, who couldn't help taking another jab. "If your friend was up to no good, I'm sure she came to a bad end."

Anguish, more than she had ever experienced, overwhelmed Crystal. The obnoxious man's lips moved, but the pounding in Crystal's ears blocked all further noise.

Suzy wagged her finger in his face and had it batted away for her trouble.

A drip struck her nose. *Had one of them spit on her?* The wet sensation sliding down her skin was cooling, not warm. Drip. Another grazed her eyelash, forcing her to blink. Drip. Drip. Raindrops. Her strained mind identified the sensation as the beginning of a rain shower. Suzy and Jasper's shouts rang in her ears, not as distinct words, but as distant echoes. Thunder rumbled in the gathering clouds, cutting the shouting match short.

The protesters fled toward the tents with the exception of the couple in the hammock, who stirred, but didn't wake. The sound of zippers filled the clearing as the scattering group took cover from the storm.

One second, Crystal could pick out individual raindrops. The next, it was the hiss of a deluge striking trees and tents. The intoxicating scent of rainfall touching down on warm earth suffused the air, snapping Crystal out of her shock.

"What do you want to do?" Suzy raised her voice over the noise of the storm.

Mind racing, Crystal latched onto the one thing she remembered. "Tyler said she's out walking." From Suzy's expression, Crystal was positive her eyes blazed with a fey light, but none of that mattered. *Olivia was in the woods.* Picking a path on the east side of the encampment at random, Crystal bolted. "Olivia! Are you out here?" She repeated her shout as she raced down the narrow trail.

Suzy's swearing faded as her swift pace through the damp forest accelerated. "Olivia, where are you?" Limbs and ferns cramped the already narrow pathway on all sides, but Crystal swept through them without a second thought. Her friend was somewhere in this forest, and Crystal would find her.

The raindrops grew in size and intensity, turning the dusty path in front of her to mud. She stumbled as her foot slipped, sending her to the ground. Her knees and palms caught the brunt of the tumble as she slid to a halt. Sharp pain informed her that she had skinned herself like her nephew Joshua did when he outstripped his toddler's agility.

A grunt of determination left her lips. She propelled herself to her feet and took off down the path again, shouting her friend's name. Turning a corner, she slowed before a raging creek, four yards across. The burbling of the fast-moving water replaced the sound of rainfall as she closed the last few feet. On the other side, the trail continued deeper into the woods, and without hesitation, Crystal started forward.

Knowing the dangers of crossing any moving body of water, Crystal took a careful step into the rush of current. It swirled around her ankle, causing her arms to windmill, but she straightened and edged her other boot in. Leaning into the flow, she took another cautious step and then another, frigid water filling her boots and creeping up her jeans.

"Crystal, what are you doing?" Suzy's voice startled her, and on instinct Crystal swiveled her head. She caught the barest glimpse of her friend's face when her foot slipped on the smooth river rocks. Before she could comprehend what had happened, Crystal plunged into the water, breath stolen by the icy shock of snowmelt closing around her entire body. Scrambling for purchase, she wrapped her hands around a slick submerged rock and twisted to get her feet on the stream bed. Standing, she heaved in several shallow, shuddering gasps of air. Crystal gathered her wits and was startled to see the tumble had swept her ten feet downstream.

"Are you okay?" Suzy scrambled through the thick brush of the bank.

"I'm fine." Crystal gasped out the words and attempted to explain the only thing hurt was her pride, but her teeth chattered when she opened her mouth. A violent trembling coursed through her, and she wrapped her arms around her body, glancing left and right to see which side of the stream was closer. In the slip and fall, she had managed to almost cross to the other side. Two more steps, and she stood on the opposite shore from Suzy.

"Do you think you can find Olivia by running around and shouting her name? You don't even know if she's out here." Suzy swiped at the strands of rain-dampened hair in her face and cast an annoyed look at the dripping Crystal.

"I...I...have to try something." Crystal forced the words past her constricted throat. Whether it was the stress or cold, she couldn't tell which inhibited her ability to speak. "It's my fault..." A lump cut off her next words. She forced a calming breath and the discomfort eased. "It's my fault she's out here. I should have never let her do something this dangerous. Now..." Crystal couldn't bear to complete the unsaid sentence.

Suzy's scowl softened. "Olivia's your friend. She may be helping you, but you're helping Roxie. It's what friends do for each other. Don't forget she volunteered for this."

The words were meant to help, but only dug deeper. "This isn't the army, Suzy. She didn't volunteer for danger and possible death. She figured it would be fun, like something from a Nancy Drew novel. In her mind, I'm sure she imagined laughing after it was all over, but she's missing. Maybe even dead."

"You don't know that."

"Why hasn't she answered my texts or calls? Why isn't she here?"

"Naked tree guy says she's around."

"We don't even know if that's her. Olivia might have come up with a pseudonym, but a Russian accent? Jasper told us she wasn't welcome and they were glad she was g...g...gone." The cold coursed through her again, eliciting a full body shiver.

Anguish caused Suzy's expression to fall, and if rain hadn't been washing down her face, Crystal would have bet she would see tears dampening Suzy's cheeks. If the implacable Suzy was shaken, Olivia was in trouble.

Crystal nodded at the path leading deeper into the forest. "I'm going to follow this trail into the woods. Why don't you search one of the other ones? No need for both of us to be drenched by this river."

"Do you think it's safe?" Suzy gave a skeptical look. "Olivia is missing, and we think these folks had something to do with it. It doesn't seem smart to run around alone. Besides, you're soaked and freezing. Let's head to the hippie commune, I'll stoke the fire, and you can dry off. Then we'll search, and those tree-hugging layabouts can help."

"I want to look a little more, okay? I promise I'll

be back soon." Crystal slogged up the bank, rejoining the path. Her socks squished with every step, and her clothes and boots had tripled in weight. She grabbed her bedraggled hair and twisted it into a quick knot to keep it from plastering to her face.

With figurative, and literal, heavy footsteps, Crystal reentered the trail, passing under the dark canopy. The constant bird calls had fallen quiet during the storm, leaving her in oppressive silence, with the exception of the white noise of the rainfall. Much of the precipitation was halted and collected by the trees, only to fall in even larger drops with the knack of landing on her neck. As she hiked deeper into the woods, her exertions paid off, and her shivering ceased as her core temperature rose. After another ten minutes, several buildings peeked through the trees. Crystal stood on her tiptoes and spotted the cabin where Frederick Baranhof had met his end, framed by the interlacing branches of two towering redwood cedars. Crystal paused to study the building where this had all begun. If one of the eco-protesters had killed Frederick, this path would have led them to where they set up camp. Not a bad getaway. The trail was constantly stirred up with rain and feet, so footprints would have been difficult to trace. Unless you ran into someone else, no one would ever know you were here. As she contemplated the scene before her, something odd caught her attention.

The rain forest floor was coated with an even detritus of rotting leaves, pine needles, and other assorted vegetation. However, in between a grouping of sword ferns, the residue had been scraped together. Her heart clanged to a halt. The pile was mounded in the shape of a human body.

Chapter Fifteen

"No!" Crystal's heartbeat started again, but now with a furious pounding, filling her ears with intensity. "No, no, no." She chanted the mantra as she approached the pile with trepidation. Gouge marks, still present in the soil despite the persistent precipitation, made it clear a frantic someone had flung forest debris over what lay beneath.

Crystal trembled as she stared at the mass, afraid to uncover what she had stumbled upon. If it was Olivia's body, how could she ever face her best friend's mother, much less live with herself? Falling to her knees in the damp soil, Crystal forced herself to shift the top layer. Piling it to the side, she scooped two more handfuls. Picking up speed, she found herself casting armfuls aside in her pursuit to find the truth.

Her hand struck solid earth and she stopped, confused. She had dug where the body's torso should be but held only handfuls of moist mulch to show for her effort. Two smaller piles remained after having divided the middle of the body-sized pile. Crystal was about to chalk the anomaly up to an animal making a den when she spotted something.

A long strap dangled from one of the remaining leaf mounds, snaking into the area she had cleared. Grasping at it, Crystal tugged. Inch by inch, more of the fabric came free. Clambering to her feet, Crystal lifted what she'd found, sending a cascade of leaves falling to the ground.

It was a bright yellow sundress decorated with tiny pastel polka dots. Giving it a shake, the last of the forest duff fell. What at first glance had seemed a mud stain around the midsection, actually had a reddish-brown cast to it, the color of dried blood. Spreading out the material as best she could revealed distinct images of hands wiped on the fabric. This was the exact type of dress Olivia would wear.

Crystal crumbled to her knees, and bile burned its way up her esophagus. She fell to all fours, her whole body convulsed, and she vomited where she had been digging moments before. Retching noises filled the forest as the tragedy poisoned her soul. Sticks dug into her palms and knees as her body continued its attempts to reject the bloody confirmation of her friend's demise. After a last dry heave, she sank onto her feet, panting. The saltiness of her tears touched her lips, and she dropped her face into her hands.

Her best friend had been murdered in these woods, playing investigator. Crystal had pretended they were qualified, not believing they were in danger until too late.

Waves of cold, worsened by her tumble in the creek and the persistent rain, tore through her body, and she began shaking. Clasping her arms around her, she rocked back and forth. Her shivering grew worse, and nausea swept through her again.

A harsh, guttural voice from behind froze her in place, "Why don't you give the dress to me, and in turn I won't blow your pretty little brains all over the Olympic National Forest?" Her body continued trembling from the shock it had taken, but the rest of her motion ceased at the threat.

"Did you hear me? Drop the dress, step away, and go home, safe and sound. No one gets hurt."

Crystal mustered herself and stood, uncoiling her spine as she straightened in what she hoped was a nonthreatening fashion.

"That's right. Nice and slooow." The dark voice dragged out the word as Crystal confronted him.

A menacing figure loomed over her. Muscles bulged inside his black sweatshirt, the hood tight over his head, the ties lashed in a knot to keep it in place. Large wrap-around sunglasses, speckled with rain drops, reflected Crystal's ashen face. Camouflage pants completed the intimidating effect, not to mention the massive silver handgun pointed at her head.

"Wha…what do you want?" Crystal couldn't stop shivering.

"Just the dress. Hand it over."

"Why do you want my friend's dress? What do you know? What happened to her?" Crystal tightened her hand around the straps. He wasn't getting anything until he gave her some answers.

The gun roared, and there was a flash of light.

With a small scream she fell into a half crouch, cradling her head in her arms. Her left ear throbbed in pain, and the gunman was shouting.

Ringing drowned out his words. Crystal cautiously unfurled her arms that were forming the protective shell around her head. She stared at the crease of her left elbow, expecting it to be soaked in blood from her being shot in the ear. She didn't feel any pain, but her nervous system wasn't functioning at its most optimum.

No bloodstains marred her clothing, so the gunshot must have been a warning.

The man's voice sounded like the tenth echo from a canyon, faint and distant, but still distinct. "Quit stalling. Hand it over."

"What type of sicko are you?" Fury replaced terror in Crystal. "You murdered my friend and stripped off her clothes. What did you do with her body?"

The man's lips curled into a sneer. "You don't have the foggiest damned clue what's going on. You'd think setting fire to your tent would have taught you to mind your own business. Since you don't want to hand over the dress, I guess we're doing this the hard way."

The click of the hammer cocking cut through her stunted hearing. He leveled the gun again but twisted his head to peer down the trail Crystal had come from. His lips formed several curse words, but Crystal couldn't hear them. With one last glare down the path, he swung the pistol at Crystal's head.

She yelped in alarm, spinning away from the blow. The butt of the gun thumped against her temple, rolling her over repeatedly into the ferns, but her momentum protected her from the worst of the damage.

Shaking her head to clear the pain, Crystal managed to get on her hands and knees in time to see her attacker sprinting down the path with the dress, the grisly trophy dangling from one hand, the revolver still clutched in the other.

She lunged to her feet, intent on giving chase, but her balance betrayed her, and she staggered to the right, crashing into the trunk of a tree and sliding down its rough bark.

Suzy burst into the clearing. "Crystal! What

happened? Why didn't you answer my shouts?"

The tinny words echoed in her damaged ears. "I didn't hear you. We have to go after him." Pointing down the path, Crystal attempted to get to her feet, again. She lurched forward, and Suzy caught her elbow, steadying her.

"Go after who? The person who fired the gun?"

"Yeah, the guy in black and camo. The guy who killed Olivia." The last words slipped out of her mouth as a whisper. She couldn't believe it was true.

Suzy's tanned face went as ashen as Crystal's had been in the man's reflective sunglasses. "You found her?"

"I found her sundress buried in a pile of leaves. There was blood covering it."

Suzy squeezed her eyes shut and tears began pouring out the edges. "I can't believe it. This can't be true."

"That's why we have to go after the guy. He took the dress. It's the proof we need to get the police here. Not the local ones. Real policemen, who want to get to the bottom of this. Ones who will want to solve Olivia's mur…" She couldn't finish the word. Choking back the pain, she continued. "I think I'm ready to go after him."

Sympathy radiated from Suzy's tormented expression. "We can't chase an armed murderer through the forest. You can barely stand."

"I'm fine." Crystal started off to prove her point, but she stumbled in the leaf pile.

"You can't. We can't. He'd kill us, even if we could somehow catch up." Suzy wrapped Crystal in a hug, both restraining and comforting.

Sinking into Suzy's arms, Crystal sobbed, her tears

mixing with the rainwater already drenching the fleece. The warmth and love offered by Suzy helped draw the toxic hysteria from her, clearing her mind, but the ache and pain was too much to bear.

"What's that?" Suzy's dull voice was more audible as Crystal's hearing cleared from the gunshot blast.

"What's what?"

"That." Suzy thrust Crystal away with a gentle arm and pointed at her feet.

"Looks like a sandal."

"What's it doing here?"

"I'm not sure."

"Is it Olivia's?"

"Maybe. I didn't see anything she packed."

Suzy picked up the white sandal and set it on a rotting log overgrown with moss. She shoved her hands into the pile of leaves and swirled her arms around.

Her searching hands halted, and a quizzical look crossed Suzy's face as she fished something from the leaves. "It's the left one." Sure enough, the other sandal dangled from Suzy's hand, dirt and leaves clinging to the strap.

Crystal sniffed and rubbed her nose on her sleeve. Suzy laid out the second sandal beside the first and they inspected them. In the corner of one, the same reddish hue as from the midriff of the sundress stood out from the dirt.

Crystal stared in numb shock. Why did this happen? She'd only been trying to help Roxie.

"How do we handle this?" Suzy's nearly whispered words broke Crystal's daze.

"What do you mean?"

"With the police. They are nothing if not

suspicious of us. How are they going to take it when we turn in bloody evidence with our fingerprints all over it?"

"I don't know. Let's get back to town, and I'll call Roxie's lawyer. Maybe she can give us some advice.

"Good thinking. By the way, you're shouting."

"What?" Crystal gave Suzy a quizzical look.

Suzy winced and nodded. "Not so much shouting, but you're talking louder than you think you are. I think the gunshot messed with your volume control."

"Good to know. I hope it's temporary."

"You and me both." Suzy gathered the sandals, and the two set out toward the encampment and Suzy's car.

"Did you charge into the forest to save me after hearing a gunshot?" Affection washed over Crystal at the thought.

Suzy grunted, but her lip turned up on one side. "Not my brightest moment, I'll admit, but you keep getting into trouble without me."

"Your boots are sopping wet, too." Crystal's hearing had cleared enough to pick up the telltale squishing of socks in Suzy's boots.

"I had to run through the creek to get here. Personally, I chose not to fall in, but to each their own."

Crystal smiled through her tears but was wracked by more shivers. It grew worse, and her whole body began shaking as numbing cold crashed in. She braced her hand on a stump. "Let me sit for a sec to get warm." Crystal sank down.

Suzy studied her and frowned. "You're going hypothermic. I think the cold and shock are sinking in."

Crystal nodded. Her first aid training told her Suzy was right, but she couldn't manage anything but curling into a tight ball and shaking. Suzy stepped close and chafed her arms. "We need to get you to the fire in the camp. Can you stand?"

"I think so." The urgency of Suzy's tone got her to her feet, but the meaning was unclear. *Why did they have to go?* Suzy grabbed a fistful of shirt, tugging her down the path. Crystal did her best to keep up, but her feet were clumsy and her mind clouded.

Soon, they returned to the small river, and without hesitation, Suzy stepped in, urging Crystal to hold her belt loops for balance. Their footing slipped, and Suzy stumbled to one knee in the rapid water, but the two emerged, dripping, on the other side. The cold water doubled Crystal's shaking and her teeth chattered more violently than ever.

Suzy slung Crystal's arm over her shoulder and they stumbled down the path. Crystal kept insisting she was fine, but Suzy grumbled and growled, taking on more of Crystal's weight the farther they walked. By the time they stumbled into the protesters' encampment, the rain had halted and wan rays of sun peeked through the forest. Large droplets still fell from the trees, but the sunshine and the beginnings of bird songs promised returning warmth.

Suzy set Crystal down on a rock next to the fire ring, where smoke still snaked upward despite the recent deluge. Suzy shifted the wood pile and found dry tinder at the bottom. With sure, confident movements she built a teepee of fuel around the last embers. Crouching on hands and knees, she blew into the fire with a slow and steady breath. The smoke plume grew thicker and Suzy exhaled again. With a hushed wuff, flames burst around the dry twigs.

Crystal stared at Suzy's work, overtaken by erratic fits of shaking.

"Get in close." Suzy beckoned Crystal toward the fire.

Crystal sat forward with a mechanical motion, lowering her hands over the small flame. Heat stung her numb fingers and palms at first, but soon the warmth began creeping up her limbs. Suzy fed several larger sticks into the growing flames.

The zipping of tent flaps filled the hollow, and heads poked out. The first to greet them was the scowling face of the resident pain in the butt.

"What do you think—" Jasper began as he stomped in their direction.

Suzy was at the end of her patience. "You're as useless as a jellyfish in a square-dance competition. Start warming some water. My friend is hypothermic."

Jasper opened his mouth, but the slamming of car doors beyond the trees cut them off and the two arguers exchanged hate-filled stares. Jasper's, however, held grim satisfaction. "My friends are back. You should have left when you had the chance."

Suzy flipped him the bird.

Turning to Crystal, she muttered, "I probably shouldn't have done that. Get warm quick because this might get ugly."

Crystal hunched over the flame, risking getting licked by the dancing fire. Glorious warmth spread into her body, but her core still ached with the chill.

"Did you hear me?" The sound of mud sucking at Jasper's approaching footsteps filled the air, but neither Suzy nor Crystal deigned to look at the blowhard. "I don't care if you fell into a snowbank on Everest, you need to vamoose."

"For the love of all pure and innocent in this world, please be quiet, Jasper." An exasperated woman's voice cut through the air, the voice thick with a Russian accent.

"Seriously, dude, you'd think all the pot you smoke would make you more chill, but you need to up the dosage or switch to something with more oomph." Another voice, exuding California surfer backed up the girl.

"C'mon Rodrigo, Anastasia—" Jasper lifted his voice in a plaintive whine.

"Enough, amigo. I don't care what these two have done. They don't need you and your vigilantism." Rodrigo's slow tones silenced the enraged hippie.

"Here. We just came from Mother Earth Café. Have mine. It will help." The Russian, her accent ridiculous in its strength, offered up a cup of much needed warmth. However, something in the voice tickled Crystal's overwrought mind.

Glancing up, she peered into Olivia's sparkling baby blues, a grin battling its way through her best friend's composure.

Crystal launched herself from her rock, wrapping her arms around Olivia. Staggering, the two crashed to the forest floor, Crystal squeezing tight as sobs wracked her body.

"Anastasia, do you know who this is?" Rodrigo sounded ready to intervene.

"I know her not. I think she is, how you say, emotional."

"Shut up, you idiot," Crystal gasped through her tears. "You're alive."

"Kinda blowing my cover, Crystal," Olivia whispered.

"I don't care. You can't stay here. It's not safe." Crystal ignored her friend's protest.

"You're talking kinda loud."

"So I've been told. I can't hear quite right."

Rodrigo offered a hand and helped the two to their feet. Olivia's grin broke into a huge smile, and Crystal was positive she matched her friend's expression, albeit with tears streaming down her cheeks.

"What's going on with you two?" The surfer threw his towhead back with careless abandon. He stood and watched them in a forest green hoodie and floral print shorts.

Olivia sighed. "My name isn't Anastasia, and I'm not from St. Petersburg. It's Olivia, and I was born in Seattle. I didn't mean to deceive you, or anyone for that matter."

The surfer gave Olivia a skeptical look. "You made up a name, spoke in a bad fake accent, and didn't mean to deceive us?" His gaze grew steely and his jaw clenched.

"When you put it that way, I guess I wanted to, but it was before I got to know you, so it doesn't count."

Rodrigo adopted a glassy look as his brain processed Olivia's logic. Crystal knew from years of assessing Olivia's reasoning that he fought an uphill battle. His next words were even slower than usual as he tried to understand her argument. "Why did you lie to us, though? I know you pretty well now, and I can't imagine it was anything malicious."

"Get comfortable. This is going to take some explaining." Olivia found the coffee cup on the ground and handed it to Crystal. The lid was still on, but much of it had leaked out the spout. Crystal brushed the dirt from the rim of the coffee, downed the dregs, and gloried in the instant warmth seeping into her body.

More protestors clambered out of tents at the commotion, and soon close to a dozen of them gathered. Everyone grabbed a seat on a rock or chair around the fire. The flames took hold, and the wood began crackling and popping. Tyler even made an appearance, regarding them from his tree fort to watch the scene unfold.

"We're looking for the person who killed Frederick Baranhof." Olivia led with the headline, peering around at the expectant faces.

"They caught her. It was the camp cook." Rodrigo nodded like he had solved the crime.

"Her name is Roxie and she's a chef, not a cook." Indignity flared in Crystal. She was risking her life for her friend after all and wanted everyone to know who they were accusing.

"What were you doing here Anasta…Olivia?" Tyler called down from his nest.

"We were concerned someone in this group might have had something to do with it, so I joined you to investigate." Olivia's confession, delivered in her usual cheerful tone, caused several faces to scowl. Oblivious to the mood shift in the camp caused by accusing them of possible murder, Olivia continued. "I got to know a lot of you and started asking questions. It wasn't long before I figured out none of you had anything to do with it. Everyone was horrified by the murder and were excited that the killer was arrested. It wasn't Roxie, by the way." She threw a glance at Crystal, who gave a vigorous nod.

"You snuck into our group, pretended to be one of us, made it seem like we were friends, and it was all fake?" Tyler's position from up on high made it seem like judgment being handed down.

Olivia reeled at the condemnation. "When you say it like that, I seem awful. But it wasn't fake. I like every one of you. Even Jasper, some of the time."

"At least Jasper is honest." Tyler waved her objections aside.

"I have feelings, you know?" Jasper glanced around for support, but no one met his gaze.

"Maybe, it's time for you to go." Tyler pronounced his verdict and pointed out of the camp. With one last glance at Olivia, he spun and disappeared from view.

"But, wait," Olivia called out. "I think what you stand for is awesome. I'm totally on board. However, I have to help my friend."

It was too late. The crowd dispersed, many shook their heads, and Jasper sported a nasty grin. Olivia sighed, crossed the camp, and fetched her bag from a tent. "Guess it's time to head out."

It stung Crystal that Olivia was unhappy with how things had ended, but with the revelation of her being alive, warmth flooded into Crystal's body. Despite the unfortunate scene that had just occurred, Crystal couldn't stop grinning. Her best friend in the whole world shook dirt from her clothes and grumbled about stains, when only ten minutes ago, Crystal assumed her body was buried in the woods, murdered by some monster in a black hoodie.

However, Olivia being alive raised a question. What unfortunate person had the dress and sandals belonged to?

Chapter Sixteen

After having taken hot showers in the hotel room, the three returned to Mother Earth Café to discuss what they had learned. With glee in her heart, Crystal bought two chocolate muffins to go with her mocha. The first muffin she devoured before Olivia and Suzy finished placing their orders. The rich chocolate mouthfuls set her taste buds tingling and made her wonder how the awful fiend Dottie could have thrown it in the trash. This was proof-positive the police station office manager was evil.

Suzy and Olivia settled next to her with pastries and coffees of their own. Olivia had her traditional croissant and a mug that consisted of more whipped cream than espresso. Suzy was making her way through a cheese Danish and what appeared to be plain black coffee.

Olivia spoke up at the sacrilegious sight. "Suzy, this is the Pacific Northwest and you're in a coffee shop. They have more options than plain drip." It was downright weird to see the brown liquid without anything to dress it up.

"It's what I like. When I want a cup of sugar and milk, I get a milkshake." She adopted a baleful look, obviously weary of an old argument, but willing to take up the fight if needed.

"Fine." Olivia threw up her hands. "Just thought

I'd let you know."

"Have you even tried a mocha?" At the startled looks from the other two at the table, it was clear Crystal still hadn't zeroed in on the correct speech volume. Everything sounded muted, but she had been certain she had lowered her voice to a reasonable level. Several glances from the occupants of nearby tables confirmed she hadn't.

Suzy waved her off. "Froo-froo crap. This is good coffee, though." She took a deep swig of her drink to the astonished looks of the other two.

"That's like a thousand degrees." Olivia stared as the steaming liquid disappeared.

Suzy set her coffee down with enough vigor to splash some over the edge. "Can we discuss anything other than my coffee-drinking habits? For example, why the hell didn't you return Crystal's texts? She's been worried sick. Literally. She puked in the woods."

Crystal clarified the statement. "Any sort of message may have helped when I found what I thought were the clothes you'd been murdered in."

"Well, first, in regard to texting. I checked around for power plugs the first day, but there weren't any, because it's a *friggin' forest*. My battery died within hours of arriving. You know how ancient my phone is, and when I did come into town with the others. I realized I'd left my power cord in the hotel room. If you'd noticed, my sleuthy friends, you might have figured it out."

Crystal massaged her temples. How could a forgotten phone charger cause so much agony and heartache? "Well, whose clothes did we find and what is wrong with that guy, Jasper? He made some ominous sounding statements when we were there."

Olivia fiddled with the napkin in front of her. "Jasper has a huge man-crush on Tyler and gets a little overprotective of him. But I think Tyler liked me. I'd go up to his perch every night and we'd talk for hours. He's a sweet guy and is trying to do good things."

"And the clothes?" Crystal urged.

"How should I know? They're not mine. However, I have spotted the creepy guy in the forest snooping around. I kept going for walks to catch him in the middle of whatever he was up to."

"You wandered the woods, stalking a giant dressed like the Unabomber?" Crystal directed this at Olivia before turning on Suzy. "And you charged into the woods after hearing a gunshot?" The other tables were now staring. Crystal's mouth split into a huge grin. "I'll question your wisdom until the day I die, but no one could have asked for better friends."

Her friends' cheeks pinked at her proclamation, but whether it was due to the praise or the fact the entire coffee shop now gawked at them, there was no way of telling.

"What size was the dress, anyway?" Olivia asked.

"I don't know. I didn't check before the guy took it, but I'd guess a size four."

"Hmm...how about the sandals?

Suzy produced the plastic bag containing their find from under the table. She peered inside, rustling the bag as she inspected them. "Looks like size six and a half."

Olivia glanced askance at Crystal. "You know I have big feet. You should have known those weren't mine."

Crystal sighed. "I'm not the best private

investigator for Roxie, am I?"

"Not true. We know there is way more going on here than we thought, and this," Olivia tapped the bag, "will prove it. Call Roxie's lawyer and see what she has to say."

Crystal found Isabella Contreras in her contacts. Glancing around, she made a snap decision. "Let's do this outside." They were still getting a lot of sidelong glances, and Crystal could tell others were straining to overhear their conversation.

Suzy and Olivia nodded and the three bussed their table. Crystal left with her mocha in one hand, and phone and extra muffin in the other. They wandered over to Suzy's car, and Crystal sat on the bumper, flanked by her friends, who stationed themselves like the Secret Service around her.

Crystal tapped the call button, and on the third ring, Isabella answered.

"Crystal. I've been waiting to hear from you. Tell me you have something to help with Roxie's case."

Taking a deep breath, Crystal filled her in. She described the encounter with Emerson, the shady business dealings of the Laughlins, and possible corruption of the Forks police. She finished with her discovery in the forest and the confrontation with the gun-wielding man. As she unloaded her story, Suzy and Olivia would glare at anyone who walked too close to her, causing them to invariably veer away from the suspicious stares.

"Are you still in possession of the sandals?" Isabella asked at the end of the retelling.

"I have the sandals. That's why I'm calling you. What should we do with them? If the police here are corrupt, I don't want them to dispose of the evidence."

"I'm glad you called. Without proven corruption, the local police still have jurisdiction, but I will be in contact with the FBI. They handle oversight when public officials may be suspect. They will make sure everything is on the up and up, and the fact they are involved will expedite the DNA testing of the blood, if it is indeed blood."

"How long until I should give this to the police?"

"The sooner, the better. I'll make the necessary phone calls right now. I'll start with the Forks PD, so they'll be expecting you."

"Thanks, Isabella. This means so much to have your help."

"Thank you, Crystal. This might just be what we need for Roxie's release. Good luck." The call clicked as Isabella hung up.

"Did you both hear what she said?" Crystal glanced up at her two defenders.

"Enough of it. We're going to the police station." Suzy's face was grim.

"What's wrong with the police station?" Olivia asked.

Crystal sighed. "Get in the car. Have I got a story for you."

****

"I can't believe you got arrested," Olivia said, climbing out of the car at the police station parking lot. "I'm out of your life for a couple of days and look at the trouble you got into. You were kicked out of a resort, arrested for being a stalker, tested for drugs, and were almost shot."

"Suzy said something similar. I want to argue with

you, but I'm thinking maybe I do need a permanent chaperon."

The front door of the station swung open, and Dottie bustled out like a Kansas tornado. "What is wrong with you? I just got off the phone with a lawyer." She flashed air quotes at the word. "She told me some cockamamie story about bloody evidence and FBI oversight. What are you playing at? Do you want another night in the holding cell? That can be arranged."

"You need to back off, Dottie." Suzy stepped between Crystal and the approaching police secretary.

Dottie ignored her but did stop in her tracks. "I've called my husband. If you know what's good for you, you'll be gone before he gets here."

"Wow. You've been making new friends while I've been gone. Why does this lady hate you so much?" Olivia asked in a stage whisper.

"She took the last chocolate muffin I had my eye on and then threw it away because it wasn't bran like she wanted."

Olivia gave a sage nod at the quirky reasoning. "If she's as uptight as she looks, she could use all the fiber she can manage."

Dottie spluttered at the comment, but Little Tony's bulky frame hustled out the door. "Dottie, why don't you go inside? I'll handle this."

Dottie's expression transitioned from outraged to gleeful. "I'll get the cells ready."

"Dottie. Go." Tony's voice switched from de-escalation to stern in an instant.

Dottie opened her mouth to say something, but snapped it shut at a glare from the officer. With an angry flounce, she beat a hasty retreat, her curls bouncing in time with the stomp of her feet.

Not until the door clicked closed behind the angry station assistant did the policeman relax.

"She is going to be the downfall of us." With a shake of his head, Little Tony refocused his attention on Crystal and Suzy. "An FBI agent told me you have some evidence in your possession."

Crystal patted the bag with the sandals, holding it up for him to see.

"Why don't we go inside. I'll take your statement, and log it in."

Crystal nodded. "You aren't going to arrest me again, are you?"

Tony grimaced. "I can see why you'd ask." He gave her a strained look. "With such a small police force, we lean on Dottie more than we should. She was put in a position to overstep her boundaries, and that's on us."

"On you? That was the worst night of my life."

"Which is why I don't blame you for calling the FBI."

Trusting Isabella knew what she was doing, Crystal gave a curt nod and followed the officer into the station. The fluorescent lights and Dottie's glare greeted her, but Crystal did her best to ignore all of it, drawing support from her trailing friends.

Following the officer down the hallway, he led them to an office with the nameplate Anthony Wilford riveted to the door.

There was only one extra chair in the office. Crystal took it, and her friends stood behind her. Papers were stacked in tidy piles about the desk, and several half-finished cups of coffee fought for space next to pictures of the man's wife and children. Several citations for service decorated the wall, along with a snapshot of him posing next to a swordfish he had caught. The officer grabbed a pad of paper and a small recorder from a drawer. "Why don't you start from the beginning?"

Taking a deep breath, Crystal told the story again, the details fresh from having recently shared it with Roxie's lawyer. The officer wrote down copious notes and asked questions throughout the process.

"This guy in the woods. How tall was he?"

"Very tall. Not as tall as your partner but at least several inches over six feet."

"Between six-two and six-ten. What color was his hair?"

"I couldn't tell. He had a hood over his head."

"His eyebrows maybe?"

"He had wraparound sunglasses on. I couldn't see them."

The officer made notes. "How about his build? Bulky? Thin? In between?"

"Bulky, but in a muscular way."

"What type of gun?"

"I don't know much about guns. Silver and loud."

"Did it have the spinning part in the middle?"

"Yes."

"That makes it a revolver. The loud noise is tough to say. Probably not a twenty-two, but it could be anything else. Can you show me where you found the clothes?"

"Of course."

"We'll go, but first I'm going to log this in and

227

lock it up. We'll overnight it to the DNA lab in Seattle."

The officer stood and left. He returned ten minutes later with two plastic wrapped kits. "You said you touched the sandals?" He pointed at Crystal and Suzy. They both nodded. "I'll have to do some cheek swabs to rule out your DNA. The lab will identify whoever's blood this is if they're in our database, and we can put a name to the missing person."

The officer donned a pair of blue nitrile gloves and swabbed the inside of their cheeks, documenting each on a set of paperwork after placing the Q-tip in a corked plastic vial. "Next, prints." Each finger was scanned on a small portable device produced from his desk. Part of Crystal worried this would be used to implicate her and Suzy in Frederick's murder. However, they had handled bloody clues near a murder scene, so she could understand the need.

They left the station, driving to the fateful Baranhof log cabin, followed by Little Tony in his police cruiser. They gathered in the driveway, the policeman carrying a large roll of caution tape.

Crystal picked the path leading in the correct direction, and after a few twists and turns down the damp trail, they arrived at the scene where Crystal had been attacked.

"This isn't how I left it." Crystal frowned at the mass of leaves. "These are more spread out, like someone sifted through it even closer than Suzy and I did."

Suzy nodded. "Someone's been here. Look. You can tell this log has been upended."

The moss-covered fallen maple Crystal had sat on

to compose herself was flipped, revealing the rotten underside.

Tony nodded as he took in the scene with an intense stare. "It seems someone returned for what you two found. Good thing you handed it over to me first."

Drawing down a branch, Tony wrapped the end of his tape in a simple knot. Unrolling it, he walked around the clearing, enclosing the area.

"Isn't this like closing the barn door after the horse left?" Crystal waved her hands around the chaotic setting.

"More than likely; trace evidence often doesn't last long in a turbulent environment like this, but we might get lucky. It's all part of the investigative process."

"Can we help?"

"Nope. We'll take it from here. I suggest…Well, I'd suggest you go home and wait for news, but I tried that once before. You do what you want to. I'll be in touch with the FBI and the lawyer you're working with."

Crystal milled around, at a loss for words. *Should she hand over her investigation? Wait and see what they found out? Did she have a choice?*

She started walking from the clearing, followed by Olivia and Suzy.

"Crystal?" the deep voice of the officer called out. "Thank you. You're helping solve a murder in my town. I appreciate that and wish we could have started off on a better foot."

Crystal's heart lightened. "Me, too. Good luck with getting to the bottom of this. I hope you can help the woman's family find peace."

She received a solemn nod in response.

"What now?" Suzy glanced around like she was looking for the next obstacle to overcome.

"We go home and wait."

Chapter Seventeen

Crystal worried she might pass out. Her heart beat at a rhythm rapid enough to give a cardiologist cause for concern, and every time she didn't remind herself to breathe, she forgot to inhale. She sat on a bench by the water's edge of Lake Union in Seattle, waiting for Conner to join her. This spot was where she had seen the Facebook post of him with the redheaded tramp from his past. Did he have to be so cruel to break up with her where he had been cavorting with *her*, days earlier? He'd been nothing but a stellar boyfriend. Kind, understanding, supportive, and trustworthy, but now? Now, he wanted "to talk." Crystal had broken up enough times to know the meaning of that particular code phrase.

Where had they gone wrong? From Crystal's point of view, it had been the most fulfilling relationship ever. Built on trust, sharing of lifestyle, common goals, but most of all, love. His warm heart, gentle nature, and the way he joked with her led her to believe he'd been happy, as well. She must be blind, because all she could recall was how he made time for their relationship and been there for her as she learned to be a wilderness guide. Her entire family had told Crystal how lucky she was to have met him, with not a single caveated, "He seems nice, but…" qualification she had received with past relationships.

Her blood began a slow simmer in response to her stewing. Conner had played her emotions worse than she'd ever experienced before. How dare he invest so much into their relationship, make her love him with every fiber, and then throw it all away the second he got some alone time with Samantha-freakin'-big-boobs.

The object of her ire appeared at the top of the cement stairs leading down to her location. His left leg was locked straight with a brace secured above and below the knee, and with a grimace he started an awkward jump-skip down the stairs while holding the metal railing on either side.

Crystal's initial impulse to rush and help was reined in when she reminded herself how furious she was.

After what seemed like an eternity of watching his exertion, her heart attempting to hammer out of her chest the entire time, he finally landed at the bottom, panting from the effort. He took a few awkward steps toward her, a light sheen of sweat glistening on his brow. It was obvious he was struggling because his inhuman constitution from nonstop outdoor activities typically gave him unflagging energy.

"You're difficult to get a hold of." His cheery manner was like a razor blade to her nerves. The least he could do was pretend to be somber.

"I've been busy."

"So I hear. I got some of the low down from Suzy last night after you rolled into town. You must have fallen asleep early because you weren't answering your texts."

She'd been ignoring them but didn't have the fight in her to throw that at him.

"Arrested, shot at, and run out of town. You don't do things half-assed."

"Why are we here?" She couldn't stand the idle banter. Not now.

"Curious, huh? You have never, ever been able to stand an unsolved question. I should have known better than to lay it out there in such a fashion. I'm assuming that's why you're all business."

"I'm not all business. Spit it out."

"You're also cranky. They say prison changes a person, and they weren't kidding." Conner grinned at his own joke.

"I know you're breaking up with me." There. She'd said it. Better to go out on her terms.

He flinched and recoiled, a bewildered expression crossing his face. "How do you *know* that?"

"I'm not stupid, Conner."

"Well, let's assume I am. Why would you say that?" Conner's face had paled, but his words carried heat.

"I want to know where it went wrong. Please don't use the hackneyed expression, it's not you, it's me." Hot tears welled, blurring the image of him, before rolling down her cheeks. She lashed at them with her sleeves, angry at her emotional weakness this soon in the conversation. Unhappy how he peered down at her from his vantage, she stood.

Conner took that moment to drop down on the bench, extending his injured leg ahead of him. "Let's get one thing clear. I didn't ask you to meet me here to break up. Why would I want to break up with you? You're the best thing that's ever happened to me."

Crystal's butt hit the bench before she was aware

that she'd sat. Several different emotions and questions all scrambled to seize control of her body at once, causing her to open and close her mouth several times like a landed fish.

"You still haven't answered my question. What gave you the idea we're breaking up? Aren't things perfect with us?" Conner leaned forward, his face grave.

"I saw you on Facebook with *Samantha.*" Crystal put an extra dose of disdain on the full name. "When you said you were hanging out with your friend Sam from Search and Rescue."

Conner blanched. "Oooh, I can explain. I did try to trick you, so I can see why you're steamed. I didn't know she'd post anything on Facebook."

Crystal sat up a little straighter and shot a sidelong glance at him. "That's what you're worried about? The selfie you took looked like you were having the best time ever, and then you send me a mysterious text saying we need to talk."

Conner nodded. "We do need to talk. What's wrong with talking?"

"It's code. It means you want to break up." Crystal studied his face, looking for a clue as to what was going on in his head.

Confusion overrode his expression, but his lips quirked in irritation. "Says who?"

"Says everyone."

Conner scowled. "Everyone's a moron. Why can't it be something good?"

"Look." Crystal withdrew her phone from her pocket and sent a group text to her family and friends, asking what they thought. "I'm taking a poll. I'll show you."

Conner gave her a lopsided smile. "I'm sure you will. Still, I'm kind of mad you thought breaking up was even on the table. We're peanut butter and chocolate, meant to be together."

Crystal's phone chimed. Her sister, Heather, had already responded, asking if Conner was breaking up with her.

Her phone trilled several more times, causing Conner to glance at the screen. "Says here your mom and dad think I have something important to discuss."

Suzy's answer popped up, putting them in a tie.

Olivia's answer caught her off guard. She replied with—*Just talk to him for crying out loud.*—

"Happy?" Conner shifted his leg, grimacing.

"Not in the slightest. If you didn't ask me here to break up with me, then what are we doing here and why did you lie about spending time with Samantha?" Crystal still couldn't help but say the woman's name mockingly. How could she detest a person that she'd never met?

Conner scowled at Crystal's combativeness. "Why we're here and what I was doing with Samantha are one and the same. I didn't tell the whole truth, but it was to surprise you, not lie to you." With a shove of his arms, he propelled himself to his feet. "Follow me."

Crystal fell into a slow shuffling walk next to her limping boyfriend. He stretched out a hand to grab hers, and she almost yanked hers away. However, her fury was cooling, and she controlled her instinct.

"You know you could have phrased your text in a different way." Her words made it clear she wasn't completely over the trauma.

Conner frowned. "You could have trusted that I love you." Ouch. Score one for him. To his credit, he softened the sting. "However, I want you to know Samantha is and always has been just a friend."

A seagull perched on a railing by the lake cocked its head at them and started its raucous lilting caw.

Sullen words slipped out. "Suzy said she had a crush on you when she worked at Emerald City Outfitters."

Conner nodded. "She asked me out on a date on her last day. I turned her down."

"Why? She's gorgeous."

"She's not my type."

"What is your type?" The long, silky red locks, emerald eyes, and buxom figure had haunted Crystal ever since Suzy had shown the girl pictured with Conner.

"You." Conner's simple answer stopped her in her tracks. It took Conner a step to realize she'd frozen. "What are you doing? We're not there yet."

"You just can't say stuff like that." Crystal's emotions were doing a loop-de-loop on the roller coaster of life, and she wanted off the ride. Her heart, so filled with anger and bitterness this morning, swelled with love and affection for Conner, whose blissful unawareness of his words sent her emotions spiraling to new heights. Between their relationship, Roxie's imprisonment, and her dangerous adventures, her poor nerves weren't equipped to handle the constant changes.

Conner wrapped her in a warm hug, his strong arms encircling and squeezing her tight. His chin rested on top of her head as she buried her face in his broad chest. The seagull's cry had finished, but the sound of water lapping the shore was a constant reminder of where she was. She released the pain of the last few days and nearly sagged as emotional exhaustion overtook her. They stood, holding each other for several minutes next to the lakeshore.

Eventually, Conner broke the embrace. "Not only am I going to say things like that, I'm going to show you how I feel. Come on." His arms unwrapped from around her, and he seized her hand anew. Crystal could see where her tears soaked his sweatshirt. She squeezed his hand and strolled next to him.

It wasn't but a few more steps on the shore's path when he made an abrupt left down a pier. A closed gate with a keypad barred their entry, but Conner tapped four numbers into the lock and a metallic click resonated. Conner opened the door and led her onto the wooden dock. Their feet echoed with every step, and the faint odor of creosote combated with the fresh breeze rolling in from Lake Union.

This time she grabbed his hand, and he led her farther down the pier with his thumping gait. At the farthest end she could see several people putting paddle-boards into the water and picking up body-length poles. She'd always wanted to try the sport. A wetsuit clad woman shoved off the pier, swaying a little as she caught her balance. This was a lot of trouble and effort for Conner to go through to show her a new outdoor sport. Their relationship revolved around doing outdoor activities, and it was odd he would have made a big deal trying to surprise her like this.

"So, all of the secrecy and misunderstanding was for paddle-boarding?"

"What? No." Her presumption made him chuckle. "You have to stop making assumptions."

As the water deepened, they began passing house boats, the style of home made famous in the *Sleepless in Seattle* movie, and found in the calm waters of the central lake and along the banks of the ship canal leading to Elliot Bay. Clever names, painted in flashy cursive flourishes, decorated the sides facing the pier. *The Codfather* and *Aboat Time* tickled her sense of humor. Conner dreamed of owning one of these, living in a tranquil floating community amidst the hustle and bustle of Seattle.

Now it was her turn to freeze. *Conner's dream, his life's ambition, was owning a home on the water. He was years away from saving enough. Still...*

Conner stopped and studied her. His lips twitched upward. "I'm guessing you solved the case, Detective Rainey."

"Did you buy a houseboat?" A sudden rush of shyness had come over her, and her words eked out as timid as a mouse.

"Why else would I spend the day with Samantha who happens to be—"

"A realtor." Crystal cut him off. She covered her face with her hands. "Suzy told me Samantha was in some sort of sales."

"That's right. Sam knew from our days working together that I planned to buy a houseboat. When a deal came along too good to pass up, she contacted me." Somehow, Conner kept all overtones of incrimination out of his words.

Crystal uncovered her eyes. "Can I see it?"

"That's why we're here, silly. It's right there." He

pointed to a house tied several slips away.

Crystal couldn't help it. She trotted the remaining distance and stopped next to the home with the *For Sale* sign. A sticker had been applied, stating it was *Pending*. "This one?"

"That's the one."

The vessel had seen better days, but Crystal could tell it was once a beauty. The paint of the name had peeled and flaked to near illegibility, but Crystal could still make out the word *Ocean* written in faded calligraphy. It stood two stories tall, the upper deck lined with a decorative railing. The enclosed portion of the top was half the size of the bottom, with the other half an open-air deck with several faded plastic chairs.

Round porthole windows dotted the sides, but the large central window overlooking the lake had cracked and fogged with moisture.

"What do you think?" Conner studied her face, gauging her reaction.

"I'm so happy for you." She was excited his dream was coming true, but she was still recovering from her misunderstanding of the day's intent. She wanted to be as buoyant as the situation warranted, but her emotions were still reeling. "It's beautiful, but it looks like you have your work cut out for you."

Conner nodded, his eyes sparkling in the warm rays of the sun. "I knew what I was getting into when I bought it, but the chance to get on the water ahead of schedule was an opportunity I couldn't let pass. The deal closes next week."

Knowing her simple words and stilted body language weren't enough enthusiasm for such a momentous happening, Crystal threw her arms around his neck and gave him a thorough kiss. Conner staggered backward as she leaned into him but caught himself with his good leg and gave her a powerful squeeze as he met her lips with his own.

After a few seconds, they broke the kiss, but not the embrace. Looking down at her, Conner's lips parted into a huge smile followed by a throaty chuckle. "Now, this is a little more like it. Do you want to see inside?"

"Can you do that? It isn't yours, yet."

"Technically, no, but when have you taken rules— and by rules, I mean laws—too seriously?"

"Well, I kinda got my hand slapped by spending the night in jail, but what the heck. Let's do it."

A cracked terra-cotta pot with the remnants of a long-dead plant greeted them, so dried and wilted there was no telling what it had once been. Conner tilted the pot back, revealing a tarnished silver key underneath. The boat swayed beneath their feet as a large wake passed below, the aftermath of a yacht making its way toward Puget Sound.

Crystal's balance compensated for the motion, and she found herself enjoying the creaking of wood and lapping of waves. The faint rumble of city traffic reached her ears, but the residence was truly an oasis.

The lock clicked at the turn of the key, and with a slight thump of his shoulder, Conner popped the door open.

Inside was a reflection of the outside. The scuffed wooden floor showed tremendous wear through the walking area leading to the kitchen, the hallway, and the stairwell spiraling up to the second floor. A slight musty odor filled the air, as well as the faint reek of stale cigarette smoke.

Only a single tattered recliner parked before an old box style television graced the living room. Conner explained the decor. "This was owned by an old bachelor. Hard to believe looking at the furnishings, right? When he passed, his extended family offloaded it as fast as possible. The neighbors described him as a grouchy son-of-a-gun who chain smoked on the upstairs deck and yelled at anybody making too much noise. Nice of him to set the bar so low for what they should expect."

Crystal wandered into the kitchen. The cabinets were scuffed, and one door was missing, lost to time. "It isn't the model home Suzy and I stayed in at Evergreen Resorts, but it has its charm." The houseboat swayed as another gentle swell rippled over the water.

Tickling the recesses of her mind, a memory bothered her regarding Evergreen Resorts. She'd made a mental note to look into something, but couldn't recall what, the issue forgotten in the ensuing chaos. She strained to remember as she peered into cabinets and scrutinized the scarred countertop.

"I know it's a fixer upper and won't be ready to live in for a while, but it has good bones." Conner patted the wall.

Crystal refocused her attention and studied the interior with a different perspective. The round windows drove home the nautical theme, and the ceiling consisted of sealed planks. A graceful archway framed the hallway, inviting her to explore, and a window bench on the far side called for her to curl up with a book on a rainy day. This home's cozy interior begged for a new life.

"But," Conner cut off her musing, "something is

missing. I signed the papers, not believing my luck. I'm even excited to gut and remodel the entire home, making it my own."

Despite his positive words, tension laced his voice. "What's wrong?" Conner shifted his weight between his good and bad leg, betraying his nervousness.

His gaze searched hers. "Let's talk upstairs." Conner led the way up the spiral staircase, stopping at the top to open a hatch. Whatever he had wanted to discuss in person, this must be it.

Puzzled, Crystal followed. If she didn't know better, she'd think there was trouble in their relationship, but they'd talked and everything seemed perfect. *Didn't it?*

Crystal's palms burst into sweat, and the anxiety from earlier thundered back. Conner was acting unsure of himself. For a man whose confidence was part of who he was, Crystal didn't know how to cope with this uneasiness.

Following him up the spiral staircase to the deck, she joined him leaning on the rail to study the view of Gas Works Park. The rusty remnants of the defunct oil refinery still stood, the rounded towers and twisting pipes direct from a steampunk artist's imagination.

She placed her hand atop Conner's on the railing, intertwining her fingers with his large calloused grip. "What's wrong?"

He started a bit and turned to face her. His smile was radiant, but his demeanor was intent. "Nothing's wrong. In fact, everything's perfect. So perfect, I don't want to do anything to screw it up, but I also dare to make it even more magical."

His poetic words were out of character and had the

intonation of something written earlier and memorized. They didn't help put her at ease, and the exhaustion of riding the emotional highs and lows of her life were taking its toll. Couldn't she have a normal day? Wake up, eat a bowl of cereal, and watch a movie in her pajamas? Was that too much to ask the universe?

"Crystal, I don't want to make this my home. I want to make this our home."

"Wha...?" The question lodged in her throat, her brain racing to catch up to his words.

"I love you and want you to move in with me. Here."

She stared at him, trying to find words, positive she resembled a deer at midnight staring down an oncoming semi in a mountain pass. "Conner, I..." What did she want? They'd only been dating for six months. Was this too early? Part of it felt like it was, but a good portion of her wanted this more than anything. What would she do with her condo? What about Elf? Could he live with Conner's Labrador, Maggie? Her feisty cat was temperamental at best, downright ornery at his worst. Would their young relationship stand the strain of—?

Conner interrupted her racing mind. "I know it's a lot to take in this soon in a relationship, but I want this to be ours from the beginning. With all of the repairs this needs, we're months from moving in, and we'll continue getting to know each other in the meantime, but it wouldn't be home without you."

That did it. She threw herself in his arms for the second time that day, squeezing him tight. Tears, now of the joyful variety, streamed down her cheeks. She wasn't positive she was ready to say goodbye to her condo and her own life, but every shred of her wanted a future with Conner.

Her phone rang while he held her. She ignored it at first, too caught in the moment. It chimed again, and then a third time. She and Conner split apart, with a quiet laugh as she dragged her phone out of her pocket.

"It's Roxie's lawyer." With a quick flick of her hand she answered. "Hello?"

"Crystal. It's Isabella. I've got news on the DNA testing."

"What is it? Will it help Roxie?" Crystal covered her free ear to block out the noise of the lapping water.

"Maybe. With a new technique called touch DNA, they identified skin cells on the sandals belonging to a woman, but I'm guessing that's obvious since they were women's sandals. However, that DNA didn't have a positive match to anyone in the database."

"How can that help?"

"I'm not sure, yet; but here's the interesting part. The DNA from the bloodstain didn't belong to the woman. It's from Frederick Baranhof."

"What?" Crystal switched the phone to speaker for Conner's sake.

"It puts another person at the crime scene and gives credibility to Roxie's story of walking in after the fact."

"Can you get her out of jail?"

Isabella sounded skeptical. "I'm attempting to do just that. I've requested the prosecutor drop the charges based on this new evidence, but his office hasn't responded. I'm assuming they're examining the case in a different manner to incorporate this new information into the narrative they are working on for the jury. If they refuse to drop the charges, I could attempt to have the judge do the same, but if the prosecutor can put together a story implicating Roxie, I'd be wasting my time."

"Thank you! Thank you!" Crystal cried, bouncing on her toes. "This is sensational news."

"Crystal, calm down. I suspect the prosecutor is going to move forward. Murder cases are high profile, and it always looks good to put a killer behind bars, doubly so in small communities where this is the biggest thing to happen in years. I've checked out the Clallam County prosecutor handling the case and he has some modest political ambitions. Putting the Kitchen Killer behind bars will give him a soapbox to stand on when he starts campaigning."

"Kitchen Killer?"

"I think it's a poor sobriquet, too. I would have called her the Death Chef, but he's using the nickname he came up with in his interviews."

"What can I do to help?"

"Help? Nothing more I can think of. You've given me enough to generate probable doubt. If you ever decide to be a private detective, give me a call. I'd hire you in a heartbeat."

"Nothing's guaranteed for Roxie, though?"

"Well, no. If the prosecutor convinces a jury, Roxie could get life in prison or even the death sentence, since Washington is a capital punishment state."

Conner's face paled at the words. Judging by her queasy stomach, she guessed she had gone several shades whiter as well.

"What would get her set free?"

"A confession from the real murderer or irrefutable proof. If they can track down who the sundress belonged to or the guy with the gun who took it from you, it might help. I doubt they'll confess, though. Criminals don't do that."

"Thanks, Isabella."

"Thank you, Crystal."

There was a click and the line went dead.

"What do you think?" Conner's face betrayed that he knew she was contemplating something.

"I think Olivia and I are going to Forks. I just had a revelation that I need to look into."

Chapter Eighteen

"I still don't know about this." Olivia gnawed her thumbnail as Crystal's ancient Honda sputtered into the parking area next to the protestors' encampment. Miracle of miracles, the twenty-year-old car had been up for the challenge and delivered them without incident, five hours from the city.

"You said Tyler liked you."

"He liked Anastasia, the sweet, naive Russian emigrant trying to save the earth and make her way in America."

"You do know you sounded like Natasha from *Rocky and Bullwinkle*, right? He must have known something was fishy and still enjoyed your company. Whatever possessed you to even use an accent?"

Olivia smiled around her thumb. "The couple that I fast-talked into driving me here were on their way out of town, so they dropped me off and split. Since I didn't recognize anyone from the cafe, Roxie's southern impersonation inspired me to attempt my own accent." Olivia's expression fell into a frown. "I don't know about this. Tyler's probably still mad at me for lying."

"We have to try. I have a feeling he might be able to help Roxie."

Heaving a dramatic sigh, Olivia relented. "Fine. I'll do it for you and Roxie. You owe me, though."

"You name it. Just get me up the tree to talk with

him."

Crystal and Olivia unbuckled and got out of the car. The self-appointed camp warden, Jasper, snored in his chair.

Pressing her finger to her lips, Olivia set off down the path. Crystal followed, tiptoeing past Jasper. They passed through the trees and into the quiet of the nearly empty camp. A girl sat on her heels, poking at the fire with a stick, and Rodrigo leaned against a tree, tapping a drum.

The girl brightened when she spotted them. "Hi, I'm Tyler's new publicist. Are you with the TV station?"

"Uh, no." Did she not see they weren't lugging television cameras?

"What are you doing here, then?"

"We're here to see Tyler."

"He's busy right now."

Olivia snorted at the ludicrous statement. "Busy? He lives in a tree. Is he binge watching his favorite show? Taking a shower? We don't want to walk in on him naked, after all. That would be soooo embarrassing."

The woman blushed at the sarcasm, tossed her tousled hair, and placed her hands on her hips. "He's waiting for an interview and doesn't have time for whatever voyeuristic itch you're looking to scratch."

"Karen, it's okay. I know these two," Tyler's deep voice issued from up on high.

Karen scowled at Olivia and Crystal without glancing at Tyler. After a final fierce glare, she returned to jabbing at the smoldering logs.

Crystal and Olivia made their way to the bottom of

the tree fort. "Can we come up and talk to you?" Olivia practically batted her eyelashes.

"What do you want to discuss, *Anastasia*?"

"Umm...It's Olivia, not Anastasia. I'm not Russian, either."

"I gathered, since you've lost your accent. It was a little over the top, to be honest."

"That's what Crystal said. I'll work on it for next time."

Silence fell between them. Tyler glowered, not even twitching a lip at Olivia's lame attempt at a joke.

Olivia threw her hands up in exasperation. "Look, I'm really, really sorry I lied to you, but I didn't come here to ruin you or what you're fighting for. I came to save a friend."

"The Kitchen Killer?"

"She didn't murder anyone. If you knew her, you'd know that to be true."

Tyler continued to glare.

"Please, Tyler. Roxie's a good person."

The hardness in his face relented.

"Fine, Ana...Olivia." He disappeared from the edge of the railing, and a ladder fashioned from ropes and boards was lowered. Despite its noticeable homemade and unbalanced look, Olivia grabbed onto the apparatus and started up in an instant. Not trusting the ladder to bear the two of them at once, Crystal waited while Olivia clambered up the tree. As soon as she scrambled off the ladder, Crystal stepped onto the first plank. Despite ominous creaks and groans from the ropes holding the entire thing together, Crystal crested the top after a few minutes of wrestling the swaying contraption. Getting off was the most awkward part of an already ungraceful ascent. With nothing to grab onto, Crystal managed to fling a leg up, and rolled over onto the floorboards.

She opened her eyes to a smirking Olivia. Crystal gave a wry smile. "Hey, I made it. Maybe I don't get style points, but I'm here."

Tyler stepped next to Olivia to look down at her, and Crystal got an eyeful. Her vantage from the floor gave her an intimate view of what Mother Nature had graced him with. Trying to focus elsewhere didn't help due to her peripheral vision, so she rolled over, pressing herself up with her palms.

From a standing position, Crystal was able to look at Tyler's face. His handsome features were still distracting, but not as much as the rest of him.

"Nice place you have here." Crystal began with mindless small talk. She took in the construction and was surprised by its sturdiness. Planking encircled the trunk, allowing a person to take several strides outward before reaching the railing. One half of the structure had a roof covering a cot, and there was even a tiny enclosed section. A rope tied to a carabiner clip lay coiled next to the hole Crystal had hopped out of.

"That's to send food up and stuff down. I clip it to a bucket handle." Tyler waved at the rest of the tree fort. "The entire structure is built from recycled pallets."

"Don't you get cold? We're in a rain forest after all."

"Well, I built the roof over there to keep the worst off of me, but if it gets too cold, I have blankets to keep me warm."

"Is the support staff cool with sending up food and

carrying away buckets of…stuff?"

"They are. We're all working together. They're not only helping me out physically, they're posting on social media, raising awareness for the rain forest, and contacting reporters and news stations."

"Is it doing anything?"

"It is." Tyler put a hand against the coarse trunk of the hemlock. "We've gathered a quarter million signatures on *change.org*. Once we reach half a million, we'll submit it to the state senate as part of our petition to incorporate the property in the National Park."

"That's admirable and I hope you achieve your goal, but we're here to save Roxie, our friend."

"So you've said. What makes you think she didn't commit the murder?"

"Seriously?" Crystal snorted. "You're not the type of guy who believes the system gets everything right, are you?" Crystal was fully aware her comment would strike home.

Tyler shuffled his feet and glanced out at a chestnut-backed chickadee coasting from one tree to another, singing its trilling tune. "I suppose that's true. Even so, what can I do to help?"

Crystal steeled herself. Tyler wasn't going to betray a trust for them, so she started in with caution. "Do you remember the girl who was here in the beginning? The naked one?"

Tyler snorted. "I'm not senile. Of course, I remember Misha."

"Were you expecting her to show up?"

"No, I was surprised. She hasn't spent time with us for a couple of years, but it's not unusual for someone to rejoin us after being gone for a while. We're modern day Gypsies. People come and go as they please. They're welcome when they show up but never held accountable when life carries them on another journey." Tyler settled down on the floor of his home in cross-legged fashion, inviting them to join with a wave of his hand.

Attempting not to look at his lap, Crystal sat down across from him and was joined by Olivia on the rough surface.

"Why are you asking about Misha?" Tyler's brow furrowed. "I heard about those bloody sandals you found in the woods and brought back here. They don't....they don't belong to her, do they?"

"We don't know who they belong to. They might be hers. Have you heard from her in the last couple of days?"

"No." Tyler shot to his feet and started pacing. "She left the first day after sitting with me for a couple of hours."

"When she showed up, was she wet? Like she'd been in a river?"

"Well, yeah, but we're in a rainforest. Everything's wet here." Tyler studied them with suspicion. "What are you trying to say? Is she okay or isn't she?"

Olivia spoke as if Tyler were a skittish horse. "We don't know, but if I'm following Crystal's reasoning, Misha left the scene of the crime, took her bloody dress off in the woods, washed herself in the stream, and walked into the clearing like she'd planned this all along."

Tyler stopped his pacing and leaned against the railing. Crystal would have never trusted the shoddy appearance or ominous noises emanating from the structure when his weight settled, but the naked protestor didn't give it a second thought.

"Please, Tyler," Olivia began.

He paused before answering. "I've known Misha for years. She's helped protect the Orcas, the rain forest, and the salmon runs. She's kind and gentle. You don't care about our cause, only saving your friend. Now, you're accusing *my friend* of being involved in a murder, and want me to implicate her? No way. Not happening."

Olivia's face crumbled at Tyler's accusations, and she cast her eyes downward to her hands in her lap. "I believe in what's happening here, but I don't want Roxie to be in jail for a crime she didn't commit."

The edges of his eyes squeezed shut in anguish at the words, but she pushed him harder. "It's justice, Tyler. You want environmental justice for all the wrongs you see in the world, so I know you understand. We're not asking you to identify her in court. We simply want to talk. Do you know how we can reach her?"

"I know she lives in the area. That's all I can tell you." That was all Crystal needed to confirm her suspicion. Behind Tyler's back, she tapped Olivia's hand and nodded.

Tyler didn't say another word, only continued staring out at the forest. Crystal became acquainted with what stressed and angry butt cheeks looked like, as they tensed and clenched.

Olivia put her hand on his shoulder for a brief moment. Not a muscle twitched at her touch, and Crystal began the clumsy descent down the free swinging ladder. When she reached the bottom, she held it steady as Olivia clambered afterward, touching down with a light hop.

"Are you okay?" Crystal felt terrible after things had gone so poorly with Tyler.

A brave smile greeted her question. "I'll be fine. He's a nice guy, and I feel bad my lies hurt him, but I wouldn't change a single one of my actions. Other than the accent thing. What seemed like fun at first became a pain to keep up after a while. I don't know how Roxie manages to keep in character all the time."

Olivia and Crystal wandered through the scattered tents toward the trail leading to her car. Olivia sniffled and gave her nose a wipe with her hand. "Did you find out what you need to know?"

"I did. When Tyler told me Misha lives in the area, it corroborated where I'd seen her before."

After a long pause, Olivia couldn't stand it any longer. "Well, are you going to tell me or keep it all to yourself?"

"Misha is an alias. Her name is Eunice."

"Who's that?"

"She's Kinsey Laughlin's assistant and niece. Her father is the co-owner of Evergreen Resorts, the company that wanted to buy this land from Frederick Baranof."

"Cool. Let's go talk to her and squeeze her for information like in the detective movies." Olivia began tapping the dashboard of the car, excitement coursing through the rhythm she beat out.

Crystal glanced left and right as she merged into traffic. "Well, the bad news is the witness is in the one place the police have forbidden me to trespass."

Olivia stopped her impromptu drum solo and threw

her hands in the air. "What do you want to do?"

"If we can't go to her, we'll have to lure her to us."

"How?"

"One thing I've learned about fishing with Conner, success depends on picking the right bait."

Chapter Nineteen

"Hello, Eunice. I found something you lost in the wilderness. I know you've had someone looking for it, but they aren't going to have any luck. The good news is I have it, safe and sound. If you want the rest of your outfit returned, I'm happy to give it to you. A finder's fee sounds fair, though. Five thousand dollars. Deliver the money to the Baranhof cabin at noon tomorrow, and you can start resting easy again." Crystal flipped over the cue card she had made and kept reading. "Come alone. If I see anyone else get out of the car, I'll turn over the evidence to the authorities before you can say jail time." Crystal hung up her phone.

"Nice work, Crystal. I liked how sinister you got toward the end." Olivia gave a gentle clap in appreciation.

Crystal tucked her phone in her pocket and breathed out a sigh of relief in their new room in the Quinault Bed and Breakfast. She figured it prudent to change accommodations, since too many people in town knew where she had been staying.

Olivia sat on the edge of one of the beds and faced her. "So, is the guy from the woods the one you're trying to warn away from tomorrow's meet? Any idea who he is?"

"Probably her father. I noticed him when we were getting kicked out of Evergreen Resorts. He's tall, muscular, and bald."

"You described Mr. Clean." Olivia broke into a grin.

"Not far off the mark. No earring and definitely no smile, though. What makes me think it's him, aside from the height and muscles, is remembering how close the hood of his sweatshirt hugged the top of his head. There wasn't any hair."

"If he gets wind of you ransoming something you already gave to the police, he is going to be super angry."

"Don't I know it. That's why he's not invited to this party." The tenseness of the phone message had left Crystal agitated. "Follow me. I'm having a hard time thinking straight in this closed up room." She stood and headed outside. A pair of hammocks had been strung up for guests to use near the main building where they checked in, and she hoped their gentle rocking might help with her nerves.

"What if he shows up?" Olivia trailed after, clearly concerned Crystal hadn't thought this through.

"Easy. I can watch from the cabin window. If I see anyone else other than Eunice, I'll hightail it into the woods, like she did the day she killed Frederick."

A small footpath led through the grounds to a clearing clustered with ferns. Crystal found the hammocks tied to towering cedar trees in the center of the peaceful spot.

After several tries, a few muttered expletives, and almost being dumped in the dirt, they managed to clamber into the swaying devices. Stretching her legs, Crystal stared up at the canopy. A high, clear piping call caught her attention, and she glanced up the tree holding one end of her hammock. Her knowledge as a wilderness guide identified the red and white head as belonging to a pileated woodpecker. It finished its call and proceeded to hammer at the trunk. The staccato thumps vibrated down the massive tree through the ropes of her hammock.

"Your scheme seems straightforward, but I feel like something could go wrong." Olivia's fretting exacerbated Crystal's own fears.

Crystal forced some bravado into her voice. "All plans work if you follow KISS."

"The rock band?"

"Umm, no, not the rock band. KISS stands for keep-it-simple-stupid. Less things can go wrong if your plan is simple, right?"

"I suppose so." Olivia didn't sound convinced.

"What I need to know is whether I should move in with Conner on his new houseboat."

"Wait. What?" Olivia twisted in her hammock.

"He asked me yesterday."

"You've only been dating six months."

"I know, right?"

"But I've never seen you happier."

"Really?"

"Of course. Maybe it's partially the new job, but I know a large portion of your newfound happiness is because of him."

Crystal blew out a hearty sigh. "You're right."

"Then you best go for it."

"That's all you got. Go for it?"

"Keep it simple, stupid." Olivia's grin betrayed how much she enjoyed throwing the concept back at Crystal. "You have been known to overthink everything you do in life."

"I do not." Crystal's voice rose in protest. With another cry, the woodpecker darted for a quieter tree.

"Yes, you do. Right now you're thinking a lifetime alone in your condo with your rotten cat might be a better choice than shacking up with the love of your life."

"What am I going to do with my condo? If it doesn't work out between us, I'll need it to move back in, but if I don't sell it, it will seem like I'm going in with half a heart."

Olivia snorted. "Thanks for proving my point. Look at all of the overthinking and worrying going on in your head."

Crystal folded her arm over her eyes and groaned. "That still doesn't answer the question."

"How's this for an answer: I move into your condo and pay the mortgage. You shack up with your amazing boyfriend on a fairytale houseboat and live happily ever after."

"If you'd seen the state the boat is in, you'd know it wasn't a fairytale. However, it does look like three bears lived in it for a spell."

"Sounds like more worrying. Fix it up. It'll be like one of those cute movies where you paint each other's nose and end up laughing and kissing on the floor."

Crystal swayed in the hammock, breathing the moist earthen scent of the forest. She pondered her future in silence. *Was she ready for this? Was their relationship ready for this?* She wasn't positive it was.

****

Crystal paced in the front room of the Baranhof cabin, constantly glancing out the window through the barely parted blinds. What if Misha-Eunice hadn't listened to the message? What if her father showed up instead and Crystal had to flee out the back door? Her tennis shoes were laced tight and double knotted, and she had dressed in a pair of running shorts and a tight top that wouldn't snag on the brush encroaching the potential escape route. She double-checked the Go-Pro camera she had borrowed from Suzy. It was positioned and recording on the bookshelf in as inconspicuous a place as possible. Isabella's comment in respect to getting confessions had made her think ahead to this moment when she would have a chance to talk to Eunice. Hopefully, this recording would be the proof she needed to save Roxie. She studied the hiding spot and tilted several books in an attempt to better mask its presence. Go-Pros were meant to record outdoor action in all conditions, but they weren't exactly spy micro-cameras.

The clock on the fireplace mantel gave twelve soft chimes, but it took several more restless minutes of pacing until a black Corvette appeared, its throaty engine growling loud enough to fill the forest.

Crystal glued herself to the window, staring in nervous anticipation at the doors of the sports car. The windows were tinted black and she couldn't see anything going on inside. She risked a quick glance at the back sliding door, confirmed it was unlocked and ajar, ready for a quick getaway. Crystal checked her other avenue of escape, the hallway to the room where Frederick had been murdered. The window in the room was also unlocked and opened, ready for her to jump to the ground, a couple of feet below.

After several heart pounding breaths, the driver's

door swung open and Eunice's head popped up over the body of the car. The object of her investigation heaved out a black bag, presumably the ransom money.

Eunice scanned the parking area, wary of being watched. Like Crystal, she had arrived dressed for potential action. Her long silky hair was stuffed beneath a ball cap and threaded through the back in a ponytail. She wore white sneakers, black yoga pants, and a formfitting top. Crystal would have preferred if Eunice sported another pair of sandals, but if it came to it, Crystal judged that she could outrun her.

Eunice halted before the front door covered in police tape, stretched out a hand to knock, paused with a puzzled expression, and then turned the knob. In all fairness, were you supposed to knock in these situations? It wasn't as if Miss Manners covered ransom meeting etiquette.

Crystal turned from the window to watch the front door opening. Eunice froze when she spotted her blackmailer.

"I'm glad you came." Crystal did her best to speak calmly.

"You didn't give me much of a choice." Eunice's voice was high and strained. She ducked under the yellow tape barricading her way and flung the bag at Crystal's feet. "Here's your money. Where's my sandals?"

This wouldn't do at all. Crystal didn't want the money. She needed a full confession, especially one the camera she had borrowed from Suzy could record. She and Olivia had bought a dummy pair of sandals this morning, but they were in her car trunk. If Crystal didn't get a confession now, she planned to set up a second meet to ostensibly transfer the evidence in another attempt to elicit the information she needed.

"They're somewhere safe. Why did you do it, Eunice? Frederick Baranhof never did anything to you." Crystal glanced at the camera, then out the window at the Corvette, keeping a lookout for any support Eunice might have brought with her.

"This isn't a social call. I'm not telling you anything." She shoved her chin out and took a step closer.

"Then I'm not giving you anything, and you can keep your money."

"Why do you care?"

"Frederick Baranhof was a friend."

"If he was your friend, why don't you turn me in rather than ask for money you claim you don't want? And why aren't you calling him Fred or Freddy? You expect me to believe your bullshit story?"

Touché. Crystal darted a glance out the window. Still clear. "It seems odd that you risked everything by murdering a man in cold blood, just to secure a piece of land for your family, Eunice."

"Don't call me that!" Grabbing a lamp from an end table, Eunice yanked the cord from the wall, and flung it against the brick fireplace. Crystal flinched at the crash, shoulders raising to protect her head on instinct.

Silence filled the room, and Crystal snapped her attention to the unhinged killer. She mustered what little calm she had left in her psyche. "Why shouldn't I call you by your name?" Crystal lowered her shoulders, but her other muscles tensed for action. This girl was on the brink.

"I loathe that name. It's a damned family name my

father gave me when I was born. He insists on calling me Eunice."

"Well, change it."

"He threatened to cut me off if I did. Can you believe it?"

"Umm, no. Still, it doesn't answer my question. Why did you do it?"

Eunice threw her hands up in exasperation. "I was trying to impress my father. He always tells me I'm not smart or tough enough to run the business. We knew old Baranhof wasn't likely to sell to us, so I blended into Tyler's group of protesters, made my way through the forest, and went into the cabin to convince him. I knew if I could talk him into letting us purchase the land, my father would be proud." She snorted with contempt. Crystal wasn't sure if it was for the idea she could convince Frederick or that her father would be proud.

"You attempted to persuade him carrying a knife?"

"It was just an impulse. I saw it in the block in the kitchen, grabbed it, and hid it behind my back in case I needed to protect myself."

"How did you know your way through the forest?"

"Please," Eunice snorted at her ignorance, "my family's been here for generations. During the summers, my dad would dump me here at camp for weeks on end to be rid of me. I know these woods like the back of my hand."

A deep, raspy voice rumbled agreement. "Yes. We do."

Crystal whirled to the sliding glass door. Her mystery assailant, dressed in his same ominous outfit from the woods, flung the slider open.

"What the hell are you doing here?" Eunice retreated a pace. "How did you know I was here?"

"You should delete your voice mails if you don't want anyone to know what you're doing. It's on the company phone, for crying out loud. It's like you want to be tracked."

"You checked my voice mail?" Eunice shrieked.

Crystal edged her way to the hallway. This whole time she'd kept watch on the Corvette, too arrogant to think of someone sneaking in the back when she was distracted.

"You also took five thousand dollars from the company account. You don't think the bank calls when withdrawals that size are made? Your mother would be disappointed if she were here to see you today."

"I wouldn't be in this situation if I wasn't trying to impress you, but you're such a contemptuous bastard, I never will." Spittle flew from her mouth when she threw her insult.

Crystal's heart pounded a million beats per second in response to the argument unfolding before her. Her brain agreed this was a bad situation and screamed it was time to go. Her gut, however, told her she needed to stay and listen.

Grant Laughlin gave a derisive chuckle. "You thought murdering the property owner was a good way to negotiate a transaction? You didn't get your brains from me or your Aunt Kinsey, that's for sure."

Eunice flushed a deep red and stamped a foot. "I've told you. I went to his room to talk to him and when he took a threatening step toward me, I pulled the knife I'd hidden."

Her father blew a raspberry.

Eunice flushed deep crimson at his disrespect. "When he came at me, he impaled himself on the knife. I didn't kill him, he killed himself."

"That's the defense you've come up with? He killed himself on the knife you were holding? You aren't to blame at all? It's a good thing you finally told me the whole story, so I can clean up your mess. Again." Eunice's father slid the door shut and moved his hand to the waistband in the back of his pants, where the butt of a familiar revolver poked out.

A furious expression contorted Eunice's face at his condescension and she seized the now empty end table beside her. Her father had managed to tug the gun free when Eunice let fly the small piece of furniture, crashing it into his head.

Three things happened simultaneously. The struck man staggered, throwing his hands out to catch himself against the glass door, Eunice screamed "You're the worst father ever," and Crystal's feet were given leave to get her the heck out of there.

She bolted for the location where it had all begun, Frederick Baranhof's room. Crystal slammed and locked the door behind her. Quickstepping over the bloodstains on the floor, Crystal threw a leg over the windowsill.

The knob jiggled, and Grant's voice bellowed. "Open the door, Crystal. Give us the sandals and no one has to get hurt."

Crystal didn't believe him for a second. Throwing her other leg over, she slid from the open window, dropping to the packed earth below.

A crash resounded from the cabin she had just vacated. Crystal put her head down and sprinted the short distance to the trees, pumping her arms. Cursing and stumbling emanated from the open window, but she didn't dare look.

Fear urged her past the trees flanking the entrance of the trail and into the cool air of the forest. Confronted with the first turn, Crystal took a sharp right toward her destination. Straining her sense of hearing, she listened for the telltale sign of following footsteps, but her own heavy tread and panting breaths drowned out any chance she had for tracking pursuit.

Branches slapped against her passing limbs, but the trail was dry, and her footing was firm. She took a right at the next split.

What had she been thinking? How did she ever think she'd outsmart locals on their home turf? She stole a glance behind her. A flash of black caused her overtaxed adrenal glands to pump another gallon into her veins, urging her flagging legs to pick up the pace. How had he figured out where she was going? A stitch developed in her side, but she ignored the pain.

Feet pounding, she zipped between two alders and jumped over a small moss-covered log. The cramp in her side seized up and she stumbled, gasping for air. She thrust her hands out to steady herself, but her foot caught on the knob of a root. Before she could react, she was face down on the path, breath driven from her with the impact.

Run! Her lizard brain impelled her to take action. She thrust herself to her feet, wincing at the ache in her side.

Grant appeared around the last corner. His hood had fallen back, exposing his bald scalp, its deep red hue matching his flushed face. Sweat beaded and dribbled down his head, and his expression was manic as he closed on the object of his hunt.

She couldn't outrun a bullet, so she darted into the forest, ducking under branches and scrambling over deadfalls. Her feet skidded on the slick rocks and tree limbs covering the forest floor, but her luck held as she managed to navigate through a copse of sword ferns and dart behind a Western Hemlock.

"Crystal," Grant wheezed, "we…can come…to an….arrangement."

Crystal labored to keep her own panting under control as she leaned against the tree, the large swaths of damp moss soothing her overheated body. However, when she forced her breath into a normal pattern, her body would exert control, and she couldn't help but draw in deep gasps.

"It's a pity what happened, but it was an accident. No reason for my careless daughter to go to jail." Her pursuer's own breathing was evening out. The snap of a twig revealed he'd taken another step closer.

Her frantic glance fell on a lichen covered tree limb sticking out of the duff, roughly the shape of a bat. She crouched down, sliding a hand toward it.

Grant continued shouting into the forest. "What's it going to take? Do you want the five thousand? Well, I need assurance you won't come for more later."

Crystal's hand closed on the end. The spongy outer layer crumbled at her touch, but the inner core was solid wood. With patience she wasn't feeling, Crystal dragged it closer.

"Because I found your hidden camera. I can't imagine why you'd want a recording, unless you planned on double-crossing us!" The last words were roared as he charged her hiding place.

His heavy steps and clumsy shout gave away his position, and she timed her swing. She'd never played baseball in her life, but this better connect.

Chapter Twenty

It didn't even come close. The limb she had seized was rotted through from the rain forest's ongoing decay, and when she swung, the top half spun over Grant's head and into the brush. He ducked and twisted to avoid the missile. His foot planted on a slick log, and his leg shot down the length, dropping him to the ground.

Taking advantage of his misfortune, Crystal bolted deeper into the woods. The wall of a cliff, twice her height, loomed out of the dense vegetation. Instead of slowing, she quickened her pace, trusting in the rock-climbing skills she had learned from Suzy and Conner. She picked an ascension route and grabbed onto the first outcropping within reach. The handholds were slick with moisture, but she clambered a few feet up before the crashing sound of her pursuer approached. She stretched for a granite protrusion above her head and heaved herself several feet higher.

A calloused hand seized her ankle. She yanked her appendage from his grasp and lashed downward with her heel, striking flesh. Grant cursed and released her, giving Crystal enough room to scramble from his clutch. Desperation drove her to dig deeper. She grabbed onto a large rock protruding over the edge of the cliff and muscled herself up.

Her weight was too much, and the stone she was

lifting herself with rocked forward over the cliff. Crystal didn't even have time to scream.

Breath exploded from her lungs as she crashed into the moss and ferns of the forest floor. She wrapped her arms over her head, knowing the stone she had been holding tumbled after. There was a muted thump, and Grant crashed down atop her.

Air refused to pump into her lungs, but she kicked her attacker off and scrambled to her feet.

Grant lay still on the ground, face up and eyes closed, the fallen rock beside him.

Managing a pained, panting breath, Crystal stared at the limp body for signs of deception. Not seeing a twitch, she jabbed his stomach with a stick but didn't get a response. Realizing she needed to hit him in a more sensitive spot, she rapped his nose, hard. He grunted but didn't budge an arm to protect himself. At least he wasn't dead. Crystal didn't need that on her conscience.

A nasty lump rose on his forehead where the rock had struck, red, swollen, and painful looking. If he was playing possum, he deserved an Oscar for his acting.

Where was his gun? He'd kept it tucked in the waistband at the small of his back, but he was on the forest floor, face up.

Mustering her courage, she knelt, keeping watch on his face for any telltale indications of awakening. Shoving her hands under him, she hefted, turning the upper half of his body over. Twisting around, she put her shoes on his shoulder blade and shoved. She slid back a few inches but flopped over his entire limp form.

There wasn't a gun. It must have jostled loose in their mad dash through the old growth forest. Crystal exhaled a sigh of relief. She didn't want it, but she sure as hell didn't want him waking up and using it on her.

Crystal stared at the unconscious man, wondering what to do. She could call the police, but what did she have? He'd found Suzy's camera, so it was almost certain that either he or Eunice had grabbed it in the scramble to chase Crystal, and any confession was potentially lost.

Crystal knew the truth of Frederick Baranhof's murder, but that didn't mean anything to the police, judge, or jury. She was here to get Roxie's name cleared, and that meant she had to see if she could retrieve the recording.

The easiest way to accomplish her goal was to keep following the path she was on to Emerson's job trailer, where Olivia waited with her car. They would drive to the cabin, and if Eunice's Corvette was gone, Crystal would risk the dash inside to grab the camera, if it was still there.

Mind made up, she abandoned the helpless Grant Laughlin and retreated to the path. The distance to the logging camp was short, and after mere minutes the forest brightened ahead and she entered the clearcut.

Next to the job trailer sat her car, boxed in by Eunice's black muscle car. Olivia faced Crystal with her hands in the air, Eunice pointing her father's massive revolver at her back.

"Come join us. We have a few things we need to hash out." Eunice's taut tones cut through the fifty yards between them.

Crystal couldn't believe Olivia's life was in danger again because of another of her half-baked schemes. She swore she'd do whatever was needed to get Olivia out of this predicament unscathed.

Crystal picked her way through the brush and dangerous footing, mindful of Conner's accident. "How did you know where I'd run?"

"Despite all of the crisscrossing trails from the camp, they all either end up here or the place Tyler and his friends are encamped. I waited with them for a while, and when you didn't show, I headed here."

Crystal cleared the last of the undergrowth and scrambled up the embankment to the graveled road next to the two.

"I'm sorry, Crystal. If I'd known, I would have done something." Olivia's voice cracked.

"What do you want, Eunice?" Crystal faced her, unflinching.

"I want my sandals, and I want you to leave me alone." Her voice rose at the end, and desperation coupled with hysteria took over. "I just want to be left alone," she repeated in a soft whisper.

"Don't you care someone else is in jail for what you did?" Crystal didn't use the term murder. Tears trailed down the distraught woman's cheeks and her hand twitched. With the gun pointed at Olivia, she didn't want to push Eunice over the edge.

"I don't want to go to prison, okay? Why is that so hard to understand? Now, where are my sandals?"

"They're in my trunk in a gym bag." She and Olivia had scoured a thrift store and found passable matches to what they'd given the police and a bag to keep them in. Any sort of close inspection would reveal they weren't the real ones, but with any luck the nervous woman would grab the fake pair and leave.

"Open the trunk." Eunice waved the pistol at

Crystal.

Crystal sidled to the car, holding her hands wide to keep Eunice calm. She found the latch by the driver's seat and popped the trunk.

"Get the bag."

Crystal edged around her car, flipped the trunk open, and lifted the black and white striped bag.

"Show me." Eunice found a measure of confidence as Crystal complied with her demands, and more steel entered her voice every passing second.

Crystal unzipped the bag, and briefly flashed it open for Eunice.

The nervous woman wasn't willing to take her scrutiny from her hostages long enough to make sure they were the real deal. She only nodded, and Crystal zipped the bag shut, handing it over. Refusing to grab it, Eunice pointed at her car with the gun. "Put it on the passenger seat."

Crystal trudged to the Corvette, a fine coat of dust from the dirt road covering the immaculate paint job. Crystal opened the passenger door and spotted Suzy's camera on the seat. She snuck a peek at Eunice to see if she could stash the GoPro in her pocket, but every move was watched with frightening intensity.

Even though the revolver was still leveled at Crystal and Olivia, Eunice's tense muscles eased. "I hope your friend gets out of jail, but I'm not going to take her place spending my life rotting in a cell because of a stupid accident that happened because I tried to impress my un-impressible father."

"Eunice—" Crystal began.

"Call me Misha." Her hand tightened on the gun. "I told you, my father calls me that. He tells me I'm a failure and compares me to my dead mother. Nothing's good enough for him."

As far as Crystal could see, he had a point. Her simple stunt to convince Frederick Baranhof to sell his property had ended in murder and false imprisonment.

Eunice ranted on. "I'll show him. Where is he now? I've got the evidence and the money. The only lingering problem is you two."

Panic flared in Olivia's expression and Crystal knew it was mirrored in her own. Crystal held her hands out in a stopping motion. "Do you want to turn an accidental death into two real murders? You got away with it the first time, but if they open a new investigation, it only takes one person pointing out your extremely noticeable car leaving the scene of the crime." Crystal mentally patted herself on the back for the quick logic, despite her brain focusing on the barrel of the revolver pointed at her head.

"Fine. Have it your way. But I won't have you tailing me." Eunice squared up, braced her legs in a wide stance, and with two hands, swung the gun to point at Crystal's rear passenger tire. The gun roared and her tire blew, echoing in the forest. Several angry crows answered, taking flight and cawing their agitation at the noise.

Eunice controlled the recoil with her shooter's stance. The gun had bucked, but she had it under control in an instant, once again training it on her hostages.

"That was so you don't follow me." She squared up again, firing a round into the front tire this time. Now that she was aware of what was happening, Crystal considered jumping her, but Eunice fired the round and had the gun repositioned so fast Crystal didn't see an opportunity.

"That's because you've pissed me off. Leave me alone. And good luck getting to town with two flat tires and one spare." She swung her ponytail in a defiant toss and strode to her sports car, keeping the gun trained on Crystal and Olivia.

The door slammed shut and the Corvette thundered to life. The engine growled louder, and the tires spun in the mud and gravel, spraying Olivia and Crystal. They covered their faces and pivoted away from the barrage, peppered by stinging hits. The tires found purchase and the powerful car rocketed down the rough road, bouncing with abandon as Eunice celebrated her victory.

Crystal and Olivia stared until she disappeared and turned their mud-spattered faces toward each other.

"That didn't go as planned." Crystal found her jaw ached from how hard she had clenched it in frustration.

"Did you get anything on the camera that can be used?"

"Everything I needed was there, but they found it. I spotted it on her car seat when I threw the bag in. I'll have to buy Suzy a new one."

"Well, poo." Olivia flopped on the hood of Crystal's Honda.

"I hope Isabella has enough to free Roxie, because this ended up being a bunch of nothing." The weariness of it all struck Crystal, and her shoulders slumped.

"Do you have cell reception? We need a tow truck." Olivia threw an arm up to shade her vision from the sun's glare. Crystal found her phone tucked in the center console where she'd left it.

They must have been close enough to town because Crystal's phone showed several bars. She called a local towing company, gave them directions to their location, and sprawled out on the hood next to Olivia to stare at the sky.

A hawk coasted above them, riding a thermal. The logged area allowed them to observe a few soft, pillowy clouds dotting the azure sky, so difficult to view from the shadowed depths of the rain forest where they had spent so much of their time.

"Can you keep trying to find proof of Roxie's innocence?" Olivia asked after a minute.

Crystal squinted as the cloud masking the sun drifted away. "I have to go back to work. Amelia has been understanding about my absence since Roxie is her friend too, but the company won't keep paying me now that I've used up my vacation and sick time."

"Do you think Roxie will get out?"

"No idea. Maybe. I hope so." Crystal heaved a sigh. "It sounds like it's going to be dicey in court."

"Are you going to move in with Conner?"

Crystal sat in silence, mulling over the question. She hadn't taken much time to consider the topic since their talk. *Why wasn't she sure she wanted to move in with Conner? What held her back?* She loved his adventurous spirit and easy manner. She had no doubt he loved her with all of his heart and felt ridiculous for ever doubting him.

Was it simply worry keeping her from committing like Olivia suggested? Was there something else telling her to slow things down? Crystal explored this concept as a cloud shaped like a bear passed overhead. Olivia sat in companionable silence, letting her friend work things through.

Crystal's brain seized on something. It wasn't worry making her doubt moving in with Conner. It was a much more sinister word. Fear. Fear of it not working out. Fear of losing Conner. Fear of starting over in love.

Fear had never worked out in Crystal's life. Fear of chasing her dreams had landed her with a useless English degree in a corporate cubicle because she'd made what seemed like safe choices. The one time she had faced down her internal dread, she had become a wilderness guide, a path that had realized her nothing but fulfillment, joy, and love. It was all so clear.

"How do you think Elf will react to living on a boat?"

"Now you're talking. He'll probably scratch you, Conner, and Maggie, but maybe not in that particular order."

Crystal gave a deep, satisfied smile. "He probably will."

"You and Conner are going to be so happy." Olivia clapped her hands in excitement. "I can't say I'm not jealous, but you two are perfect together."

Crystal's phone chose that moment to ring.

"Is it Conner? Tell him the good news."

"It's probably the tow truck driver wondering where we are. It's not like a clearing in the woods down a dirt road are great directions in these parts." Crystal checked who the caller was. Tapping the answer button, Crystal greeted their friend. "Hey, Suzy, what's up?"

"Are you okay?" Suzy was frantic.

"We're fine. What's going on?"

Her measured answer did nothing to calm Suzy. "You were chased by the man from the woods. How could everything be fine?"

"Are you here?" Crystal stood on the rust pocked hood of her car, shielded her eyes, and twisted left and right, searching.

"What? No. I saw it on my phone."

Crystal dropped her hand and put it on her hip. "Suzy, you're not making sense."

Suzy growled out the next words with a deliberate, slow cadence. "Were you not surprised by the scary dude in the Baranhof Cabin, and were you not forced to run into the woods to escape?"

"How do you know that?"

"Aren't you listening?" Suzy's exasperation was reaching new heights.

"You said you watched it on your phone. How?"

"The GoPro auto-downloads videos to my phone if it's connected to Wi-Fi, and there's an open network at the cabin. Once the recording was stopped, it uploaded to my phone."

Euphoria started as a warm sensation in Crystal's stomach before radiating to her fingers and toes. "You have the whole video? With the confessions?"

"That's what I've been trying to tell you."

Epilogue

Crystal handed her parents each a glass of champagne. A glance showed everyone now held one on the crowded deck of Conner's—no—their houseboat. They had made the home as presentable as could be expected in the few days after the sale, but the renovation work hadn't begun to make it a livable home. The sun made its afternoon appearance as Seattle's marine layer of low clouds and cool air dissipated. Friends and family were chatting with each other, admiring the view of Gas Works Park, and already sipping the bubbly beverage meant for a toast.

Even her nephew, Joshua, had been given a sippy cup of sparkling cider, but downed it immediately after his first taste of the sweet treat and was burning off the sugar high by swinging on the metal railings. His father stood close, keeping watch on his rambunctiousness, but grinning from ear to ear with pride as Joshua showed off trick after trick.

If Eunice's father had showed the same amount of pride in his child, this whole disaster could have been avoided. His cruel judgement and withholding of love had driven Eunice to desperate measures to win his approval.

Suzy and Olivia were talking in the corner while gazing out across the water. Sail boats, kayaks, and canoes dotted Lake Union, the gorgeous day luring

Seattleites out of their winter hibernation as spring took control of the weather. The two had become fast friends through the experience and were recounting the crazier happenings of the last weeks. Ethan joined them and judging by Olivia's snorting laughs, his conversation was at least entertaining. Suzy had given fair warning of his love-them-and-leave-them attitude, but despite that, Olivia was clearly intrigued.

"I do hope ya'll are hungry." Roxie carried a plate of ribs up the stairs. She had been grilling on shore at the pier's communal picnic area, and the smell of smoke and barbecue had been tantalizing their taste buds for the last hour.

The Clallam County prosecutor had dropped the case against Roxie after the DNA on the sandals was linked to Eunice. He had taken up the case against her and her father, dubbing Eunice the "Evergreen Executioner." The guy had a thing for alliterative nicknames. With motive, a confession from the GoPro recording, and DNA working against them, Eunice and Grant were looking at a pair of long sentences.

"May I have everyone's attention?" Conner spoke above the chatter, causing the conversations to die down. He raised his glass, and their friends and family copied the gesture. Crystal sidled up next to him and he put his arm around her waist. "It means so much for you to join us on this happy occasion. Today, we are starting a new chapter in our lives, literally, building a home together. We are beyond elated that our friend Roxie is here with us and are grateful to our coworkers who helped by either being in Forks or covering our jobs as Crystal sought proof of Roxie's innocence."

"Cheers," the entire gathering called out.

Roxie stood, holding back unshed tears, and raised her glass. "You are the best..." Whatever she was going to say was lost when her voice choked. She opened her mouth to speak once more but gave up and settled for hugging Crystal instead. Crystal's own vision misted as she squeezed Roxie.

Roxie hadn't even cried the day she'd been released from prison. Crystal, Conner, and Suzy had been there to greet her as she walked through the prison gates, a free woman. Roxie had whooped with joy and pulled them in for one humungous bear hug. After promising to cook them the best meal they'd ever had, she shouted, "Let's blow this joint!" It appeared the emotion of her ordeal had finally overcome her.

After a heartfelt squeeze, Roxie released Crystal. They both wiped away tears but shared a warm smile.

Isabella tilted her glass in Crystal's direction. "You made my job easy. Let me know when you decide to change professions, and I'll start sending PI work your way."

"Now, now. No poaching my employee. I only just got her back," Amelia spoke up from where she was seated on a deck chair.

"Wouldn't dream of it." The lawyer reclined in her chair, basking in the sun with a soft, pleased smile.

With the exoneration from Frederick's murder, Roxie was now in line to inherit a sizable estate, and Isabella's work had gone from pro-bono favor to lucrative representation. The official reading of the will was a couple of days hence, but due to the information released during the investigation, Roxie knew she wouldn't have to worry about money for the rest of her life.

Drawn by the scent of the ribs, Maggie, Conner's black Labrador retriever, joined the crowd. Maggie's tail whipped back and forth as she received pats or had bites snuck to her.

"Do you have a plan for the rain forest land?" Ethan asked Roxie.

Roxie shrugged. "I'm not sure. I was approached by the Nature Conservancy who want to turn it into a campground and educational center. I think Freddy would have liked that."

Ethan nodded, and an impish grin teased the corner of his mouth. "The most important question is, who's going to be the chef at all of our destinations? We've been spoiled all these years and are going to miss you."

Crystal, Amelia, Conner, and Suzy all raised their glasses in agreement with Ethan's words. "To Roxie," Conner toasted. They all echoed the praise.

Roxie broke into the first broad smile they'd seen since she'd been released. She kept in her southern character. "Bless your hearts. Did ya'll think I was gonna retire? I'd find myself in a heap of trouble if left to my own devices."

Cheers greeted the proclamation. Their world was realigning after almost falling apart. Glancing around at the gathering of her loved ones celebrating in the new home she would share with Conner, Crystal corrected herself. Her life hadn't only come back together, it was better than ever.

The party broke up as the evening wore on. Her sister and brother-in-law were the first to depart, each toting a sleeping child. The others trickled home, eventually leaving her and Conner sitting on deck chairs and watching the city lights flick on as the sun disappeared below the horizon. Conner fetched them a blanket to share as the temperature dipped and a light breeze picked up. Crystal snuggled next to him, leaning her head on his shoulder. Maggie circled several times and was soon snoring by their feet, curled into a ball.

Conner spoke, his voice husky with emotion. "I know my aunt and uncle raised me with all the love parents should, but I always felt like something was lacking, no matter how much I tried to convince myself otherwise. Now, I know. This is what I was missing."

Crystal hugged him tight, communicating, without words, how much she loved him.

After another long moment of quiet calm, Conner broke the silence. "What do you want to do tomorrow?" His voice had returned to its usual affable nature, but soft, reflecting the quiet around them. Crystal would have never guessed this calm haven existed in the heart of the thriving city.

"Part of me wants to tackle refinishing the floor, but paddle-boarding could be fun to try."

The contentment in Conner's voice told the entire story. "Why don't we wait to see what we feel like in the morning? We have all the time in the world, and our adventure is just beginning."

A word about the author…

ML Erdahl lives amidst the trees of the Pacific Northwest, where he pens humorous cozy mystery novels set in the wilderness he has spent his lifetime exploring. The only thing slowing him down is when his adorable rescue pets, Skip, Daisy, and Deucser demand to be cuddled on his lap while he types.

When he's not working in front of a computer, you can find him gardening, hiking, or grumbling to his wife, Emily, about the perpetual Northwest winter rain that prevents him from going outside.

Thank you for purchasing
this publication of The Wild Rose Press, Inc.

For questions or more information
contact us at
info@thewildrosepress.com.

The Wild Rose Press, Inc.
www.thewildrosepress.com